Praise for *The Radio and Other Stories*

"In *The Radio and Other Stories*, the scholar and the storyteller converge. The stories stir our emotions even as they prod our intellect. This is a fascinating collection that celebrates the tenacity of memory. In the end, the narrator presents a complex continuum of disparate realities that are made wholesome by his ability to impose a humane melody to the cacophonous inheritance falsely labeled as a postcolonial state. The prose flows seductively with stylistic versatility, and the reader is bound to return to this collection over and over again for engaging reflections."
—Joyce Ashuntantang,
Author of *Beautiful Fire*, University of Hartford, USA

"These short stories, pulsating with the real, register the experiences of a child of today's global space, navigating the local and the global. The multivocal, intertextual perspective is ingenious and innovative. Simply brilliant!"
—Eunice Ngongkum,
University of Yaoundé 1, Cameroon

"A fascinating life-narrative that humorously explores serious personal and collective experiences. The narratives are both affectively and cognitively stimulating and captivating."
—CJ Odhiambo,
Moi University, Kenya

"Gil Ndi-Shang weaves a sequence of tales that are funny, touching, humorous but also haunting, unsettling and unnerving. It is a testament to life's frail wonder and a rich lesson on the commonality of our humanity in an increasingly interconnected world."
—Victor N. Gomia,
Delaware State University, USA

"This book is fraught with dangerous depths, menacing walks and spectacular escape routes... Gil Ndi-Shang has twisted an instant classic for students in African studies. A must-read for the students of African literature, critical theory, philosophy, sociology, psychology, media and cultural studies."
—Moulay Driss El Maarouf,
Sidi Mohamed Ben Abdalla University, Fez, Morocco

"A great semi-autobiographical piece which puts the reader at the very heart of the storyline, gluing their attention to each line from start to finish. The perfect use of the second person singular (YOU) makes each reader a full part of the storytelling; a model of reader-centred writing."

—Ras-I Mackinzeph,
Lyricist and Pedagogic Inspector of Philosophy,
Centre Region, Cameroon

"Sensitivity and keenness to detail are the hallmarks of this rich collection by Gil Ndi-Shang, in the same way as his travel memoir, *Letter from America*. In both, he successfully intertwines the local and the global. Moreover, through creative juxtaposition, the narrator oscillates between familiar landscapes in Cameroon and the ones he encounters during his sojourns in Europe and America. *The Radio* can be read as the entanglement between self and community, self and nation as well as the political consciousness of a global citizen."
—Samuel Ndogo,
Moi University, Eldoret, Kenya

The Radio
and
Other
Stories

Gil Ndi-Shang

SPEARS
BOOKS

SPEARS BOOKS
AN IMPRINT OF SPEARS MEDIA PRESS LLC
7830 W. Alameda Ave, Suite 103-247
Denver, CO 80226
United States of America

First Published in the United States of America in 2021 by Spears Books
www.spearsmedia.com
info@spearsmedia.com
@spearsbooks

Information on this title: www.spearsmedia.com/the-radio-and-other-stories
© 2021 Gil Ndi-Shang
All rights reserved.

ISBN: 9781942876755 (Paperback)
ISBN: 9781942876762 (eBook)
Also available in Kindle format

Cover Art: Alain Kojele
Cover designed by Doh Kambem
Designed and typeset by Spears Media Press LLC

*Any references to historical events, real people, or real locales are used fictitiously. Other
names, characters, places, and incidents are the product of the author's imagination, and
any resemblance to actual events or locales or persons, living or dead, is entirely coincidental.*

Distributed globally by African Books Collective (ABC)
www.africanbookscollective.com

To life and, of course, death

"To find a point where hypothesis and fact meet, the delicate equilibrium between dream and reality, the place where fantasy and earthly things are metamorphosed into a work of arts, the hour where faith in the future becomes knowledge of the past, to lay down one's powers for others in need, to shake off the old ordeal and get ready for the new, to question knowing that never can full answers be found, to accept uncertainties quietly, even your incomplete knowledge of God, this is what man's journey is about, I think."

The Journey (1954), Lillian Smith

CONTENTS

PROLOGUE

As a child, you confronted the world with a series of puerile presumptions: that Heaven was above and Hell was below; that Israel, Jerusalem, Palestine, Damascus, etc. were heavenly places; that if you read too much, your head would explode; that biscuits, sardine and Fanta brought happiness to the soul, such that shopkeepers were the happiest people in the world; that the grey and blurred image in the full-blown moon was that of a man splitting firewood; that if you stood on the tip of the Kaa Mountain in Luh, you could touch the sky with your fingertips; that the sweetest thing in life was to drink fresh water on a cocoyam leaf; that it was sinful to say, 'I swear to God,' because no human can create even a single strand of hair; that the masquerades were made up of wood and that Life was a gift from God. But, believing that babies came to the world through a woman's anus, you wondered why a divine gift should take such a route; why your Sunday school teacher told you God had special love for children but at the same time claimed that man is born already with scales of sin on his skin; why you were always cautioned that eating too many sweet things like sugar endangered one's health; why you rarely got ill, thus deprived of the full bottle of Fanta which your mum offered to your luckier siblings whenever they fell ill and why tablets and drugs that cured headache and stomach ache were always bitter. And so, one day, you asked your mum: "Mum, when shall there be Life?"

THE RADIO

I hear her voice
In the mornin' hour, she calls me
The radio reminds me of my home far away
And drivin' down the road I get a feelin'
That I should have been home yesterday, yesterday
("Country Roads", Olivia Newton-John)

M oving out of the student room to a larger apartment in the
Bavarian town of Bayreuth was symbolic to you in a very
specific way. You were taking off the cloak of student life for good.
From parental home through a series of student rooms in Cameroon
to Germany, now you were in an 'apartment'. The trajectory seemed
deceptively simple and straightforward. On unpacking one of the
book-filled cartons amongst your cargo in your new apartment, you
found this stereo radio, helplessly pressed to the corner by a mound
of books. You rescued it, contented that it was not damaged in any
way. You had thought it was amongst the things you disposed of as
you cleaned your student room upon moving out. You had decided
to part ways with any furniture or household item you did not find
useful or that did not earn space in your new apartment. For instance,
aided by your Kenyan friend, you threw into the trashcan the heavy
analogue TV screen bequeathed to you by a Burkinabe friend. In
the student hostel, the TV screen was amongst the commonest 'gifts',
since most of the students returning home could not take it along.

But it was not always easy to have someone kind enough to accept the inherited gift.

As you dusted the radio, almost half-heartedly, wondering if you needed it at all, you said to yourself: "Truly, the radio keeps tracking me, like the woman I shared with my father." You had bought that radio as one of your latest strategies for learning German. The language seemed to you like a hydra and one needed to keep overhauling old methods and devising new tactics in order to apprehend it. In addition to that, you enjoyed sleeping to the tunes of Radio Bayern that most often played pleasant RnB music all through the night. Then, for some time, you had gotten so busy with your thesis that your laptop took precedence over any other appliances in your room. Whatever radio programmes you still followed, like your long-time companions BBC Afrique, Focus on Africa and BBC News Hour, you did so on your laptop. But here was the radio again, in its physical form, accompanying you to your new apartment! As you held it in your hand, wiping it, you realised that, in many ways, you were a child of the radio, that the radio ran through your veins, that she lived in you and you could not deny her. Sometimes, when someone asked you what you missed most from home, you often answered: "The radio." Of course, that often sounded like a rather weird answer to an earnest question.

You grew up in a distant village in the north-western part of Cameroon, and the radio was to you the only cord between the here and the there, the now and then, the homely and foreign. It was in fact the main vista through which you viewed the world, a constant reminder that there was a world beyond your immediate home, out of reach, yet not unattainable. It was the Tantalus of your infant desires. She spoke of the world beyond the Kaa and Nchindong mountains that guarded the eastern borders of your village. She instilled in you a longing for the not-yet-seen and not-yet-known, making you develop a certain instinctive sense of homeliness in foreign spaces and instant affinity with foreigners. The radio of your upbringing was your father's four-battery, copper-coloured JVC.

"When I was posted to Subum, I needed a powerful radio that could enable me to stay abreast of the news. When my brother Sam went to Nigeria to sell kola nuts, I gave him 200 frs to get me a nice radio set. That was a great amount of money by then. In Nigeria, you certainly needed a *Ghana-Must-Go* bag to carry such a huge amount!" Noticing your sense of disbelief, he changed the analogy: "Yes, you could even woo a woman with that amount in those days."

"Is that how much you gave to grandad for letting you take away his jewel?" quipped your kid sister, Mameng. Virtually everyone was in tears, giggling in a chorus. Mameng was fond of teasing your dad even when he meant to be serious. When the spate of laughter subsided, he continued.

"But my elder brother got into some problems in Nigeria and only came back after many years. So, I travelled to Subum with a two-battery transistor radio I bought in the late 1970s during one of my early trips to Yaoundé. But it was not very strong. When Mangwang was born, a colleague of mine, Mr Tame, offered me this JVC as a birthday gift for my daughter. Mr Tame was both a teacher and a trader and he used to travel to Nigeria during holidays to buy goods." All eyes turned to Mangwang who assumed an instant sense of pride, as the radio's alter ego in body and soul.

"Subum remains one of the best places I have worked in during my entire working life." Your dad continued with his narrative. "The people were very kind to us and the land was very fertile. We even had a cocoyam farm there. We did not buy food in Subum. We produced everything by ourselves, excluding the numerous gifts that neighbours and friends offered us. That was when teachers were still held in high esteem, not like nowadays. But the only problem was the effect of the hot climate on the kids, especially Nshie."

"I kept singing into his ears to look for transfer. At first, he resisted but finally gave in," your mother stepped in, with a sense of plaintiveness that perhaps came close to capturing how much your father resisted her insistent plea back then.

"In fact, it is your mother who put pressure on me to seek for transfer." Your dad conceded, in earnest. "I applied unsuccessfully and I had to write a personal letter to the Divisional Delegate of Education for Menchum Division. By then it was a certain Mr Gowon. One evening, while I was preparing my lesson notes on the veranda, your mother called me from the parlour, telling me that they were reading the list of transfer cases on the radio. I abandoned my notes, hurriedly followed her and we listened keenly to the names. When they came to Menchum, we held our breath, and then... Actually, the journalist mispronounced my name so much so that I didn't even recognise it, if not for your mother's ever-sharp ears."

"The journalist read as if he had burning charcoal in his mouth and we almost did not get the name," your mother added.

"I was redeployed to Government School Taku, where I had earlier taught in the late 70s. We started packing a week later, not without a hectic send-off evening organised by the staff members and class seven pupils. Given the nature of the roads, we did not leave Subum with much property, apart from the JVC and some other things that we could take along. To change locations with four kids was a difficult task in the first place." That was in April 1982.

Your father continued to narrate to you and your siblings how Subum had never left him and how he maintained contact through letters with some of his friends and neighbours. But the most dramatic part of the story was that four years after they left Subum, there was the Lake Nyos Disaster: a lethal gas explosion from the lake led to the death of more than two thousand inhabitants and about four thousand livestock. Subum was within its deadly twenty-five-kilometre perimeter. The disaster was somewhat heralded by a swarm of locusts that destroyed crops in the Lake Nyos area around 1980 and caused great misery amongst the population. Each time your parents recalled those moments, their sullen faces communicated the weight of that tragedy in their lives. *They* were lucky enough to have left just four years before the disaster. But then, the memory of friends, neighbours and colleagues sometimes moved them to tears. Your dad returned to Subum a year after the disaster and found the place abandoned and decrepit; a place that used to bustle with life had become a wasteland. He jealously kept a picture which he took during that visit. There he was in trumpet-shaped trousers as was fashionable in his days, leaning on a motorcycle, with a rather forlorn demeanour. As children, even in the background of a sombre story, you used to bombard him with questions to know what happened to his motorcycle and why he would not buy one anymore for the family. As he and your mum tried to recall the names of some of their Subum neighbours, you asked them:

"And what about Mr Tame, the one who gave you the radio?"

"Oh, he also sought for transfer after we did. But was not as lucky. He died in the tragedy, with his entire family. He actually hailed from Subum." As your mum responded to your query, your dad suddenly became pensive, apparently touched by the memories. You felt rather guilty for striking on an uneasy chord.

Your mind came back to the JVC, one of the few relics from Subum. Whenever your dad came back for the holidays while you were out of home, perhaps playing football in a nearby makeshift pitch, the sound of the radio was the first signal of his presence. He used to place it either on a stool on the veranda or sometimes took it with him to the kitchen. The sound of the radio meant that you were going to have bush meat on the menu for weeks since your father had the ill-luck of always being transferred to bush places. But the sound of the radio also meant physical labour and discipline. For your dad, your entire compound was a perpetual work-in-progress and whenever you did not meet up with his work schedule, you needed to devise your own trajectories in your six-room house in order to avoid the sound of his voice and that of the radio.

Since you always did your best in carrying out the tasks he assigned to you, the radio was often a point of accord between the two of you. Depending on the circumstances, you used to sleep either with the kerosene lamp or with the radio by your side. After the evening meal, you would wait for the right moment to take control of the lamp and disappear with it to your parents' room to select a book to read for the night. The book-filled trunk also contained an outdated record player, accompanied by a set of plates of musicians such as Prince Nico Mbarga, Sonny Okosun, Evi Edna, Bongos Ikwue and the Groove, Eric Donaldson, Sonya Spence and Ginger Williams. At a time when the Philips analogue magnetic tape was fashionable, these plates, some of which were impeccably intact, as if surprised by the quick succession of sound technology, remained great reminders of the heydays of your parents. In his light-hearted moment, your dad would promise to fix the record player, which he claimed only had a slight technical problem. But that was one of the few promises he never fulfilled.

Your family had two lamps but at any one time, there was always a problem with one of them. The lamp was your only source of energy as your family only used the generator during important football tournaments like the African Nations Cup/FIFA World Cup and on days with interesting Cameroon Radio Television programmes. In the 1980s, the magic box created in the 1920s by John Logie Baird in Britain and Charles Francis Jenkins in America finally made its way to Luh. Special programmes on Saturday (Dance Cameroon Dance, Télépodium, Papa and Kids, as Cosby Show was known in your local setting), Sunday (Tam-Tam Weekend), and Monday (Jake and the Fat Man) held everyone spellbound. It was very costly using the generator on a daily basis given the constant hikes in the price of petrol. On the rest of the days, you had to make do with the hurricane lamp. It was not an easy thing to deprive the household of a single lamp. Your parents, in particular, had the habit of staying longer in the kitchen after evening meals. As you stood close to the kitchen door, impatiently waiting for them to grant your request for the lamp, your mother would admonish you:

"There you go again; if you're not sleeping with the radio, it's with the lamp. When shall you ever have rest, this son of mine?" To such a rhetorical question, you just mumbled, trying to let her know that you had something important to read that night. Your father would not meddle in your discussion. Staying quiet meant he was in your defence.

Most often, however, your dad also needed the lamp to go through some of his readings or to prepare his lesson notes in advance on the eve of school resumption. On such occasions, he would concede to you the JVC. You would dash with the radio to your bedroom and begin the bittersweet task of tuning it for a favourite station. In those days you had difficulties receiving FM stations in the village. The shortwave was relatively the most functional mode of reception. Most often the available stations were the foreign ones. You became a faithful listener of BBC World Service, VOA Africa, Deutsche Welle, etc. at a rather young age. Some of your cherished presenters were VOA Daybreak Africa's 'King' Richard Kotey, Network/Focus Africa's Robin White and BBC Letter from America's Alistair Cooke. When you visited Ellis Island in New York decades later, Cooke was your imaginary guide. As you boarded the ferry at Manhattan to Ellis Island, you could still hear his voice, with its majesty, magic, life and transcendence. His voice captured American culture through the practices of everyday life. His historical accounts, delivered in impeccable journalistic idiom and measured pauses, were brought to you at the fringes of the erstwhile British Empire by your father's JVC.

The JVC came to mean everything to you. While the TV turned your family's parlour into a public space, the JVC belonged to your private realm, at least at night. Your dad's TV was SHARP. But that was the name of the mark and not a description of its image and sound. For the TV signals to procure basic visual comfort was an arduous task, characterised by a prolonged and tortuous adjusting of the fifteen-metre-tall aerial antenna pole beside the house. Still, that hardly mollified the interfering rice-like figments that usually chose the most suspense-laden moments to run their course. That often left the telespectators to complete with their own imagination what they saw and heard on the SHARP 14C-C1F. Thus, whenever Cameroon was playing an important game, the telespectators had to sit in front of the screen with their transistor radio sets on, to complement the information emerging from the epileptic TV signals. Even slow-motion replay at times did not settle the confusion caused by the poor images, leading to serious arguments amongst the telespectators. Perhaps that explains why the 1-0 victory of Cameroon against Argentina in Italy 1990 remains for you the greatest misinformation in football history. You counted 11 goals against 0, in favour of the Indomitable Lions of Cameroon!

The TV broadcast used to start at midday and prior to that time, the screen bore the boring and vexing image of a multicolour globe with a ticking clock at the base. Whenever there was to be a live football broadcast, the clock was slower than usual and snailed indifferently as worms churned in your stomach in anticipation of the game. The redemptive moment often came when the globe would gradually disappear, followed by a musical intro. That is how you got to know 'Siwo' and 'kolé séré' (Jocelyne Béroard); 'Umqombothi' (Yvonne Chaka Chaka), 'asimbonanga' (Johnny Clegg & Savuka), 'cicatrice d'amour' (Tshala Muana), and 'Kazet Gazette' (Mahlathini & Mahotella Queens). Sometimes the intro was 'wakoka', 'pam pam be', 'yowiyo' or 'la musique' (Rum Tah). Whenever a nice music clip struck a particular chord in your puerile sensibility, you would develop the sensation that the musical career was your calling. And for every child of your generation, Rum-Tah was the paragon of achievement, happiness, and fame. The Rum-Tah youngsters made you dream. Like the indomitable Lions, they represented the bright colours of the nation in your imagination. But there was always the lingering doubt as to whether that future was accessible to and attainable by all the sons and daughters of that nation. The failing

TV and radio signals were telling signs of that marginality. The waves of the nation only reached Luh in dribs and drabs. The Rum-Tah were the centre of the nation, while you were the periphery and you looked up to them, dreaming of the day when you would be fully part of that ideal nation called Cameroon, the only bilingual country in the world, apart from Canada. Being a bilingual country was presented to you in primary school as a rare feat only achievable by Cameroon and Canada. There were primary school songs that made the fact of Cameroon being divided into ten provinces sound like a country with a special status. But the electoral crisis of the nineties and the political violence in your community caused immeasurable damage to your affective attachment to the nation, a damage which the euphoric aftermath of Italy 1990 and the mournful, soulful and interminable jingle of dima dangwa Yerusalem on national TV that followed the death of the country's First Lady, occasionally mitigated but hardly could repair.

Your cousin, Nfoninwe was fond of disciplining your habits through the TV regime. He would shout at the younger televiewers in your parlour to take their evening bath before sitting down to watch the evening news or any dance programme. Even you, otherwise privileged children of the TV home, were not spared. This meant that during TV time, you somewhat became strangers in your own house! While others, having complied by the rules, were watching TV in the parlour, sometimes you went back to your room, in your bed, turning the knob of the radio in what seemed like an extended foreplay. She accompanied you in those nocturnal private moments, between sleep and wakefulness, sharing with you stories far removed from your immediate environment, stretching your imagination to places and people that sharpened your curiosity. Whenever you woke up in the morning, you were unable to distinguish between your night dreams and memories of news items that seeped into your half-conscious mind at night. When later in life people asked you, as they did to Chinua Achebe, in what language you dreamt or in what language you experienced orgasm, you found the question doubly intriguing. Sometimes due to the erratic nature of the frequency modulation, the volume of the radio would increase exceedingly at night while you were asleep, making it audible in the other rooms and even to the night sojourners since your house (and especially your room) was a few metres away from the road. Your mother would remind you grudgingly the following morning that she had to come to your room to turn off the radio while you were asleep. Some passers-by confessed having heard the sound of the radio from your house very late in the night, making them wonder if your dad ever slept at all. With such complaints, you promised to turn off the radio before sleeping. In vain.

Most often, in the middle of a very important news bulletin, the waves would gradually grow febrile and eventually fizzle out. That was usually the case during the rainy season. You would helplessly pin your ear against the JVC's perforated frame that contained the speaker, to catch the last puffs of the vanishing voice. Most often, you felt, with anxiety and desperation, the voice of some of your favourite presenters disappearing into the background, not without leaving you with the torturing trail of names like Boutros Boutros-Ghali, Helmut Kohl, Nelson Mandela, making you imagine what the news was all about. You strained your imagination to infer the unsaid and the possible denouement of vital information of which the JVC had left you with mere fragments and innuendos. Sometimes, in a bid to force the radio to perform, you would turn off on the red button and then the green, to turn it on again. Other times, you would simply hit the radio hard, hoping that would trigger some forceful cable connection or disconnection that would help recover the vanishing voice. Sometimes it effectively worked, fired up by the half-dead Hellesens batteries which you used to recycle by sunning them on the cemented veranda. When that was done correctly, the batteries were born again, giving new life to the radio.

Most often after the hitting, an unrepentant cockroach would fall from the crevices of the radio and disappear under the bed or the cupboard. Thus, when turning the knob with scientific precision, you were unable to clearly make out if the subtle hissing sound that came out of the JVC was the promising sign of the voice of Robin White, Julian Marshall, Alistair Cooke, Richard 'King' Kotey or that of an infant cockroach entangled in the wireworks of the radio. The stations that offered themselves more easily were BBC Hausa Service, Radio Malabo and Africa N°1. While BBC Hausa Service waves were strongest at night, Africa N°1 and Radio Malabo reverberated with vigour during the day. In the afternoons, these two channels would thrill you with entrancing tunes such as Mory Kante's 'Yeke Yeke', Salif Keita's 'Africa'/ 'Tekéré' and Angelique Kidjo's 'Agolo'. Amid the indescribable boredom that sometimes assailed you when you were left alone in the compound on a public holiday, these clips commingled with the currents of the Rivers Gambia, Niger, Zambezi, Sanaga, Limpopo, Nile, Orange and Benue of your primary school geography lessons, reminding you that you were part and parcel of a large mass called Africa.

The Nigerian stations were usually very clear, especially in the Hausa language with constant reference to names like Murtala Muhammed, Shehu Shagari, Moshood Abiola, Yakubu Gowon, etc. pronounced in impeccably euphonious accent. Many people and also dogs in your area bore the name 'Gowon'! On the other hand, the signal of the national radio station was much weaker, turning official Cameroon into a far-away land. But, in hindsight, you have come to think that perhaps it is because tuning the radio became akin to such a painfully sweet exercise, that when the news finally came in a lucid voice, it took the shape of an epiphany in your infant mind, making it stick in your memory like chameleon faeces, once and for all, hardly to be forgotten or wiped off, making the world part and parcel of your haptic sensibility.

Throughout your difficult romance with the JVC, some of the news items that touched the core of your being and conditioned your mood in your early teenage days were the repeated reports of the killings in Palestine-Israel: "This morning, three Palestinian students were killed as they protested against the construction of new Israeli settlements in the West Bank"; "An armed Palestinian man shot two Israeli teenagers in Jerusalem"; "Ten Palestinian protesters have been killed after a deadly confrontation with the Israeli army in Gaza. The victims include two children." Why was there so much killing in that part of the world? Was death in Palestine the same as in Israel? Such pieces of news altered the rhythm of your days and made you unusually sullen and confused, especially as you had earlier thought that Palestine, Israel, Jerusalem, Damascus were heavenly places in the same way as Babylon, Philippines and a host of others! Perhaps, when you grow old you will understand these questions better, you thought. Your mood sometimes attracted the curiosity of your mother, she who was always concerned about your well-being, she who easily noticed the slightest change in your demeanour, weight, voice, etc. Did these murdered children also have mothers? If yes, were their mothers as caring as yours? Were these also children like yourself, with hopes, dreams and aspirations? Did death mean the same to them as to you, you who had never lost any immediate relative or friend? What did it mean to lose a son, daughter, father, mother, brother, sister, or friend? News of deadly violence constituted a series of conundrums to you. You had never experienced the death of a close relative and you could not stand the mere thought of it. You could not imagine life without any of your parents or your siblings.

Such news hung over you for days and weeks, making you develop a strong vision of the world where all human beings would live together in peace. The truth is, you were a child of many worlds. You were living in the village but the JVC and your father's library opened you to a much larger affective community that immensely shaped your imagination. Years later, you nurtured the irrevocable dream of becoming a diplomat or international journalist. Earlier in your childhood, you had even contemplated becoming a musician. This was often the effect of some melodious music that struck the right chord in your being and made you feel like having found the meaning of life. But that never lasted long. You were also bent on understanding the strange languages that your JVC was best in capturing. It was a heartfelt dream that made you excel in school subjects like history, geography, general knowledge and most especially foreign languages. You developed a keen interest in world history. Before you travelled to the nearest big town, Nkambe, for secondary education, you had already travelled the world over. Your mind was already peopled with towns, cities, countries, continents and imagined faces far beyond your locality.

You remembered one other person in your village who was as addicted to the radio as you, albeit in a different way. His name was Nyakoh. He was a frequent customer of your family's provision store cum beer parlour, part of a roadside building that your workaholic father had constructed in addition to your main family house. This soon became a public space, where people would gather and share stories on various happenings, especially commentaries about the village inter-quarter football games. On Sundays, given its proximity to the Baptist Church, it was also a place where some Christians would come and buy a stick of cigarettes or gulp a litre of palm wine before going for service. Nyakoh was a huge man with a deep voice who had spent several years in Douala. When he returned, only those of his age group could retain memories of him. After all those years of plantation labour, the most valuable property he had brought home was his radio, an eight-battery set. He would carry it up and down the village main road, setting the volume as high as possible, earning him the nickname 'Nyakoh disco'. He had many other nicknames in the neighbouring villages. Most of them were derived from his eating habits. He had a palm wine bush where, in the evening, after a fruitful wine tapping exercise, he would roast a bucket of coco-yams and consume with ten litres of palm wine. In your family's provision store, he could clear down a Murtala of puff-puff, with the accompanying bowl of pepper, in only a few minutes.

In the evenings, the final anchorage of his radio was always in your family store. Nyakoh's disco set was a welcomed source of animation in your family's modest commercial space. He would pitch his mobile disco on the table and enchant everyone with music tubes by Petit Pays, Ndedi Eyango, Dina Bell, Lapiro de Mbanga, Charlotte Mbango, San Fan Thomas, Bébé Manga, etc. Usually, as one cassette tape was playing, he would rewind the next one with a BIC pen. Sometimes, in a half-tipsy mood, he would sketch a dance step, with one hand on the back of his trademark Amilcar Cabral cap and the other hand on his hip, letting you wonder what lay beyond the trailer. (But with his size and what seemed like a clubfoot, the trailer could hardly stand for anything beyond the demo.) Bébé Manga's 'Mot'a Benama' was one of those clips that more than often threw him in such moods of solemn ecstasy. During such moments, he would say, as if pricked by a sharp swathe of idyllic nostalgia that bordered on solitude: "Oh, when I was in Disangue…" Then he would release puffs of smoke from a stick of Bastos cigarettes. Sometimes, he sang along in Duala language (God alone knows whether it was really Duala) and would go ahead to tell you stories of how he met some of the above artists, especially Petit-Pays, face to face. Some fellow returnees would confirm the story, of course in a bid to pave the way for reciprocal confirmation of their own narratives of their former lives and exploits at the coast.

Cameroon was the coast and the capital. Anyone who had ventured to these spaces had an unlimited license for stories upon return. Usually, not before long, the big radio set brought by many a returnee was mortgaged to a local storekeeper in Luh, Ntundip or Taku village in order to sustain the life of rustic ostentation they sought to portray. In those days, the returnees were special targets of the village girls, especially during market days. Nyakoh went back to Douala and after close to five years during which no one had information about him, he returned to the village, bringing with him a very slim and strange-looking woman. Many called her 'white woman'. She was a fellow smoker and her presence aroused all kinds of rumours in the village. Not long after the lady went back to Douala, he fell ill and was brought back to the village where he died shortly afterwards. The village BBC rumoured that the lady also died in Douala not long after Nyakoh's death. Such information was usually transmitted by mothers during *bofah* (farmwork by self-help groups); by young boys gathered around provision stores to comment on local and foreign news as well as by young women as they plaited hair on the veranda. In the same way that they combed the hair before plaiting, so would they comb the latest social news in the village.

Radio sets like Nyakoh's came and went, but your father's JVC remained a constant member of your household. After several years abroad, you returned home. As you alighted from the car and embraced your relatives and neighbours, something caught your attention: it was the voice of the JVC coming out from the living room. Her voice was even much clearer than in the yesteryears and you felt the urge to ask your dad if some seasoned technician had repaired it or if the satellite antennas in Ndu and Nkambe had gradually improved the reception capacity of radio waves in your village. But that was not the time for worldly questions. Later that evening, your mum asked you to accompany her to the narrow yard that separated your house from the main road, where you used to play football as kids and early teenagers. With a stretch of the hand, she pointed to what seemed like a small rectangular garden, with a mélange of flowers, splaying their petals to the languid and disconsolate sunrays of home.

There lay she that was the agemate of the radio. She was your sister, she was your friend, she was your classmate, she was your adversary, she was your ally. As with the radio, sometimes you quarrelled, sometimes you fought, but it was all out of love.

THE SHOE

ESTRAGON sitting on a low mound, is trying to take off his boot. He pulls at it with both hands, panting…He gives up, exhausted, rests, tries again… (*Waiting for Godot,* Samuel Beckett)

Amongst the things you found as you unpacked your boxes in your new apartment was a small flat cylinder labelled *KIWI Quality Shoe Polish*. You carefully opened it and were greeted by its strong naphtha scent, coupled with the smell of bottled time. It was still usable, it seemed. You had brought that *KIWI* to Germany from Cameroon almost six years ago but had not used it beyond the first two weeks of your stay. Its accompanying brush was certainly missing. During your first weeks in Germany, you had the habit of going to the university in suits and well-kiwied shoes before you got used to your new context and went in for shoes that hardly needed polishing. It is also true that the colour of dust and mud in Germany was not the same as in your homeland. Your new home greatly altered the 'shoes make a man' mantra of your secondary school days when shoes were a great distinctive factor given that you all wore the blue-black trousers and a sky-blue jacket as uniform.

Though some students went in for a zipped instead of the official buttoned jacket, the single instead of the double vent, the Pierre Cardin, Velours or Tergal trousers instead of the more common material trousers, it was the shoes that made a veritable difference.

Non-black shoes constituted a violation of the school rules which often brought the student into collision with the DM (Discipline Master). In the dry season, however, that regulation made little sense given that all shoes, like life, assumed the colour of dust. Wearing assorted shoes was a mark of grandeur at a time when some measure of notorious character procured occasional popularity, bravado, and the tag of a 'strong man'. Shoes represented class and a sense of non-conformism, not to say outright rebellion. That was the time of *JOHN GOODECKER, LAMBERT, BUTIONS, MERCURY, DIA-DORA, SEBAGO, FILA, REEBOK and FUBU* shoe brands. *FUBU!* There was one student who was nicknamed *FUBU* because of his addiction to the *FUBU* shoe brand. Another one was known as *CHASSANT*, the name of special Tennis shoes that were awkwardly but fashionably longer than their wearer's size and whose tip gained independence from the toes, tied by a shoelace that demarcated very clearly the end of its content. These shoes seemed to announce the advent of their wearer in advance in any space. There is a Form One classmate whose name or face you do not remember clearly, but whose shoes stuck in your mind. It was an all-weather and trac-tor-shaped pair of shoes, with a perennial dust colour, rugged to the core. The shoes left you in Form Two or Three for a different institution and you never met again.

In secondary school, most male students went in for the very best shoes en vogue and shoes were the most conspicuous assets in their student room. Always well arrayed and when one was to receive a female visitor, one had to make the best impression out of nothing, even if that meant starving afterwards. One always had to make sure the thirty minutes or one-hour visit was a success. Sometimes, when you look back at the different phases of your secondary school life, you can only succeed by tracing the various brands of shoes you had at a particular time. So, the great shoe tradition was part and parcel of you. Thus, when you furthered your education at the University of Yaoundé 1, you maintained the tradition against all odds.

But something was going to happen that shattered the tradition. In those days, the newly appointed Dean of the Faculty of Arts, Letters and Social Sciences implemented innovative measures to give new life to the intellectual tradition of your faculty and also to enable it to respond to burning societal issues. One of the new reforms was the institution of the so-called *Mercredi des Grandes Conférences* (Wednesday Grand Conference). This was a moment of a great gathering and scholarly illumination and for once you felt you were in an academic hub. You had the unique chance to listen to the great professors, many of whom you knew only by name. Some were advisers at the presidency or held prominent posts in various ministries but remained heads of departments, vice-deans, vice-rectors, etc. and continued to rule by proxy. Impressive myths circulated amongst students about the intellectual prowess of such professors. Sociology and anthropology students were especially fond of boasting about such luminaries, giving you the impression that they would be sure candidates if ever anyone discovered a missing line in the will of Alfred Nobel that hinted at a Nobel Prize in fields such as Anthropology and Sociology.

But there was another side to the *Mercredi des Grandes Conférences*, a more beautiful side. There were many a student who attended it for the sake of the intellectual discussions. But others came for something more, the after-conference refreshment simply referred to as the 'post'. The name 'post' came from the fact that during defence periods in your faculty, there were often extra guests, students and non-students who roamed the corridors of the faculty waiting for the refreshments that followed such academic activities. These ones, sometimes so well-dressed beyond any suspicion that food could be their problem at all, brought a particular ambience to the whole show. The rapturous applause and ululations that followed the declaration of the final marks of the candidate by the jury was often the work of such self-invited guests, often more zealous than the real guests.

After each session of the *Grande Conférence*, the eminent professors would be treated to a sumptuous dinner in the staff room of the faculty building, just one floor above the Dean's office. Formerly, the moderator of the debate used to announce at the end of the whole exercise that there would be some refreshments reserved exceptionally for panellists and members of staff. Well, in a university where students were fond of social gate-crashing, such an announcement was a recipe for mayhem. Thus, to dissuade the usual adventurers, in subsequent debates, there was a discretionary silence on the part of the organisers as to the "post-conference". Nevertheless, die-hard Thomases would always hover around the faculty building, just in case... So, you who had often come for the intellectual promise of the debates decided one day to also join the bandwagon. You left the house, dressed like a proper gentleman going to a highly intellectual event. You put on your favourite black shirt and tucked in a blue-black pair of trousers. You were drawn to the symbolism of dressing in black when you studied the life of Giuseppe Mazzini in secondary school. It was the colour of revolutionary idealism and endurance. You added a red tie to the combination, not forgetting your brown pair of shoes, well-oiled and shining. You had been battling with that pair of shoes for many months. Its sole had peeled off but you had to do everything possible to keep it going. So, a cobbler in the student neighbourhood gave it a thorough facelift and it became new again. The shoe tradition was well respected and you were in time for the *Mercredi des Grandes Conferences*.

The debate on that day was on mob justice and went on for a protracted time. Some two professors particularly monopolised the discussion, delving into deep theoretical discussions on the French justice system. You wondered why they took such pains to lecture you on the French system while the issue at hand involved the Cameroonian legal system. Some students began clapping insistently when any one of those two took the floor. In Ngoa-ekelle, that was a way of telling the speechmaker that their time was up, that they needed to cut short their prolegomena and pass on the microphone. Well, they seemingly mistook that for popular approval of their ideas and went on and on with their long treatises and tirades; and by the time they finished, a cross-section of the audience had left the amphitheatre. However, the more 'committed' students stayed behind, and like in a dream, the debate finally came to an end. Nothing was announced, you were invited to the next session in two weeks. That was disappointing, but not for the Thomases. Is it not Achebe's Eneke who says since hunters have learnt to shoot without missing, birds have also learnt to fly without perching? So, it came to pass that two friends who had bidden each other farewell at the frontage of Amphi 700 would accidentally meet some minutes later in front of the Faculty building, no longer at ease, but having to face the reality of student life.

Upon leaving the Amphitheatre 700, you thought of taking the road that passed in front of the Rectorate and the Court of Caiaphas, but later changed your mind because you wanted to avoid coming across someone who might know you. The Court of Caiaphas was the name a good friend of yours versed in Biblical matters gave to the scoreboard, popularly known as *babillard* in French. It was a place where anyone who had passed through that university must deny themselves at least three times. You are gripped by the aura of that mythic wall of tribulations. *Le babillard.* Walls of agony and tribulations. Anxiety incarnate. Sometimes, before facing that wall, you murmur a confidential prayer, a sign of the cross (even though not a Catholic). You might have written the exams with utter self-confidence, you might have burnt the midnight candle, one truth remained permanent: the wall had its say, irrespective of your desires. The wall decided your fate. Sometimes you left the scoreboard with light feet, poised to conquer the world, crossing *Carrefour Condom* and *Parlement* with music in your heart.

Most often, the wall's decision converted its victim into a doppelgänger. Checking your marks on the board, stretching your neck, disbelieving your eyes in broad daylight, hoping to be mistaken, wishing something could change even in the act and process of looking, pinning your finger on the name, dragging it past the matriculation number, percentage, coefficient and final mark columns. You cannot deny your name. It is yours. It is you. Self-fragmentation. De-familiarisation. Self-alienation. By your side: someone jubilating, ululating, ejaculating for their, sometimes surprisingly, good results. By good results, something like an 11/20. Resigned to your fate, you look around and wonder like Skeeter Davis "why people around you go on existing, why the birds in the sky go on singing when it is the end of the world, of your world..." There you stand, like a fallen albatross, wings clipped, forced to complain to the merciless Ngoa-ekelle gods. *Requête, i.e.,* an official letter of complaint to the course instructor or Head of Department, hardly leads you anywhere. The wall produced thousands of casualties. Some were forced to go back home in partial delirium, not knowing what to explain to themselves or to their parents.

> *Yea, though I walk through the valley of the shadow of death, I will fear no evil: for thou art with me; thy rod and thy staff they comfort me. Thou preparest a table before me in the presence of mine enemies: thou anointest my head with oil; my cup runneth over. Psalms 23:4-5*

So, you finally took the road that passed through Jerusalem in the rear of the main library building. Jerusalem was the name given to the public space in front of the Theatre Arts Amphi and Geography Amphi (opposite the Rectorate) during the student revolution, the place where Minister Jacques Fame Ndongo was soaked by rain as he sought to appease protesting students who were demanding improvements in student conditions and a clear and radical redefinition of the statute of university students in the entire republic. In hindsight, it was a wise decision because the area was deserted. You found yourself rather timidly amongst the amorphous multitude in front of the Faculty building. Amorphous because, whenever there was an opportunity to eat and drink on campus, all the Twelve Tribes of Israel gathered: there were regular students like yourself; there were those who had been weeded out of the university ecosystem by the irreversible verdict of the ever-unpredictable scoreboard; there were those whose marks had disappeared into the Bermuda Triangle of the University and who, after fruitless letters of complaint, led limbo lives, not knowing for themselves if they were still students or not; living and partly living, leaving and partly leaving; there were those who had simply given up university studies and entered the visa networks that flourished in the student quarter, looking for ways to leave the country and there were those who had simply never sat in a lecture hall but who were 'friends' of the university and could find ways of eating regularly in the school restaurant. Most of these people lived in the student quarter or its vicinity. Some of them would sniff the scent of free rice and beer kilometres away and in less than no time, arrive at the scene, more confident and better dressed than the actual guests. The University of Yaoundé 1 was a grey area and since it had no end-of-year convocation ceremony, unlike the Anglo-Saxon University of Buea, no one knew who was in and who was out, or who was progressing and who was regressing. Those who came to that institution with emerging embryonic high school identities found themselves totally ground by the centrifugal grinding mill of 'fac' realities, with their lives taking unforeseen paths, for better or for worse.

> They have mixed it all together
> Everything! They have mixed everything!
> And how can I find it when they have mixed it all
> With so many things?
> (*The Beautyful Ones,* Ayi Kwei Armah)

As you waited, the coast began to clear. There were promising signs. There was *the service traiteur* (catering service). Different shapes and sizes of silver pots were being offloaded from the bus in front of the faculty building and taken by some hefty men to the third floor of the building. The lecturers and support staff started streaming in. It was clear that most of the lecturers who made it to the dinner were not even present in the debate hall. On the contrary, only few of the panellists bothered to come for the refreshments. You say that without any fear of contradiction because you were amongst the first students to line up at the entrance to that building, counting those who climbed the steps of promise. Perhaps the ministerial Professors had more urgent business to attend to. But they had ready-made replacements. So, you hovered around, waiting. During the waiting, some students, especially the female ones, had their eyes fixed on their phones, smiling responsively in the process as if they were responding to romantic messages from their loved ones. By then, mobile phones were not so common and to receive a call (preferably during a public ceremony) was a mark of social distinction. Those who owned phones were either from well-to-do families or were some of those ladies with a 'fiancé' or 'fiancés' abroad. You did not own one, but you owned a desktop (which was still a rarity amongst university students), thanks to a correspondence programme with one school in the UK. But apart from its vital function, the mobile phone was also a way of passing time, of showing partial interest in one's surroundings and of zealous idleness, so to speak. However, even the phone modernists cast a casual but loaded wink on the third floor of the faculty building to scrutinise the state of affairs.

The period of waiting was an occasion for the parade of power, of knowing who's who in the faculty. Apart from the faculty support staff, who always acted as if they were more important than the Dean and the academic staff, there was another breed of intermediaries who reminded you of your place in that particular context of power.

They were the go-betweens, student assistants of the professors who were often on errands in the faculty building, enabling them to build ties of affinity, friendship and sometimes complicity with the faculty support staff. Occasionally, one of them would approach the well-guarded precincts and smile at the security man:

"Mon commandant, c'est toi?" (My dear commander, is it you?)

"Oui c'est moi, mon docteur." (Oh yes, I am the one, my doctor)

Well, that was a form of mutual massaging for none of them was *commandant* or *Docteur* yet. Yes, these *Docteurs* were deans in the making, even though they were already acting like them. They came and passed. Sometimes, one of them would answer (or claim to be answering) a phone call, nodding his head to the rhythm of *"Oui, Monsieur le Professeur" "Oui, Monsieur le Directeur"*. Time passed and bellies began to bubble as they imagined what was on the menu upstairs. On the second floor of the faculty building, it was taking an eternity for the coast to clear. You waited. Some of the feasters in the Upper Room, a kind of Cenacle, especially the young 'chefs', added insult to injury by bringing their plates closer to the balcony, making the multitude throw glances at them from below, with a mixture of admiration, imploration or outright outrage. At the entrance, even the half-distracted ones who usually pretended to be waiting for some superior motif than food increasingly ran out of patience.

At dusk, no amount of artifice, especially by those idly busy on their phones, could conceal the fact that they were all waiting for food. Those who had sat far away, under the popular jacaranda tree above the English Department, started closing in like locusts as it got darker and darker, making it more and more difficult to distinguish faces. *"La nuit, tous les chats sont gris"* (At night all cats look grey). Just like in the school restaurant, there was the usual humiliation of the female students who were seen as intruders into the male world of the intrepid hunt for public food. So, many a female student was greeted with the usual *"ushhhhh, on me donne je coupe la tête, je prends le bas."* (ushhhhh, if they offer me that one, I will cut the head and take the bottom). And then the giggles followed, even amongst those who had preferred to solve the head and bottom equation in their hearts and minds. But there were always the rowdy boys, who from the very beginning, made no secret of the fact that they were there to eat, and nothing else. They often defied all social etiquettes when their bellies ran out of patience. One of them shouted:

"Mais, nous on veut seulement manger. Ces mêmes gens ont fréquenté à l'époque où le gouvernement leur donnait à manger njo. Ils ne payaient même pas de pension. Et de surcroît, on leur donnait même un salaire." [1]

Others laughed, corroborated, or merely sighed in approval as if the guy had just expressed their mind. However, such protests did not move anyone. The professors seemed to take their time. Some were even fearful that such foolhardy statements could jeopardise an entire evening of waiting. By a mere look, they implored such rowdy elements to keep calm and have faith that the mountaintop was within sight; that they would all reach there and have their feast in due time.

"Weyyyyy les gars, même les Profs mangent comme ça que nous les étudiants pauvres très affamés on va faire comment?" [2]

Came another salvo, unpredictably and in a rather shrill voice. That occasioned a wave of laughter that rippled across the impatient and expectant mouths. In those days, the term *"étudiants pauvres très affamés"* (poor and severely famished students) became a buzzword of self-derision amongst students. That was due to the country's reaching the completion point of what the Bretton Woods Institutions called 'PPTE' (HIPC) i.e., heavily indebted poor country initiative. The attainment of the completion point was a great cause

---

1. In English, it could be translated thus: "But, the only thing we want is to eat. These same people went to school at a time when the government gave students food for free. They never even used to pay school fees. More so, they were entitled to a salary."
2. "Weyyyyy guys, if professors eat in this way, what more of poor and heavily hungry students like us?"

of celebration by the regime and its cohorts. The National Radio and Television reported it as a great success for the regime and above all, that of its eternal leader, Paul Biya. Motions of support were addressed to the president, asking him to stand for the next elections for that great achievement. Some state media journalists made a career as specialists of the HIPC initiative. In those days, everything was dependent on the HIPC completion point. But that is another story.

As it approached 7:00 PM, you wondered if you should renounce the yearning for the official dinner and hurry down the University Restaurant with your remaining 100 frs for a plate of rice and chicken. Nevertheless, the aroma coming down from the Cenacle and the imagination of the delectable menu made you consider the option not worth taking. You had hope. The University of Yaoundé 1 was a school of endurance, resistance and patience. Good things come to those who wait, says the Bible. *"Mouiller c'est mouiller, il n'y a pas de mouiller sec"*[3] say the students of the University of Yaoundé 1.

The waiting continued. Now and then, one professor would call one of his closest students whom he identified in the multitude downstairs to come up. The student in question would explain to the guard that he was responding to the call of *P-r-o-f-e-s-s-e-u-r* (Professor) so so and so or that *"Monsieur le doyen"* had called for him *p-e-r-s-o-n-n-e-l-l-e-m-e-n-t* (personally). After some moments of doubt and hesitation, the guard would let them cross to the green zone. So, the lucky one would climb the stairs with the gait of those responding to some serious official business. Seeing someone sail through the green zone was always a source of envy for all and sundry. At such a moment, the army of worms in your stomach croaked with renewed violence. Well, does not the Bible say that many are called but few are chosen?

Soon, the coast began to clear. The clearest sign came when the

---

3. An expression that stresses the need to assume one's choice and not to give up midstream.

Dean descended the stairs with his aide and was moving towards his office, on the second floor. You always had respect for him; he was a man of dignity and from every indication, his appointment as Dean was not going to change much about his characteristic simplicity. It was one of those few appointments that any objective person in the entire faculty greeted with excitement. It was well deserved, which was rare amongst many cases. He taught you French poetry in your second year. He would rebuke the entire class: "I am reading a stanza from Baudelaire's poem and you guys remain so indifferent? What kind of students are these?" Even when he rebuked or sounded bitter, there was always a lovely affect around his personality. Well, of course, many of you enjoyed poetry and did well in the exams. But then, he had to understand that students had different problems. While in class, their minds were sometimes not preoccupied with the likes of Baudelaire's 'albatross', 'cat', 'spleen', 'correspondence', but rather, with very practical, prosaic and worldly things. They were the things of everyday life that made Baudelaire quite distant and obscure.

As if appalled by the number of students waiting downstairs, the Dean retreated and asked the security guards:

"What is happening here?" He asked as if he hailed from a different country, or a different planet altogether.

"They want to eat, *Son Excellence Monsieur le Doyen!*" One of the guards responded.

"Then let them come in," said the Dean as he walked into his office in his usual gentle and carefree manner.

The students responded with euphoria and all sorts of compliments were showered on the Dean. At that time, you felt like Ali Baba at the mouth of the vault of fortune even though in hindsight, you found the Dean's order a bit rash and populist. He made the guard seem like an overzealous and sadistic servant. There needed to be some order, given that the multitude could not enter the staff room at the same time. The number of students waiting had indeed diminished due to impatience, but it was still considerably high.

The two guards, accordingly, freed the entrance and everyone rushed in, elbowing, smashing and pushing one another along the way. The Dean had just encouraged the storming of the Bastille, inadvertently. As you made your way upstairs amidst the hubbub, you felt your feet lighter than usual. You developed muscle cramps. It felt as if you were suspended in the air and your entire body had lost a sense of distinction and individuality amidst the crowd. It is only when you arrived at the corridor of the staff/dining room on the third floor and had the adequate space around you to examine your entire body that you noticed that your right sock was hitting coarsely on bare cement: the outsole and the heel of your right shoe had completely peeled off during the scramble. You were distraught. Should you adopt a specific gait and still make it to the staff room, and at least give meaning to the sacrifice or should you simply succumb to your outrageous fortune?

The truth is: even those who had reached the mountaintop, after scavenging through the pots and plates on the long table that lined the wall, could only find crumbs of jollof rice and half-full bottles of Coke and Fanta. There was no wine left and no miracle could turn empty plates into rice and empty bottles into wine. It was Yaoundé, not Cana. It became more and more evident to you that your cause was lost. Sigh answered sigh and curse answered curse amongst the multitude as even those who scraped the bottom of the silver pots and emptied the plates for professorial rice and spaghetti left more disappointed than those who had not been able to make it into the staffroom at all. Gradually, like a masquerade returning from a poorly entertained funeral on a rainy day, you descended the stairs, trying to look for the disintegrated part of your shoe on the half-lit staircase to no avail.

You began the long march home, with a heavy heart, sobbing to yourself. Your home, or rather your room, was not far from the campus. Nevertheless, homecoming was the Great Trek. Matters were made worse by a vexing drizzle. You removed the sock from your right foot and pocketed it while holding part of the shoe in your right hand, making sure it did not come close to your black shirt. At some point, you felt like throwing the shoe into the surrounding thicket. But then you looked at its brother, seemingly very strong and you consoled yourself that the right foot could be repaired subsequently. You made sure you put the pressure of your gait on the left foot, the shoed one, to lessen the burden on your right foot. The precaution did not help much and as you walked down the road, you recalled the eloquent statement by the Minister of Higher Education, Jacques Fame Ndongo, a veritable wordsmith, speechifying during the conferral of the *doctor honoris causa* to Abdou Diouf, then Secretary-General of La Francophonie by the University of Yaoundé 1: "Welcome to this citadel of science where every gravel on the Ngoa-ekelle hill is a crystal of knowledge." That was true. But the gravel meant nothing abstract or metaphorical to you as you trekked home. It was a concrete reality.

As you trudged down, the gravels under your feet connived with the worms in your stomach and the desolation in your heart to create a rather contrary effect on the diplomat in black or the Giuseppe Mazzini that you were. You knew your night was going to be longer than usual. The stores selling bread and chocolate in the student residential area were closed for it was getting to 8:00 PM. The University Restaurant had also closed. Even the makeshift puff-puff/beans bistros in the neighbourhood were vacated earlier than usual due to the rain. Otherwise, you would have moved into one of those bistros and confidently order for the usual equation of beans for 35 frs and puff-puff for 65 frs. Like Mami Julie, those bistro sellers called 'la mère' irrespective of their age, were always willing to sell on credit. It was not uncommon for a typical student to enter the bistro and in a confident mode, pass his order: *"La mère, haricot de 35 et beignets de 65. Avec le piment du village"*. After eating, he would, in an almost philosophical attitude, tell *la mère: "On gère ça demain, la mère. Tu ajoutes ça à celui d'hier et demain on va gérer les deux. Tu comprends non, la mère?"* Like Kourouma's Salimata, the many *la mère* in Bonas never got tired of selling on credit. Whether students always honoured their commitments is a different story.

Your frustration was compounded by an incident that had occurred to your dad the week before. After twenty-seven years of service, he came to Yaoundé to "follow up" his pension dossier in the Ministry of Basic Education. He spent two weeks with you in your student room, going to the ministry daily. However, his dossier could not even be traced. On one occasion, he was told by the official that he (the official) did not understand your father's English. The next day, you opted to accompany him to the ministry to act as his interpreter. After a long day of waiting in the queue, you were told to *"revenir demain"* (come back tomorrow). It was said in the usual way that ministerial functionaries spoke to their subjects; in the manner that distinguished between those who mattered and those who were pure matter; that turned the one-metre square office space into a national territory where the occupier could give or take life at will. From experience, you had expected the officer to at least ask you for a long list of photocopies. Sometimes, when one had all the required photocopies at hand, one could be asked to bring a photocopy of oneself. Instead, you were asked to come back tomorrow. When you sought to explain the case further, you were interrupted by a slim woman covered in a forest of wig and in shoes reminiscent of 18th century colonial administrators' housewives. Her zealousness was typical of secretaries in Biya's republic. She made it clear to you that the orders of her boss needed to be followed without protest nor complaint. The following day, you had classes the entire day. Your father carried his Cross alone.

At about 6 PM you got a phone call inquiring if you were the son of Mr.… *"Ton père est au CHU. Chambre numéro 219), il a eu un petit incident. Mais, c'est léger. Néanmoins, si tu peux nous joindre là-bas maintenant ça serait bien."*[4] This could as well be a false assurance for a critical situation. With a thumping heart, you left the campus and boarded a taxi to the University Teaching Hospital. When you arrived, your dad seemed fine. He had been knocked down by a car at a road junction on his way from the ministry and had sustained some bruises, especially on his knees. After two hours of treatment, you left for the student quarter where you lived. The hospital bill was settled by the driver who acknowledged his fault in the incident. Your father swore never to come to Yaoundé again for his retirement benefits. The following day, he was on his long way home to Nkambe, with nothing but a bunch of ministerial decisions related to his dossier. Everything was in French. At the travel agency, he handed you the last ten thousand francs note he had in his pocket but you refused to take. You preferred to manage the leftovers of your pocket allowance while waiting for the end of the month. Upon returning to the village, the accident took its toll on him and he visited the local health centre for an entire month.

With these thoughts in mind, you arrived at your student hostel, took a bath and tried to bury your head in your books, to no avail. You proceeded to perform thorough archaeology of the pockets of your trousers and shirts, including those that you hardly wore. That was a childhood habit that only rarely yielded any results. You turned on the desktop to tame the worms with some tunes of Dolly Parton, Kenny Rogers or Norah Jones which you had saved in the music files of your IBM Pentium II desktop. The machine produced a long-drawn beeping sound and went off. You removed the sloppy floppy disk and tried turning it on again but the White Horse squealed and refused to boot. Night.

---

4. "Your dad is hospitalised in CHU (University Teaching Hospital). Room number 219. He had a small incident but it is nothing serious. However, if you could meet us there now, it would be fine"

THE BELL

Le temps adore les malheureux. (Time adores the unlucky)
(*Anté-peuple,* Sony Labou Tansi)

"You can wipe off these words if you like. I just thought, perhaps, just perhaps, the person coming in could also be a Wagner fan like myself," Thomas mused as he showed you the writings on the wall. He and his partner were handing you the keys to what would be your new apartment after close to five years in the student residential area in Bayreuth. You had rented the apartment in anticipation of the beautyful one with whom you were going to walk down the aisle.

"Do not bother, for me it's okay. My colleagues and I offer a city tour of Bayreuth and it is often about Wagner. So, I am part of Wagner's inner clique. But even if I wipe the expression on the wall, I cannot wipe the view of the Wagner *Festspiel Haus* from the horizon of that window!," you said jokingly, as you moved close to the window.

"Oh yes, it is one of the things I like about the location of this apartment," Thomas' partner responded.

She moved close to you at the window, to behold for the last time that wholesome view of Bayreuth's cultural peak. Before now, she had assumed a silent presence as Thomas showed you around the house. Gradually, she became more involved and expressive, chipping in one or two comments about the state of the apartment they were handing over to you.

From the window of the living room, one could have an impeccable view of the imposing *Festspiel Haus*, the opera hall which hosted the annual Wagner Festival in the Bavarian city of Bayreuth. When they left, not before you signed some paperwork on the state of the apartment at the time of handing over, you took a second tour around the apartment. When you came back to the living room, the expression on the wall shone again with energy and sharpness: "*Die Musik ist die Sprache der Leidenschaft.*" (Music is the language of passion). It was crafted in dexterous calligraphy, with musical notes at the end of the sentence. In black against a white background. Under it, the name of its author in smaller characters, *Richard Wagner*. You moved close to the window and took another view of the daffodils of rooftops in its purview.

Not far from your dwelling were the tower of an old church building and the minaret of a mosque. Further afield, beyond the snow-covered rooftops was the sumptuous structure of the *Festspiel Haus*, perched on top of a hillock. As you stood there looking at the structure, it seemed to you both like the beak of a bird and a coxcomb, or perhaps a giant red feather pinned on a black cap, a symbol of distinguished achievement. But its towering and bristling edifice also seemed like the tip of a ballistic missile pointed at the city of Bayreuth. You had never really come close to that structure. You imagined how the interior could look like. You learnt that to get a ticket for the annual Wagner Festival, one needed to book it some years before the actual event. You did not know the exact figure but guessed it would be a luxury for anyone.

As you looked once more at the imposing structure that settled comfortably like a giant duck on the distant hill, you recalled an entry in the diary of Edward Said about his surprise at the letter of invitation to attend a meeting with Jean-Paul Sartre, Michel Foucault and Simone de Beauvoir in early January 1979: "At first I thought the cable was a joke of some sort. It might just as well have been an invitation from Cosima and Richard Wagner to come to Bayreuth, or from TS Eliot and Virginia Woolf to spend an afternoon at the offices of the *Dial*. It took me about two days to ascertain from various friends in New York and Paris that it was indeed genuine, and far less time than that to dispatch my unconditional acceptance".

While the Bayreuth of Richard Wagner remained a desire for Edward Said, Wagner's Bayreuth was your reality for several years. It was the city that opened its arms to you on 25th April 2010 when you spent your first night in a foreign continent on the premises of the Red Cross. There had been a communication lag with the university assistant who was supposed to pick you up from the train station upon arrival. As a result of an Internet blackout in parts of Yaoundé on the eve of your departure, you had not read the email in which he gave you some directives. On the whole, everything happened in a blitz: within two days, you withdrew your new passport from the DGSN[5] in Yaoundé, submitted it for the visa, obtained the visa, booked the flight ticket and travelled. But a situation that made you initially anxious soon turned into one of your first experiences of xenophilic warmth and assurance, thanks to the hospitality of your circumstantial hosts.

The following morning, after serving you breakfast, one of the workers walked with you up to Geschwister-Scholl Platz[6], the seat of your doctoral school. Little did you know that on the precincts of that structure, you were going to experience a community of African and non-African colleagues that became your new academic and human family. But it was later on, after having pitched your luggage in the secretariat of the institute and attended your first German class with "Guten Morgen" as your only foreknowledge, that you were taken to what would become your home for the following half-decade.

Bussardweg, the student residential quarter, your new home, was a curious place. As you entered the compound through the main

5. Délégation Générale de Sûreté Nationale.
6. Named after the two Scholl siblings, Hans and Sophie, who were members of the White Rose peaceful resistance movement against Nazism. They were guillotined in 1943 by the Nazism regime for distributing anti-establishment flyers.

entrance, the nearby bus stop read 'Rheinstrasse' (Rhein Street), but you had to enter the space through the backdoor to unearth the somewhat obscure signpost that read 'Bussardweg'. It was after some days that Frau Fteimi, your German language teacher made you understand that 'weg' meant 'road' and that 'Bussard' was a hawk-like bird of prey. You enjoyed the sense of good neighbourliness and friendships amongst the international students in Bussardweg. But there were always these disturbing moments when the same European friend with whom you had boozed in the general kitchen and talked passionately about life in 'Africa' and their country the previous night would meet you the following morning in the yard or along the corridor of Bussardweg and totally ignore you or, simply pre-empt the encounter with a ten-metre distant 'hi', accompanied by a two-millisecond long smile. No more, no less. While you were there, wreathed in smiles. Apart from such weird moments, some international relations and friendships were born in Bussardweg, some lasting less longer than others.

Since your room was close to the yard that separated the three main blocks of the residence, your windowpane was constantly caressed by hybrid sounds of German, Amharic, Swahili, Turkish, Arabic, English, French, Spanish, Czech and Portuguese produced by its student tenants. You might not have understood everything (or anything) from some of these languages, but what filtered into your room underlined the beauty and diversity of human cultures. In your new home, you began to miss those voices and their sweet fusion in your mind. Bussardweg stood for invaluable memories of time spent with colleagues and whenever any Bayreuth alumnus travelled the world for conferences, they were likely to meet an African researcher in the humanities who would tell them nostalgically about their time in Bayreuth and in Bussardweg specifically. The experience with the language was often one of the most memorable encounters, for many of you had not studied the language before coming to Germany. Whenever one was faced with a real-life situation requiring linguistic interaction, in front of the supermarket cashier, for instance, the verbs and nouns they had learnt and domesticated in their very initial German class flew off sarcastically, leaving them barely with prepositions and interjections that could not flesh out their thoughts to the point of comprehension. For some, the adaptation phase was short, but for others, it took a bit longer.

But, after a few months, the language took its revenge systematically on everyone, coming back and sending equivalents in other languages packing, replacing them with German cognates. Thus, certain spaces in Bayreuth brought back specific memories of colleagues while some German expressions had specific (and in some cases existential) meaning to many an international student trying to adapt to a new environment and culture. They included *Entschuldigung* (I'm sorry/Excuse me); *genau!* (exactly!), *Angebot* (special offer), *Mülltrennung* (waste separation), *Polizei* (police), *Hausmeister* (caretaker), *Flohmarkt* (flea market), *Staubsauger* (vacuum cleaner), *kostenlos* (free), *Fernbeziehung* (long-distance relationship), *verborten* (forbidden), *Vorsicht!/Achtung!* (look out!), *Super!/Prima!* (fantastic), *echt?* (for real?), *typisch* (typical), *nein* (no), *immer* (always), *Frau* (Mrs, Miss, Ms); *Vertrag* (contract), *Kündigung* (contract cancellation), *Doktormütter/Doktorvater* (thesis supervisor), *Urlaub* (holiday, leave), *Ausländeramt* (immigration office), *Umsteigen* (change of bus), *Lieblings-* (favourite…), *normalerweise* (normally), *Verspätung* (delay, as with the train/bus), *kein Problem* (no problem), *Krankenversicherung* (health insurance), *Grieß* (semolina), *Gleis* (platform), *Suppenhuhn* (stewing hen), *Wasser mit/ohne Kohlensäure* (carbonated/non-carbonated water), *Termin* (appointment), *Fiktionsbescheinigung* (fictional certificate), *Geschenk* (gift), *Fahrschein* (ticket), *Rathaus* (city council), *gerade aus* (straight ahead), *Bitte* (please), *Moment!* (a moment, please!), *ein bisschen* (just a bit), *Überweisung* (money transfer), *Ausweis* (identity card), *Briefkasten* (letter box), *Hausaufgabe* (school assignment), *Bis später* (see you later), *Tschüss* (bye-bye). Even when students were speaking in Swahili, Arabic, French or English, such words spontaneously articulated themselves in German as if to preserve their beauty, texture and density. Mind you that in German all nouns begin with capital letters. Meaning that all nouns are proper nouns. You had colleagues who became synonymous to *alles klar* (alright), *ach so* (oh, I see), *deswegen* (that is why) by virtue of their speech mannerisms that incorporated these German words and interjections so naturally and indiscriminately.

The evenings you spent in the general kitchen under the close chronometric watch and decibel policing of the Hausmeister, telling stories and eating *ndole, eru, attiéké, ugali, injera, goraasa, palm nut soup, ogbono soup,* etc. were full of fun. Though most of you hailed from English-speaking Africa, the diversity of your Englishes came together in a delightful dissonance of accents, a befitting tribute to the illustrious pioneers of British empire-building such as Mungo Park, David Livingstone, Lord Kitchener, Frederick Lugard and Cecil Rhodes. If one agrees with the assertion of that irreverent Irish playwright, George Bernard Shaw, that the United States and Great Britain are two countries divided by a common language, then one is close to grasping what that means. And so, *months* became *menses, snacks* became *snakes, girls* became *galls, pepper* became *paper, back* became *bag, work* became *wake, but* became *bat, church* became *chech;* while *fungus* became *foungous,* usually with exciting and hilarious (but also inauspicious) consequences. During weekends, those evening sessions in the kitchen served as a preamble to disco nights in the gala hall of Bussardweg or in other disco spaces such as Borracho, Iwalewa Haus or Glashaus where 'Afro-night' parties were the order of the day.

After just a few hours in your new apartment, which was a stark contrast to Bussardweg, it felt lonely. No doubt, you had a lot of space. No doubt it was a sign of transition from student life to responsible adulthood. But it had its downside. It was all dead silent, no sign of life beyond Wagner's expression on the wall and on the horizon.

Ever since you began packing into the apartment, you did not meet a single soul in the compound. "If by some chance I forget to buy salt, I will likely eat an insipid meal, not even any neighbour to turn to." You thought to yourself. Your new home reminded you of a colleague who was studying in a Northern German town. He used to call you on the phone and describe in bleak terms his solitary life in a hostel that seemed more like a graveyard. Hardly were there students around, or most of them were engaged in part-time jobs, leaving home very early and only coming back late at night. He envied the rather communal lifestyle in Bussardweg that you described to him on the phone.

"I swear to God, bro, whenever I come back to my block every evening, I feel as if I am entering the mouth of a gigantic grave."

You sometimes felt he was dramatizing the situation but the gloomy tone in which he expressed his fate drew your empathy. Not surprising an account, though, from someone whose research topic was on pessimism in the poetry of Thomas Hardy!

Since you had not yet bought a bed in your new apartment, you spent the first night on two pieces of bed sheets spread on the wooden floor of the living room. That seemed threadbare but after such a long day of hectic packing and unpacking, Morpheus did not hesitate to stretch his welcoming hands to you. You were already deep in slumber when you heard an insistent sound of a bell. You tried to persist in your slumber but could not resist its tension. Its crescendo built up in your drowsy consciousness and you woke up and moved to the window as if to vent curses on whoever was ringing the malignant bell. Was it rung by an automated system or by the physical hands of a catechist or a parish timekeeper? By the way, why didn't Thomas and his girlfriend tell you that this sound-scape was also part of the special features of the apartment? You conjectured, in vain exasperation. You wondered how much noise pollution could be allowed in a society like Germany with strict laws on decibels. You remembered listening to a German missionary in

Ethiopia who came to your Bayreuth church to fundraise for his evangelization campaign. He needed money to beef up the sound system of his mission through a state-of-the-arts musical band, mobile rostrum and above all, some powerful loudspeakers. "Unlike in Germany where there are legal limits on sound volume depending on the time, in Ethiopia, there are no such limitations." He told the church members, with a sense of Hallelujah! When offertory time came for members to support his mission, to praise God by giving, you decided to be tight-fisted out of conviction.

The bell stopped ringing after a few minutes and you went back to sleep amidst sighs. Hours later, the drama resumed. You woke up again. It was 4 AM by your watch. That time around, you noticed it was not a single bell ringing, rather two bells answering and challenging each other. You then remembered that apart from the Lutheran Church close to your new abode, there was another church, the Evangelical Church, about three hundred metres away. You were the collateral damage of the struggle between these two churches. You stood helplessly at the window. Noticing you could not help the situation, you contented yourself with the beauty of the moon. It was in full bloom. You had not witnessed that beautiful view for many years and your mind went back to the different hypotheses which, as children, you mused and argued about the visual content of the moon: a man splitting firewood; Jesus spreading his hands; a man beating his wife and so on. Back then, you thought that when you grow old, you would be able to unravel such mysteries.

As the quarrels between the two bells subsided, you went back to your makeshift bed. But could no longer sleep. Your "bed" had lost its previous softness. Between sleep and wakefulness, your mind went down memory lane, resurrecting memories of bells that punctuated your childhood, in your home village in Cameroon.

The image of your timekeeper in primary school came sailing into your mind, a certain, Tata John. He was studious, intelligent, always first in your class. He hailed from Ngaki-Mansa quarter. You were the only one who could lock horns with him in the class tests and exams. As early as 6 AM, he was already on the school ground, ready to bang the school bell. He had a wristwatch that was offered to him by the Headmaster of your school, Mr Ngeh. You have always thought of it as a yoke because the metal works of the object formed a rather too large a structure round the lean wrist of John. Maybe it had to be that big to incarnate the time of the entire school? Well, whatever the intention to get a watch that big was, the object was more of a punishment for John's tiny wrist— a burden on his body and soul. The watch was one of the most invaluable properties of your newly opened government primary school. By then, school property meant nothing more than a few English textbooks, a football and handball and two sets of jerseys for the school football and handball teams.

John handled the school watch with absolute care, only wearing it during school hours. He was a perfect example of public mentality, of the distinction between private and public good. During the long break, as you were still making your way to the school canteen, John would stand menacingly near the bell, steadfast to sound it exactly at the appointed time: 12:30 PM. Sometimes, as break time drew to a close, he abstained from any class discussion, his eyes and mind fixed on the impending hour, minute and second. It seems whenever he didn't have enough for the break, his punctuality filled in the emptiness of his stomach. One day, during break time, you summoned a class five girl whom you wanted to chat up through one of your friends, Daniel. Daniel was an expert in such artifices. He had learnt the art of dating at an early age. Though he was not brilliant in classwork, you used to envy him for his bravado and foolhardiness. Sometimes you felt it was worthless scoring 20/20 in an Arithmetic test and being sick of a girl's love and yet lack the courage to declare it for fear of being rejected. To declare one's love for a girl at your young age was against family authority, Sunday school lessons and pastoral sermons. But in the face of Jane's beauty, the interdiction "Thou shall not commit fornication" lost its foreboding connotation. At that age, it was not clear to you what lovers do. But you knew you wanted Jane, the class five girl. You would pray for nights asking God to understand your situation, imploring His kindness, asking Him to forgive you even before you committed any sin. You sought God's complicity in your crime by convincing Him of your genuine love for Jane and by assuring Him that you were not going to commit any fornication. It was just love.

There was Jane, in front of you, fresh, oval face and innocent smile. Love stood right there for you. Unable to go straight to the point, you began by asking her how she spent her day, what she had eaten at the canteen, what she would do after school, etc. You avoided the present. You built the momentum and summoned the energy to release the magic expression "I love you" and chain it up with a carefully rehearsed love poem you had found in the *Sheldon Book of Verse*. Uttering that expression was like staking the essence of your inner self away since you did not know how Jane would react. Your heart thumped. But just as you resolved to let loose your expression of love for Jane, the Hand mercilessly fell on the Bell. If only John could imagine the damage he had done to your love, your future, your dreams, and your life.

"I have to hurry to class. Our teacher gives any late comer ten strokes of the cane!" Jane said to me, visibly poised for her class.

"Okay, see you after school hours." You said, confused, disappointed, and barely understanding the echoes of your own voice, for your voice resonated in your ears like a stranger.

You knew it was a missed opportunity because her class ended thirty minutes before yours. Baffled, you promised you were going to send her a letter. You had sent her a letter the previous week but she had not replied, telling your middleman that she wanted to hear everything from the horse's own mouth. Now, your chances of success with Jane hung on a thin thread. The wheel of time was turning and you were dying of unrequited love. You watched her hurry to class, knowing that she would revisit you in your sleep at night, to haunt you! You bore a deep grievance against John, this messenger of Time. You also had a moment when you brought time to a standstill, but the ultimate authority as far as pupil power was concerned lay with the timekeeper. You were the flag-bearer or rather the flag hoister. Hoisting the flag was a privilege. At times the flag got warped up like the tape of a radio cassette, or better still, like the nation itself, and you had to bring the piece down while the school looked on, re-knot it properly and with accelerated speed, let it clatter along the pole and then fly graciously in the direction indicated by the wind vain. Then followed the singing of the national anthem. Some verses of the anthem were virtually unsingable to most pupils. While some went ahead with *"they welfare we we we we we we we"* and *"tonkantel"*, others hummed along and then slowly joined in the less tongue-breaking verses of the anthem.

> Those who are blessed with the power
> And the soaring swiftness of the Eagle
> And have flown before.
> Let them go
> I will travel slowly,
> And I too will arrive. (*The Beautyful Ones*, Ayi Kwei Armah)

Hoisting the flag did not carry that enormous power of sounding the bell of Universal Time. Your usual competition with the time-keeper when it came to class performance was now compounded by the damage caused by his overzealous bell. Your classmates hated John. In spite of his brilliance, he was seen as anti-social and was the laughing stock of the girls. You would even say because of his brilliance, given that his performance made him the envy of the class. He was the only one who upheld the English-only policy in your class with missionary zeal and as the Head Boy, he would not hesitate to submit the noisemakers' list to the Headmaster whenever the latter asked for it. John showed no consideration for those who made language errors or could not solve a simple arithmetical equation.

Classmates nicknamed him Abraham Lincoln, not only because of the sense of integrity with which he handled school duty and property but mainly because he bore that serious and slightly contrite demeanour typical of the pioneer Republican president, whose facial wrinkles aptly captured the strain, toil and faith of an entire nation at a crucial point of history. Like Abraham Lincoln, he was a bookworm, a moralist and self-conscious bloke. Others called him Head of State because of the shape and size of his head. To your teachers, the two of you were the ideal images of the pupils that your newly created Government School required. *Discipline, Morality and Punctuality* was the motto of the new school. But in matters of discipline, he was a better icon than you. You were a backbencher and like all backbenchers, you had a way of shrugging off the watchfulness of the school authorities on occasions such as the march-past rehearsals in preparation for the National Youth Day and the National Day. While the frontliners sang the official songs, those at the defence line subverted the wordings of the songs that were meant as praise for the president.

> *I saw Paul Biya in a foreign country*
> *He was selling sugarcane*
> *He was selling two for twenty-five*
> *In the name of the people of Cameroon*

You could not recall the wordings of the original song. But these alternative verses were crystal clear in your memory—how easily the wrong thing clung to the mind!

You were the first batch of Government School Luh, the first government primary school and as pioneer pupils, the Headmaster and his staff placed on the young shoulders of the first batch the dream of the entire village and its coming generations.

"I will not accept anything less than one hundred per cent in both the First School Leaving Certificate and the Common Entrance." Mr Ngeh would vow to the pupils in the morning General Assembly, causing the imploring eyes of pupils from the lower classes to turn to you the Class Seven pupils, in admiration but also with a sense of pity.

He was the brainchild of the one hundred per cent pedigree of GS Ntundip, the neighbouring village where he had taught for many years. You were the frontline soldiers of the school. You might not win the shields in all sporting events, but you had no reason not to beat the other schools in academic warfare. Though the Headmaster's words might not have meant much to some of your mates, they always left a deep impression on you. Your father was also a Headmaster in a different locality and you always had the impression that the Headmaster had concluded a secret pact with your father to keep a particularly watchful eye on you and your sister, Mangwang.

Inasmuch as the pupils shouldered the burden of the first batch, even greater pressure lay on the shoulders of the teachers. The Headmaster was the lone Government teacher. The second Government teacher came years later. The rest were employed by the PTA. Amongst them was Mr Amos Takwa, the one who taught the very first classes in the Baptist Church when the school had just been opened. Every teacher accumulated several roles in the school and community at large. As a bricklayer and a pioneer teacher, he built the foundation of the school. In the Baptist church, Mr Takwa was the interpreter of sermons into Limbum whenever there was a non-Mbum guest pastor in your church. He used to break the gospel into Limbum as if he grew up with Jesus in Jerusalem, Galilee, Gethsemane and Judea. He was your History/Geography, General Knowledge and Civics teacher. Whenever the pupils did not show signs of understanding, he would turn to Limbum and that made the stories even sweeter to the pupils' ears.

So, it is partially in Limbum that you learnt the stories of

Sumanguru Kante of the Sosso Empire, Sundiata Keita of the Mandinka Empire, Kankan Musa of Mali, Usman dan Fodio of the Sokoto Caliphate, Ibrahim Sori of Fouta Djallon, Hannibal's crossing of the Alps, Mungo Park and the Niger River. Not forgetting the way Mr Amos would explain the Peloponnesian wars and life in Athens and Sparta - "Sparta died but never surrendered" –

> *O' la yu shine, a mba ji a toh Sparta, munkeh amlo bji ne kuhu bah pfih mntunfu or samba, oku chuar yi ningnsi ba mi nwah bjir. Ghar bi shi oku bji ba mnseng. Oki kuh waha, yu shi wowi o ring yap ku ba ba bjir i. Nwah bjir hana jim tap bar tap kah, ogi fa wowi pji sef yeni kah, pcheh bong bong kah. Ambu shi ne pmoh fa wowi o mkwingir mbo. Nwah ji bo byingi ji mba ji muje. Gini waha, imba fong a terkah. Om yehni wowi wrestling, gymnastics, ba armah bjir i. Bi ni Sparta om ring hine ha byingi shi oh tapngir chah chah kata oh bji bo shi o tapngir i. And a mba njnwe shi we tap i o tfur ar train we keh a ghar nwe.*

(In Sparta, when a male child reached six or seven years, he was seized and sent directly to the military school. Children still as fresh as freshly tapped palm wine. In that way, when they grow up, what they know best is the art of war. School courses were very hard and painful for boys. They weren't given enough food or clothing. Meaning some of them died during training. For the girls, it was a bit different but not any easier. They were taught physical education, which included wrestling, gymnastics, and combat skills. Spartans believed that healthy women would produce healthy babies. And to be a strong woman you needed to be trained when you were still a girl)

The pupils listened keenly to the detailed description of Spartan life, imagining themselves as possible members of the Spartan army at their young age. It remains to you as an inscrutable mystery how he came to know so much about Asia Minor than any history teacher you have ever come across. He had no professional training in pedagogy but was a seasoned and pragmatic pedagogue. While preparing the class for the Civics Paper of the First School Leaving Certificate, he gave your class the following advice: "When you encounter a question like 'Who is the Cameroon Minister of…?', if you do not know the exact answer, just begin with Mbarga, Owona, Oyono, Mbella, Etoundi, Fouda or Atangana[7] and leave the second name to the marker". In hindsight, you came to doubt if he really meant it. Anyway, the end justifies the means. By that time, the syllabus underwent some forms of indigenization. In the English Reader, for example, the famous John and Mary were gradually being replaced by Mr Namundo, Mrs Ekema, Mr Mbah, Enanga, Mr Ngala, Tabot, Mr Ngwa, Ndi, Tabi, Ngala and other names closer home. But, even as pupils, you asked yourselves why these names in the Reader never featured in the Civics paper. Why was the Minister of this and that never a Mr Ngwa or Mrs Enanga? Why is it that the names in the English Reader never made it to the Civics textbook? Why were Enanga and Namundo always sweeping the compound, and Mr Ndi always taking care of his goats while Mbarga, Mbella and Atangana were 'ministering' over the country?

The Headmaster, Mr Ngeh from Ndu, doubled as a Class Seven teacher and carpenter - occasionally, during his class, a bamboo bench would collapse and he would have to interrupt the class to repair it with the help of the concerned pupils. Never were the exigencies of the pioneer stretched to such limits, both for the master as well as the pupils. Watching Mr Ngeh sweating as he sought to repair the bamboo structure left the pupils with a sense of sympathy but also with admiration for his commitment. You were amazed

7. Names common amongst the Fang-Beti people, President Paul Biya's ethnic group.

by his sense of responsibility. Even though he proscribed Limbum in class, during such moments of comic tension, he would bitterly complain about the government's neglect of the school. *Nje toh jisi ha langa, me ring ha yu kah. Me sang inspector ha sang lar. Well, si bi ku ye ka ambo ibih ba.* (This country of ours, impossible to know how it functions. I have written to the inspector about the issue of benches, to no avail. Well, let us see how this will turn out.) He spoke in his typical Ndu dialect, causing a ripple of giggling across the class in an otherwise sorry sight. But the pupils could only giggle with moderation, for, even in those frustrating moments, Mr Ngeh, would warn that he expected nothing but 100% in the upcoming public exams from the pupils. Under such circumstances, his threatening wish seemed like an illusion.

Before you entered the government school in Class Five, your previous education had been in Catholic School (CS) Luh, one of the two Catholic primary schools in your village at the time and the alma mater of your dad. The latter was part of the first batch of that school. Leaving the Catholic School was not an easy transition for you. It meant disconnection from Catholic friends who could not leave, partly for reasons of denominational loyalty. It meant severance from strict religious discipline and an entire symbolic universe. Though you did not particularly enjoy the Catholic obsession with prayers, at the moment of departure, you felt the pain of separation. You looked back with regret to the beautiful songs, the school choir, and the school band of your alma mater. In those days, the dream of every young pupil was to be a member of the band. Band members commanded particular prestige amongst the pupils. Leaving the Catholic School meant losing claim to its pantheon of football legends and the numerous shields accumulated by the school over the years. Think of Tahkala, the magical striker and Gowon the goalkeeper. You remembered the praise songs that were composed in honour of those legends:

Tahkala our player

Who plays in a wonderful way heyyy

Oyeeee our player
Who plays in a wonderful way heyyy

Tahkala na wa ye
Tahkala oh oh oh na wa ye

They were the pride of the school, the icons of your generation. The last event that you attended in the Catholic School was the farewell ceremony of Father John, the white parish priest. He was the Father Drumont of your community. In preparation for the event, you were asked to contribute two eggs each for Father John. In the end, there were three white Murtala basins of white eggs for the white priest. The song you sang as pupils during that occasion remained with you over these years:

Farewell Father John Willeit,
We weep for missing you

As you are leaving us for your home
Think of us always and pray for us all

Chorus

Goodbye Father John goodbye
We will see you again
But we don't know when.

You were then in Class Four and little did you know that it was also your farewell to the Catholic school. That was a heavy cost to pay for a pioneer batch: having to invent a new tradition. In fact, given that the Baptist Church served as a classroom for the early days of the fledgeling Government School, some parents, especially the Catholics, characterised the school as a bogus invention of the Baptist Church, motivated by petty rivalry with the Catholics.

Some parents predicted the imminent fall of the Government School, considering it a scam. This claim was plausible at a time when the government had lost its credibility. The school was financed by communal contributions through the Parent-Teacher Association. Though some pupils had transferred to the Government School because of its significantly moderate fees, the endless PTA levies proved them wrong. The school, born in the manger, seemed abandoned at its infancy by its creator: the Government. It was like an egg laid by a careless hen, exposed to the crows. The Baptist Church stepped in to provide the start-up premises. Thus, as the young pupils listened with passion to Mr Takwa's stories about Athens and Sparta, the class-church walls were pervaded by chants of Jerusalem and Judea by the Calvary Choir, rehearsing in the churchyard in preparation for the Sunday service. After the first year in the Baptist Church, the PTA built two classrooms on a plain close to the River Mbim to set the school afoot. But the rainy season made things harder and while the Wall crumbled in Berlin, the walls of the new 'Government' Primary School were pulled to the ground by the wind of change that seemed to have gathered more kinetic force in the tropics of Cameroon.

There was no Father John to construct a football stadium for the new school. Hence, the ridges and furrows of the adjoining farmland were converted into a level-playing field overtime by the pupils during after-school football games. As pioneers, the soles of the pupils tasted the silted earth of the Mbohbar plains but also endured the pricks of fledgeling fern plants and spear grass. Sometimes, on missing the ball, the foot would accidentally unearth a tuber of sweet potatoes and the players would forgo the ball to scramble over the delicious tubers. So, the argument was not about who kicked the ball, but who missed the ball and unearthed the tubers, or who missed the ball that unearthed the tubers. The school played its first official game without a proper set of jerseys. One newly posted teacher, Mr Shey acted both as the team coach and its traditional doctor. But all that did not yield any results against a team like GS Ntundip whose striped Argentinian jerseys are still a source of trauma to many people who grew up in that era and area. Only Mallam Jipsi of Binka could maybe turn the tides in such a David-Goliath tussle. The drums, cymbals and flutes of the school band were the handiwork of an old grey-bearded tinker in the neighbouring Ngarum village, on the junction where the road separates to Taku and Ntundip. Despite the ingenuity of the band members, the band was out of tune, during National Youth Day competitions. The rudimentary linen of the band instruments was just too evident.

Those were hard times and the golden days of being a teacher's son were over. Teachers' children, hitherto members of the local middle class, became the princes of a declining system, bereft of any privileges. The acquisition of the school land was another issue and it took the regal efforts of the village Fon to secure land for the new school. It was therefore not uncommon that during a lesson, the pupils would behold with bemusement the image of a masquerade planting a peace plant on the farmland or escorting one or two recalcitrant farmers who resisted the eviction orders of the village authorities. Never had tradition been put so fully and effectively at the service of modernity. A generation that had gone to Catholic school on horseback was now exposed to the dust and the scorching heat of the suns of multipartyism, democracy, New Deal, and, as they came to learn later on, Structural Adjustment Programmes. But it had the specific touch of the years of solitude experienced by those born at the outset of Paul Biya's regime. But, somehow, as if by magic, Mr Ngeh got his 100%, thanks to his efforts and those of the then village chief who brought his authority to bear to make sure the new institution did not die in its infancy.

Unlike the Government School, the Catholic School had a strict culture of respect for prayers, almost stricter than the Moslems. Every sound of the bell marked a different kind of prayer. Every day, pupils impatiently looked forward to the Long Break Bell. But before they were released for the break, they had to converge at the assembly ground for prayer before the meal or what came to be known simply as Long Break Prayer. Woe betide anyone who was found with a tight mouth during such prayers. That gave room for all kinds of neologisms as some of the pupils hummed enthusiastically along, in imitation of Catholic friends, hoping to find security in numbers. Like the national anthem, the final product of the performance became an original text in its own right:

> *Bless us us lord,*
> *And bless is your gift*
> *Which we are about to the sea*
> *From Your goodness*
> *Throw Christ a lot Amen*

The fact is that some of the pupils never actually had anything to eat during the break. In any case, it did not matter so long as it was the rite of passage to the Long Break, the time of freedom to play with friends.

On Fridays, instead of the usual closing time of 1:30 PM for Classes One, Two and Three, the bell would ring at 12:45 PM for the entire school to go for prayers at the Catholic Church which was about five hundred metres away. The 12:45 PM Friday bell always came with mixed feelings. It was particularly redemptive for it marked the beginning of the weekend. But it also meant that one had to go through the purgatory of Catholic prayers before seeing the Promised Land of the weekend. Friday devotion was part and parcel of the school programme and absence was severely punished as both sin and crime. As the bell tolled, one would hurry to the church and take one's seat. The Father then started the numerous textual readings and the pupils had to repeat after him, followed by intermittent kneeling on the floor. Some of you, Baptist pupils, did not know when to kneel and when to stand up. So, you would tilt one eye open and squint at the Catholic friends to the right or left and accordingly orient your gestures and body movements. That was how you developed the prudent habit of not closing eyes during prayers even if your Baptist Sunday School teacher entreated you to do the contrary. Sometimes, when the Reverend Father was not around, the devotion was officiated by the catechist. Whenever he did, you were assured that it would last much longer and entail more kneeling. This was quite tedious but given the fact that it would be your last ritual before the homebound trek to meet the plate of corn fufu and huckleberry leaves waiting for you at the kitchen counter, there was every reason to be patient.

Friday was a day of freedom. Two more days without thinking of school! Back then, each day had its peculiar rhythm and cast a special effect on your mood. Monday was the most detested of the weekdays. As you witnessed the evanescent sunrays of Sunday evening disappear behind the Kaa Mountain, you knew it was time to face the hooded aura of merciless Monday. Monday! A Long Walk to Freedom - Friday. Beyond the delight of putting on clean, freshly ironed uniforms with razor-sharp pleats, Monday meant an impending trauma that could not be staved off. Against Monday, school pupils were helpless. On Sunday midnights, Monday would visit you in your sleep in the form of a black-and-white ogre and the following morning, you were on the gravel road to the Catholic school, with curses and swords in your hearts for whoever created the school system.

The Catechist! He was one of the most influential personalities in the village. You never knew the exact names of the Catholic Catechist. The very name Catechist stuck on him, wiping his original name off, exonerating his previous life and anointing him with the badge of religious rectitude. He was very devoted, punctual and impersonal.

Though living in the world, he was not of the world. People said he was baked in the image of his mentor, the impeccable Father John. Father John was a Reverend Father with a difference. His name inspired both fear and admiration. He was punctual, rigorous, freakish, kind, wicked and a sometimes-unpredictable character. Many a catechist and mass servant had borne the brunt of his caprices but also enjoyed his latitude. He was the epitome of a white (Reverend) Father in your community. He was the Catechist of the catechists, the Timekeeper of the timekeepers.

In Tabenken village, it was rumoured, that Father John had captured 'Mami Wata' that was under the bridge between Nkambe town and Baraki village and locked her in a bottle. Others claimed that with his camera, he had captured a group of witches and wizards bulldozing cornstalks in the form of wind. Father John's camera reminded you of Zintgraff's eyeglasses. It was rumoured that Eugen Zintgraff, the German explorer of the Grassfields of Cameroon, used to let his spectacles supervise construction work by African labourers while he dedicated himself to other personal tasks. Faced with the omni-visual spectacles majestically placed on a chair, the labourers worked their asses off. You only came to trace Father John's provenance to Germany later on. As a child, you only knew he was a European, a *nwe kimbang*, a white person, a red person.

Pa Catechist was as strange as his white mentor. You recalled the day you and your elder sister Mangwang left the house as early as 5:30 AM one Saturday to visit your aunt at a distant farmland that stood on the boundary between your ethnic group and the Noni. You spotted a tall silhouette a few metres in front of you under the moonlight.

"That is Pa Catechist," you whispered to your sister.

She nodded.

Pa Catechist must have been very intrepid to come out alone at that hour of the day, for that was the time when the most dreadful ghosts certainly roamed the village. You thought to yourself. He could not afford to be half a second too late for his ritual bell. You caught up with him on the road below the Catholic football field, just before the curve where the road to the Catholic Church parted ways with the one that led to the farmland to where you were heading.

"Good morning catechist," you greeted in a partially audible voice.

No response.

As you moved some steps past the silhouette, Mangwang hushed you down.

"At this hour of the day, you don't greet someone whose identity you are not sure of."

Anyway, Catechist (or so you thought) did not respond. Was your greeting not loud enough? Perhaps he did not want to succumb to any distraction as he went to perform the Lord's duty. About a quarter of an hour later, when you and your sister had started descending the last but one hill that led to the farmland, the bell rang. It was the six o'clock bell. That was proof that the figure you had overtaken on your way was the Catechist.

"If only he could understand the havoc he causes us every morning with his merciless 6 AM bell-hell" you said to yourself.

His bell was a source of trauma to you. It used to terrorise you in your sleep, sometimes driving you into insomnia caused by an undesirable expectation. That was because the sound of his bell was always accompanied minutes later by the unmistakable sound of your father's voice. They formed an unholy alliance, a terrific sequence in your consciousness. You still remembered your dad entering your room immediately after the bell, roaring.

"You people are still sleeping? Please, wake up and clean the compound."

The bell and the voice used to come right in the middle of sweetness, sometimes interrupting the happy end of a beautiful dream. At times you did not know which preceded the other. When you went home during university holidays, you didn't hear any bell ring.

You wondered what happened to this great church practice. Nor did your dad come to your room early in the morning to wake you up. His hitherto thunderous voice had grown frail with time. Your younger brother told you that the revered catechist had died several years ago! He was succeeded by other catechists, much younger. But none matched his devotion. Some of them were womanisers. One even went as far as having a relationship with a member of the parish youth group. The last one was a heavy drinker and sometimes he would forget to ring the bell at the timely moment, leading to sanctions against him by the parish priest.

The last time the bell had that terrifying effect on you was during your trip to Peru in 2015. You visited the Peruvian locality of Vilcaswaman, three hours' drive from the Peruvian town of Ayacucho. It plays host to the ruins of the Usnu and the Sun Temple, both of which are venerated symbolic and sacred sites of the defunct Inca Kingdom. The sun temple also acted as a clock and marked the cycle of seasons in the Inca cosmology. Above it, there was a stone-built Catholic Church. It was a current practice during the Conquista to erect a Catholic Church on the ashes of the Huaca, a site of ancestral worship amongst the Incas. In Vilcaswaman, what remained of the Sun Temple was a touristic simulation of the old temple. As you and your fellow sojourners stood around the Temple, contemplating its spiritual significance, a short and astutely dressed man walked past you in rapid strides, elbowing you as he made his way to the church bell close by. And then came the bang. It roared with barbaric intensity and almost sent you dumb. It was midday. The weight of Time.

Closer to me, Lord

Oh heavenly Father, I am on a mountain so high
Trying to send you a prayer from my heart so low
Give an ear to my voice, oh Lord!

My enemies have set themselves against me
Satan has taken away the bliss of the world
Oh Lord, declare your power over your creation
For we are in the midst of sorrow

Show us the way to eternal life, to attain your mission

Chorus

Closer to me, closer to me, Oh Lord
I am calling for you Father
Spend your time over this simple soul of mine
Let me understand your wisdom
You are the Alpha, you are the Omega
You are the Tree of Life

By King Rogan

THE BOOKS

The child is father of the man.
("My Heart Leaps Up", William Wordsworth)

After about a five-hour drive aboard a thirty-seat bus from Bamenda, the headquarters of the North West Region, you arrived in Ndu. Ndu was the home of your maternal grandparents even though they originally came from Ntundip, a neighbouring village to Luh, your home village. Your relationship with Ndu was furtive. You had never lived there, even though it is what comes closest to the expression your "hometown". Ndu and you were ships that crossed at night. But its specific scents, sights and sounds accompanied you all your life. Your first memories of Ndu were closely tied to the acoustics of the Ivorian music icon of the 80s and 90s, Monique Seka's 'Missounwa'. That was in the late 1980s, when your eyes were just barely opening to the bliss and bane of the social world. In one of your maiden trips to Ndu, you could not cease to admire how your cousins would sing and stage that clip in improvised veranda concerts, drawing admiration from passers-by. That sound had a particular grace, enhanced by the brittle vocal cords of both its original singer and those of its infantile interpreters. "Mistuwa, Mado Mistuwa..." You wondered who this 'Mado' was, who featured in many songs of that era, ranging from zouk, zaïko to makossa. Was she the paragon of beauty, a symbol of unreciprocated love, or some innocent girl that became an object of vainglorious desire which purged itself through music?

Going by its physical size, Ndu did not seem like a big town, but it had an aura and rhythm of its own and there were still elements of the town that stuck in your consciousness from a very young age. How could one forget the sound of the muezzin that chanted Islamic prayers as market women wrapped their remaining goods at dusk after a hectic market day? Or the forceful voice of a blind second-hand clothes seller shouting: *"wap ma wi vuni vu boh me ohhh"* (my mothers, come and fool me)? You remembered the fig tree at the centre of the Old Market and the legendary stories that surrounded it. Every time you passed in Ndu, the site of the Old Market seemed pathetic. You felt that the spirit of the Ndu Market had left the Old Market but had difficulties implanting itself on the new site. Something spiritual was missing from what used to be the Ndu market. Perhaps, it might be because you had been away for too long.

In the 1990s, Ndu, which means "life" in Igbo, became a flourishing hub of Nigerian popular culture in a way that was not very typical of Nkambe, the divisional headquarters. In terms of concrete trade, many wholesale traders in Ndu bought their products directly from Nigeria and Ndu had a modest population of Igbo traders, known locally, as *nga-ngwi* due to the widespread stereotype of Igbo people as 'dog-eaters.' But the Igbo influence went beyond this modest Igbo immigrant population. In the mid-1990s when someone entered the town, they were greeted with tunes by Nigerian gospel singers cum evangelists such as Brothers Lazarus/Emmanuel (Voice of the Cross), Agatha Moses, Rosemary Chukwu, Princess Njideka Ngozie Okeke, etc. vibrating from popular stores and discotheques in the Old Market. These songs were mostly in Igbo English and were usually loaded with salvation testimonies, with a single clip mutating into the next without any clear transitions, like Congolese rumba, notorious for its endless length. The zeal and the conviction in these songs were so enthralling that it is only in hindsight that one took note of the grammatical infelicities in expressions like "You alone is my Helper." One could say that Nigerian gospel sounds were major gateways through which certain contemporary religious idioms and expressions sipped into the evangelical speech patterns in Ndu and beyond. Examples included prayer expressions that nowadays seem so natural: "Lord remove every embargo on my way"; "any weapon fashioned against you shall not prosper"; "I must possess my possessions"; "Any arrow of death against you and family, back to sender, in Jesus' name"; "Any Egyptian Goliath, hindering my breakthrough, receive destruction in Jesus' name"; "Blessings shall be my portion," etc. Jesus became 'Daddy' and 'Doctor Jesus'. A community that had been used to Hebrew attributes of God - Jehovah Rama, Jehovah Jireh, Jehovah Nissi, Jehovah Rohi - now became used to Igbo attributes such as *Jehovah Chineke na enye-ndu, Jehovah Ukuchukwu, Jehovah Chukwu ma mee, Jehovah Eze ebere, Jehovah Nnukwu chi*, etc.

Most people, especially kids who grew up in Ndu in those days could sing some of the Igbo songs from beginning to finish, with a full grasp of the meaning. The choreography, dress code and dance style featuring in these Nigerian clips had an enormous influence on the habits of Ndu folks. Though most of the singers were of Igbo origin, their choreographies wielded into a single clip dress codes from the disparate communities that Lord Frederick Lugard and the founding fathers Tafawa Balewa, Obafemi Awolowo and Nnamdi Azikiwe fashioned into a single whole called Nigeria. If gospel music came to Ndu on compact discs, that was not the case with a previous wave of Nigerian cultural products which came in the form of the unforgettable video cassette. These included the prime comedy clips of Nigerian comedians, James Iroha aka Giringori Akabogu, Chika Opkala aka Chief Zebrudaya and J. Afolayan aka Jagua. And if one had to continue down memory lane, one could not forget that Evi Edna, Prince Nico Mbarga and the Rocaffil Jazz took the same road in the form of radio cassettes. In the 1990s Ndu, certain discotheques used to thrill the market area all day long with Nigerian comedy and music. As one left Ndu market at dusk, squeezed like sardine into a taxi, returning to one's village, the sound of Nigerian Gospel and the peculiarly Ndu market aroma produced by a mixture of dust, tired tyres, second-hand clothes, *bakuru, masa, maimai, akra beans, ching-ching,* puff-puff, unsold onions, garlic and ginger followed one unconditionally home.

The park for cars driving to your village had now been relocated from the Old Market to the New Market. Luckily enough, when you arrived, one car was waiting just for one additional passenger. So, you filled in the gap, squeezed into the already full car, heading for your home village. It was roughly a thirty-five-minute trip. You could not make out the face of the driver. Some of the passengers looked familiar, but not enough to tempt you into a chat that would answer the many questions that lingered in your mind about happenings in Luh over the years. You were seated in the middle of the rear seats and had to struggle to catch glimpses of the roadside features that flashed by as the Toyota Carina descended the hilly road with cautious and measured speed. Inexplicably, "Tears in heaven" and "Tarzan Boy" jostled in your mind as you attempted to reconnect those spaces with memories of bygone days. There was a third clip:

> *See you, I will see you, very very soon*
> *See you, I will see you, very very soon*
>
> *We need something in Africa*
> *We need somebody to save our people*
>
> *See you, I will see you, very very soon*
> *See you, I will see you, very very soon*

You had a vague puerile reminiscence of the video of that clip but being unable to find it on YouTube made you wonder if it was anything less than a figment of your imagination. After close to twenty-five minutes' drive, you were in Taku village, where you used to celebrate the National Youth Day in primary school, before new centres were created in each of the surrounding villages. Looking back, it was very evident to you that being a youth in Cameroon meant a process of waiting in eternal solitude.

In the early nineties, in your new Youth Day shoes that smelt of Ndu, you inhaled the sweet dust that carpeted the road from Luh to Taku village. But you were not yet youth and the sun, no matter how scorching it was, still meant hope for you. Back then, the Youth Day sugarcane was still sweet. But the year 1992, the year of the rigged elections when your people experienced the true colours of the New Deal, hastened your growth. You, the youth, became conscious that while you strained your backs in respect of the tri-colour flag and twisted your tongue in singing a very difficult National Anthem in a puerile patriotic frenzy, the president rejuvenated himself by constantly masturbating the constitution. Thus, the president, certainly the first and last youth of the country, remained young in power while the true youth aged and developed grey hair in their childhood like Ayi Kwei Armah's old man-child. Perhaps, amongst the fortunate ones were those like yourself who found a way to get out of the country. But the real success stories, the very fortunate ones, were those who charted their way into some juicy professional school through connections, the kind of public schools that enabled one to compensate for the lost years after just one year of public self-service.

The further you were from Ndu, the worse the roads became. The driver wriggled his way through the potholes on the valley that separated the village of Taku from Ntundip. When you arrived at the Ntundip junction connecting the main road from Taku to Luh, one passenger alighted and it was only then, after adjusting your sitting position, that you could breathe properly. Ntundip was smaller than Luh and Taku but its Government School was the best known in the area. If ever there was a primary school with the stature of a High School, that primary school was GS Ntundip, popularly known as *Midoh* due to its location on a flat-topped hill about a kilometre away from the junction. When it came to public exams, they simply got tired of scoring one hundred per cent in Common Entrance and First School Leaving Certificate. Concerning sports, their blue-white striped Argentinian jersey brought nightmares to their opponents. During the Youth Day ceremonies in Taku in the late eighties and early nineties, GS Ntundip had the habit of spoiling the taste of your sweet Youth Day sugarcane.

In football, they seemed to master the slanting football pitch of Baptist School Taku more than the home team. In track and field, you were convinced that their athletes deserved a doping test. Otherwise, if talent had any value in your country, that school would have been boasting of some Olympic Medals, especially in sprint. But there was an unforgivable aspect of the school: the way its fans used to humiliate defeated opponents, especially on home soil. Whenever you left the pitch after a defeat, descending the hillock from their football pitch, you could still hear them shouting and mocking at your team, at you. And even if you had plans to pass through the Three Corners Junction and buy some pieces of pepperish *katanga*[8] from Pa Katanga, you would preferably take the shortcut under the kola nut trees and re-appear on the road opposite the Luh Health Centre close to the Luh-Ntundip border. That was because whenever GS Ntundip won, Three Corners Junction went frenzy. What made defeat by GS Ntundip team the more painful was the fact that some of their best players were your cousins since both villages were bound by strong bonds of kinship.

As you gradually gained sensory control of your leg that had been mortified by the heavy hips of the just alighted passenger, your mind began to wander and wonder, engaged as it was in re-membering

---

8. Boiled goat-skin with very hot spices.

this space that was just a step closer to home. You were now in Ntundip, meaning that, as the car de-accelerated, the faces along the road became more and more familiar to you, especially on reaching Three Corners. The weather was rather misty and Three Corners looked a bit deserted, concealing the fact that it used to be a veritable hub, a place of social encounter, a physical Facebook where news virtually went viral. Located on the western flank of Ntundip village, Three Corners is only a few minutes from the boundary with Luh and Taku. In the 1990s, there was one Mr Mbi, a very enterprising health-worker of the Luh Health Centre who owned a provision store cum bar around that place. He was from Widikum but spoke Limbum with an English intonation very fluently. His bar was a meeting point, a place of local football commentary in the days of Dayi Revivers, the quarter's official football club. It was a place where multiple stories were generated. He owned a disco set that used to grace the entire locality with tunes of the latest music in town. Amplified naturally by the thick tufty maze of kola nut trees in that vicinity, the echoes of the music were heard across the borders in Luh and Taku. Those were the days when home-grown artists flourished in that part of the country, with artists like Amumba (*African Food Collection, Amumba Express, Donga Baby*), John Minang (*fine fine woman, greet the dawn, woman give me chop*), Ni Ken (*mami wata, Alingo*) Walters Tete (*give me bottom belle, Daddy lovet*), Krys Njowe (*chacun pour soi*), Lemy Moise (*Nsuung Jazze*), John Iray (*John the Baptist*) and Jisa Shafta (*kumela, mbaya*).

Dayi quarter even developed its homegrown dance style in the 1990s. With a network of shops, bars and open-air stalls, Three Corners was a place where people gathered in the evening to take a sip, to take stock of the day's activities and to comment on what made news in the local community and beyond. As they shared a *junguru* (two-litre bottle) of *sha* (corn beer), palm wine, or a bottle of beer, tongues were set loose and news got inflated beyond pro-portion. Satzenbrau was the most popular beer back then. After a boozing spree, as one left Three Corners at night on their way home to the far reaches of Ntundip village that lay east of the enormous and enigmatic fig tree or passed under the cactus tree on their way to Luh or Taku, the news they transmitted bore the imprints of their half-tipsy sensation. But Ntundip village is an interesting place altogether. Less endowed with territory than its neighbours, its inhabitants developed a near Jew-like business mentality and a highly enterprising spirit. (Dayi quarter looks exactly like the West Bank). Perhaps this explains why a generation of prominent Ntundip moguls dominated business in Ndu, Nkambe and Ako in the 1980s and 1990s, amongst them Pa Lufthansa and Pa Continental. But unlike the Jewish homeland, Ntundip has been at peace with its neighbours, even though it had to fight tooth and nail to defend its foothold in the past. Perhaps that is also why, when it came to sports, education and business, they fought with their whole lives, as if conscious that their survival depended on their human resources.

As you crossed the boundary from Ntundip to Luh village, you felt a sense of strange familiarity. You began recognizing not just the faces, but also the trees and the stones by the roadside. They had followed you everywhere you had been, forming the backdrop of your dreams, however hazily. So many years spent in the quest for knowledge had made you a stranger in your village, and even in your family. Much had happened during your absence. Since when you left for the university in the capital city, you only came back briefly and at long intervals, sometimes arriving at dusk and leaving at dawn. Thus, this was a proper homecoming for you. In the preceding days to your trip, the possibility of going home filled your subconsciousness with a preambular succession of sights and sounds: the splendorous firmament of the Kaa and Nchindong Mountains whose contours and silhouettes featured in your infant hopes/nightmares about the Second Coming; the grey coloured and gentle flowing Mbim River which washed away your sins during baptism; the irreplaceable echo of the roosters, standing on one leg as they crowed, marking the passage of Time; the evening chorus of the crickets and various birds; the joyous voices of the Baptist Church Women's Choir as they rehearsed for the Sunday service. Those Baptist choristers whose songs brought Jerusalem so near in space and time!

As the car turned the curve right above the Baptist Church, you gained full view of your family's compound, about a hundred metres away. But just a glance at the frontage of that stony structure, the House of God, opened the floodgates of childhood memories; memories of hope and faith; of your early attempts at a pious life; of the self-castigation for what seemed to you as life below divine expectations; of Pastor Nyong's sermons about hellfire as the inevitable price for a sinful life; of his persistent claim that even you, little children, were born sinners. The deserted nature of the churchyard crowded your mind with a plethora of memories and anxieties. You remembered how, stepping out of the church door on Sundays after agonizingly long sermons, you would make a promise to God and yourself to be different, to throw off the mantle of sin, to give in to Christ once and for all. But there was the fear: the fear of the unknown waters of Christ; the fear of losing friends; the fear of being labelled "born again"; the fear of being seen to have gone too far even by your pious mother. There were Sundays when you would leave that church door uncertain about the next Sunday, even the next day, certain about and fearful of the intervening Rapture.

The pastor's house adjacent to the main church made you recall Mathew, the pastor's son and your childhood friend, a Don Juan at an early age, an early master at combining a flirtatious character with apparent zeal for the Word of God. You loathed and admired boys like Mathew who knew how to tread on these two worlds with an in-born sense of freedom. He and others like him seemed to inhabit the frontier between sinfulness and righteousness with much tranquillity of heart, a clear contrast to your tortuous moral limbo and dilemma. How did he manage to tame his conscience so easily?

Were not pastors' children supposed to be good examples for those like you? Didn't the fervent words spoken by his dad, the pastor, on Sundays have the same unsettling effects on him as yourself? You would ask yourself, believing wholeheartedly that God always spoke through the mouth of the pastor. At times, as a teen, you thought your conscience was a barrier to your self-expression and proper exploration of the natural fruits of your age. Still, whenever you resolved to let yourself loose, that very conscience enthralled you and dictated its will on your actions. Perhaps, now, as a grown-up, you understood people like Mathew much better. You came to terms with the fact that some people are born with that inner freedom to perform, while others, like yourself (or as you used to be), strive to match their actions, perhaps unsuccessfully, with what they profess. Who would be life's victors? Looking back at those days, you realised how much the hedge separating the dusty road to Heaven from the macadamised highway to hell had been largely bulldozed and blurred in your conscience by the Caterpillar of Time.

The driver slowed down at the entrance to the Baptist Church, now just about fifty metres away from your compound. The junction that separated your family compound from the church looked deserted. The only figure standing there was the signboard of GS Luh, your alma mater. The inscriptions had peeled off, almost rendering the 'G' (which stood for 'government') nearly invisible. Close to the Baptist Church, there used to be a single room building that was used by the Men's Fellowship as a palm wine or corn beer drinking spot after church service. But at one point, it was rented out to a tailor. You recalled the whirring sound produced by the SINGER as the taciturn tailor cut through the seams of the black fabric, tapping his feet philosophically on the foot pedal. The end results were the uniforms of King Solomon Choir, those black gowns with white lapel that made the choristers look so angelic. Thinking about that tailor made you gauge the immense impact in your community of the SINGER sewing machine, invented by the failed-actor-turned-inventor from Schaghticoke (New York), Isaac Merritt Singer. It changed the dress codes across several generations in your community. The trumpet-trousers (popularly known as *apaga*) and the jumper with four bucket-like pockets were some of the trademark products of the SINGER machine. For kids' jumpers, those bucket-like pockets were good for storing enough quantity of fresh groundnuts on Sunday afternoons, after church service. Groundnuts bought with money meant for offering.

The family house had undergone a facelift. It was now painted in a deep blue colour and the three front windows were covered with protectors. The zinc on the left-hand side of the frontage was covered by a solar panel. Where the tall wooden pole of the TV antenna had once stood was now canopied by the huge petals of a parabolic antenna, suspended on a two-metre-tall spindle. The faces of that house reflected the phases of your childhood and teenage. Before being reconstructed by your workaholic dad into a rectangular block in the early nineties, it used to be an L-shaped structure with a shop facing the road. The shop was run by one of your uncles. You remembered it for its bonbons and the French baguette, *boulangerie*, which, as leftovers, tasted like boiled cocoyam. You recalled yourself playing during a rainy afternoon alone on the veranda as the rain railed against the zinc roof. It was one of such days when a heavy downpour turned the sky grey and precipitated nightfall. Your father had connected a long bamboo stick onto the elbow of the L-shaped roof, thus funnelling water into a huge jerrycan that sometimes got full and the water would stream over to the veranda before receding into the drainage on the veranda edges. There you were, playing with rainwater, fetching its drops directly from the zinc roof with your cupped palms, allowing the water to gurgle in your mouth with absolute puerile pleasure before finally releasing it down to your oesophagus and feeling it spread to your bloodstream. It was fun, but there were consequences: the pain you felt in your throat after the exercise and the scolding you received from your mum for wetting your clothes.

It was getting close to 4 PM. The driver knew your compound, so he stopped without you having to notify him. It was then that, on stepping out of the car, you saw your dad come out of the main door of the living room. Noticing you were the one, he hurried towards the car and jumped on you with incredible agility. He is still very strong, you said to yourself. You had worried much about his health. You did not know how to react to that expression of paternal joy. Your father had always been a very measured, rational man, not one to flare up so easily. But that was a special moment. Like a child, you held him for a few seconds in your arms, before letting him down.

"Dad, you are still very energetic," you said as both of you followed the driver to the carriage to offload your luggage.

"My son, here I am, we thank God."

With the help of the driver and one of the passengers, your father transported your luggage to the living room. You tarried longer in the compound, waving at your neighbours from the compound across the road. They had come out as the car stopped to drop you. Many of the people around seemed not to make you out, which was normal, for you left the village when many of them were not yet born or were mere babies. You could find on their faces an attempt to relate your identity with what one of your nieces or nephews might have told them about their uncle who was in a foreign country. One aged woman joined the group of kids and you quickly recognised her.

"Welcome oh, my son."

"Thank you, Mami Julius. Happy to meet you again," you responded, waving.

In front of your father's second building, which used to host your family's small provision store, much closer to the church, there were more pairs of eyes looking at you. You could recognise a number of them. How some had grown big and old! They just greeted you at arm's length, perhaps to allow you and your father enjoy the intimate family moment while they might come later in the evening to welcome you properly. You walked into the parlour where your dad had taken his seat.

"How was your trip?"

"It was great, dad. In Ndu, I did not have difficulties in finding a connecting vehicle to the village. That is why I have arrived a bit earlier than I thought."

"I see. These days there are many vehicles available since places are still dry today. The past days have been very different."

A moment of silence followed. As you spoke, it seemed to you as though his voice was gradually losing steam. The initial fervour was gradually simmering. You were not willing to strain him much further. You knew your father, you knew what change of tone, pitch, and decibel in his voice meant and the emotion it conveyed or concealed. In the course of the journey, you had calculated a series of scenarios, figuring out how you should approach your parents upon arrival, what kind of bearing to adopt, what to ask or not to ask, what to say or not to say, how to say and how not to say. You attempted to solve a situation that was still to unfold, to answer questions that were not yet asked.

"Your mum has gone to the farm at *Njeng*. We knew you were coming today but not the exact time. I called your sister Nshie last evening and she supposed you would surely arrive here later in the evening. Since we were not certain, we decided I stay home, just in case you come earlier."

"Yes, I was also not sure of the time because I did not know how much time I would spend in Bamenda or Ndu. I was equally surprised by how easily I could get a taxi. So, I did not waste time in Ndu."

"Welcome once more, my son. I imagine you are tired and need some rest. Perhaps, a bath too?"

"Not now dad, no problem. I would like to go to the farm and meet mum."

"Really? Are you sure you can still trace the road?"

"Come on dad, I can't forget that easily! I know it has been long, but this is my village. It is my farm; it is where I grew up." Indeed, the farm was some thirty minutes' walk from your compound.

"Let me get some fresh water from the kitchen."

"Ok, it is open; you just need to push the doorknob."

You did not have to behave like a stranger. After all, your dad was the only one at home. It was all quiet around the house, nothing like those primary school days when your family home used to look like a crowded dormitory, especially during holidays when your cousins would come visiting from Douala. You visited all the rooms and a number of them had been transformed into storage space for yams and beans, certainly your mum's merchandises. She was never tired of doing business. You entered the kitchen and were welcomed by that indelible scent, that aura of the fireside that was part and parcel of your upbringing. The pans and plates you used during your childhood were still there on the counter. The set of china was still sparkling as if no one had used it for twenty years. If they were truly made in China, then they certainly defied the widely held view about the short lifespan of Chinese products in Cameroon. Those china plates reminded you of the first seasonal beans that always had a special taste. Whenever your mum dished beans for you in those plates, they took a special savour. You used to battle with your siblings as to who earned the rights of entitlement to this or that china. Sometimes the loser (never you) would decide not to eat as a sign of protest against your mother's decision.

Your dad called from the parlour, in an inquisitive tone.

"Yes, dad."

"Have you found drinking water in the kitchen?"

"Dad, do not bother. I will." Intercepted by the memories, you were actually in no haste to drink water anymore.

"Look for it in the Murtala at the top right-hand side of the counter."

"Yes, dad. I have found it. It is ok."

You found the Murtala[9] basin. The Murtala! It varied in shapes and sizes, an indispensable feature in the parlour cupboard of almost every family in your area. It bore the bust effigy of a handsome and plump man in green and profusely decorated military uniform. It was a romantic image of a military leader, a one-time Nigerian president. Your family's was a medium-sized basin. In your household, your mother used the Murtala as an efficient disciplinary measure. All the niceties from the Ndu Market in the form of *ching-ching*,[10] puff-puff, soya (steak), were kept in the Murtala. When your mum fried puff-puff, the leftovers were usually preserved in the Murtala. And leftover puff-puff was usually more tasteful than when it was still hot or warm. Not forgetting the take-home pieces of meat from the monthly meeting of the Teachers' Wives' Union to which she belonged. Anyone who desisted from chores would not taste of the Murtala. You worked hard, waiting impatiently for the moment she would send one of you to the Murtala. By then, certain Nigerian products were sometimes treated with the same distrust and considered as "counterfeit," like the Chinese products. But most Murtalas were very durable. Your family's had survived all the weather. It had only sustained a few bruises at its rim, prompting it to be transferred from the parlour to the kitchen. But the face of Murtala Muhammed had surprisingly survived the passage of time.

Unlike your elder brothers who gradually estranged themselves from the kitchen space when they became real boys, you remained a kitchen mate to your mother. Sometimes your father would rebuke you for always keeping close to food, a trick to dodge real men's work with him, he who was always mending fences, trimming cypress, if not filing cutlasses in preparation for work. You always wondered what he would have been had he not become a primary school teacher. You grew up thinking that being close to your mother in

9. Refers to the name of the Nigerian General, Murtala Muhammed, president of that country 1975-1976. The Murtala basin bore his bust effigy and was a major Nigerian export to the North-western part of Cameroon in the 70s, 80s and 90s.
10. Croquette made out of wheat flour.

the kitchen was a way of preserving your moral uprightness and shielding yourself from the temptations of early teenage life.

"Have you found it, my son? If it is not clean enough, you can get it directly from the tap."

"Dad, the water in the Murtala is quite clean." *Directly from the tap*, how sweet it sounded!

At the right corner of the kitchen was a raised slab with a steel faucet perched over a laundry sink. In your primary school days, your mum was the treasurer of the village water project supported by a Swiss NGO *Helvetas*, apart from the valuable contributions to the project by the village folks. You felt proud to see that the fruits of her efforts had endured for that long.

"Dad, let me now go to the farm."

"Ok, when you reach there, you people may just return instantly. I am not sure they were doing any tedious work today. You might even meet them on their way back."

"Maybe, in any case, we will be back soon."

You took the path leading to the farm. It looked abandoned, partly covered by undergrowth. The ranger boots you put on were appropriate for the nature of the path. You passed under the kola nut trees of Pa Johnson that produced some of the most tasteful kola nuts in the village. As children, you would leave your houses very early in the morning to pick fallen kola nuts. Nowadays, everyone seemed to have headed for the towns.

As you were about to turn the corner, you heard a humming voice, mixed with the whistling and hissing sound of a radio set. Under the shadows of the coffee leaves, the mesh of sound quickly concretised into the figure of a man walking stealthily from the opposite direction. He had a leather bag hung to his shoulders and the small transistor radio held tightly to his ear. It was Mungo Park. "He never gets old." You said to yourself. Though his hair was rather systematically grey, it only added beauty to his turgid stature. You tried to pre-empt his questions and sketch your answers beforehand.

"Barake, how are you?"

"I am fine, uncle," you answered. Should you correct him? He was neither the first nor the only one to make that error.

Many people had always confused your name with that of your elder brother. It was not unusual that someone, wishing to see your mother, would tell you or any of your siblings, "Go and tell Mama Barake that I am looking for her, please!" Sometimes, you would tease your mum by referring to her as "Mama Barake" and would tell her "Mama Barake, so so and so is looking for you." Mungo Park, not realising his mistake at all, went on with the conversation.

"When did you come back?"

"I arrived just today and I am hurrying to the farm to meet my mum."

"Welcome, the climate over there suits you."

"Really? Thank you, uncle."

"How long will you be around?"

"Just for a few days."

"Ok, you have abandoned some of us. If I did not meet you here you won't have even thought of me at all. Anyway, I will come to the house in the evening to greet you and take my share of what you have brought."

"No problem, I will be at home. See you then." You responded, with a reassuring smile.

"My son, I am sure your mum will be very glad to see you." This was an obvious assertion, but under certain circumstances, it carried added meaning.

"That is true, uncle. I too can't wait to meet her."

You and your peers called this man *uncle* merely out of courtesy. He was a far distant relative. One thing about him that you had never forgotten was his habitual spoonerism. He would say *geogaphry* (for 'geography'), *cerfiticate* (for 'certificate'), *thief of service* (for 'chief of service'), *sacrifice* (for 'satisfy'), *apartheid* (for 'appetite'), *high potential* (for 'hypertension') with so much self-assurance that it was hard to realise the lapses. You remembered vividly how he once told you in your family's provision store, "I am *respecting* (instead of 'expecting') some money from Ndu in the coming days" in a very confident tone, in a way that the 'respected' money would solve all his problems. He used to go to his palm bush in a three-piece suit and a brownish white Sekou Touré cap, which we used to call mboko[11] cap. He was nicknamed Mungo Park in your primary school days because his habits were quite out of step with the trends, but he had a certain sense of self-conviction and an explorer's disposition. He had something akin to Mungo Park when the latter returned to Scotland on 22nd December 1797, after being thought dead during his exploration of the Niger River. In those days, school lessons provided school children with character types to re-name the world around them. Thus, they peopled the village with nicknames from distant beings who tussled in your minds as a result of your primary school history classes.

These characters ranged from army generals who fought in the Peloponnesian wars, through early Portuguese explorers like Vasco da Gama and rulers of the ancient empires of Western Sudan, to colonial officials in Cameroon like the British "Too late Hewett" and the German colonial consul, Gustav Nachtigal. It was not uncommon for the schoolchildren to nickname any pair of rivals in your village primary school as Sumanguru and Sundiata. Mungo Park's mythic radio was his one and only friend. Even when he was tapping raffia palm wine, he always had his radio glued to his left ear, animating the palm bush and thickets around with exotic tunes or with news in some foreign language. You only came to discover later on that some of these languages were German, Chinese, Spanish, Dutch, etc. The only 'radio' languages you could identify in those days were English, French and Hausa. Your village has a Hausa quarter inhabited mostly

11. Mboko refers to a linguistic variety spoken amongst urban youth. "Mboko Tok" was popularised by the Cameroonian musician Lapiro de Mbanga in the eighties and nineties. It incorporates aspects of French, English and other prominent languages (not excluding neologisms), meanwhile the syntax is mainly built on pidgin English.

by Moslems while French was one of your official languages. You knew by then that Cameroon and Canada were the only bilingual countries in the world!

As you went further down the road, every step you took, every kola nut tree and any coffee farm by the roadside spoke to you in a distinct voice, recalling moments, people, sights, sounds, scenarios, a whole world of experiences buried under those leaves. You came close to the small path leading to the pond. Before the advent of pipe-borne water, it was the main source of drinkable water for the entire quarter. Even though you were in a haste to meet your mum, you could not resist the temptation to move down and see what had become of the pond. It had shrunk into a small puddle at the foot of the steep clay hillock. Carefully, you descended the hillock, recalling how sometimes you would slide and fall on the steps, pouring the entire basin of water, thereby dirtying the pond altogether as the water gushed down to its source carrying twigs and debris along. It usually took at least thirty minutes for the water to clear again. As kids, you and your peers would ski down the slope on your buttocks, occasionally tearing your shorts. Some of the scars on your body, especially your knees, originated from that exercise. The big stone on which you used to scrub your clothes was almost swallowed by sprawling green grass while the bottom of the pond was carpeted by a warped network of spirogyra and algae, strewn with rocks and pebbles; broken branches half-in and half-out of the water; leaves floating on the water's surface and minnows and tadpoles swimming in the shallows. The little birds, the *rkansa* disappeared in between the dark creek, *mbung*, as soon as they heard your footsteps.

The place looked mossy, abandoned, serene, nothing of the buzzing noise of those days. Most often that was where you did your group assignments from school, using your water vessels as tables and drums at the same time. Sometimes as kids you would play football right into the night, forgetting to fetch water until late into the evening. To evade the wrath of your dad, you would leave the football pitch, collect your container and make it straight to the stream. The croaking tadpoles and hissing insects from the thickets under the coffee plants used to produce a peculiar nocturnal chorus. But the stream was also a site of desire and frivolity. It was the starting point of teenage adventures for those with little patience for the pleasures of elderly things.

You reached a point where the road branches northwards to a lonely compound uphill. The path leading to the compound was invaded by sprawling grass. Perched on the hill, the aura of that cottage in your mind could only be paralleled to the likes of Thomas Hardy's Max Gate in Dorchester; Jane Austen's Chawton Cottage in Hampshire; The Brontë sisters' Haworth Parsonage and Wordsworth's Dove Cottage in Lake District. Your heart leapt at the thought that Kingsley, a self-made poet of limited formal education but of unbounded talent that inhabited that house, was no more, having joined the "heavenly choirs" (as he used to say in his poetry) ten years before. Kingsley was a memorable character. He used to wear a cowboy hat modelled on Don Williams'. Kingsley had many nicknames, certainly due to his curious character. His pen name was King Rogan, but his popular names were King Angesse and King Lebro. "Lebro" was a rendition of 'level', for as a primary school pupil in the 1980s, he made news in a track and field competition in Catholic School Luh and was forever named the king of level land. At the sidelines of the village inter-quarters football competition, King and others would engage in a mock one-hundred-metre sprint race in raincoat and Wellington boots, to the hilarious ululations of amused spectators. As a self-taught guitarist and one addicted to his Sony transistor radio, he mastered many of Don Williams' songs: 'Amanda', 'Listen to the Radio', 'You're my Best Friend', 'I Recall a Gypsy Woman' and 'We Should be Together'. His love for Don Williams' music was only comparable to his passion for Lucky Dube, Tracy Chapman, Evi-Edna, Bob Marley and Eric Donaldson, especially the latter's 'Come Away' and 'Lonely Night':

Here she comes - alone in the night
She looks in your eyes while she's breaking your heart
And her smile - Mona Lisa style
She lends you her heart
Lets you think you're the only one
But she'll leave you...

Lonely in the night
She breaks all her lovers' hearts
Lonely in the night
Dreaming of a love that fades away

When she wants - she gets what she wants
She looks in your eyes and you give her everything
So demure - so insecure
Oh how she conceals - all that she really feels
And she'll leave you...

King Rogan was a poet and a songwriter and composed many lyrics for Mbum artists such as Jisa Shafta. He was an avid reader of Shakespeare and other classics. Though he had not even completed primary school, he could analyse Jonathan Swift's *Gulliver's Travel* with incredible mastery. King delighted in taking the back seat to observe the society from a twilight vantage point. In your family's provision store close to the Baptist Church, he was fond of sitting at the corner, late at night, almost unrecognised by the consumers of palm wine, many of whom did not often notice his humble presence. Once in a while, he would intervene with his guitar, taking everyone unaware. On one occasion he was joined in the singing by a dreadlocked Rastafarian who lived and cultivated his ganja on the border between Luh and Kuvlu. Many considered him mad but whenever he started narrating the history of Christianity from

Genesis through Malachi to Revelations, everyone was marvelled at how much he had read. He was a stamp carver and a gifted artist and is the author of the painting on the front wall of Luh Baptist Church. The ad-lib performance that evening combined King's mellow guitar with the rhapsody of the Rastaman. You closed the provision store later than usual as even people passing along the road stopped by to listen to the music.

King Rogan wrote and like a solitary reaper, sang with all his heart, but long after, he was heard no more. You continued your way to the farm and came close to this plane, a large strip of level land which reminded you of the 1993 Bible Conference in Luh with the theme: "Living no longer for self, but for Jesus Christ" in line with Galatians 2:20 – "I have been crucified with Christ and I no longer live, but Christ lives in me. The life I now live in the body, I live by faith in the Son of God, who loved me and gave himself for me." The conference usually lasted for three days and it was a time of great Christian fellowship, spiritual nourishment and mass conversion. The first day ended well, but God was still preparing a surprise for His children: on the second day, the heavens were let loose of grasshoppers that fell on that level farmland. As a result, the conference centre was nearly deserted, as faithful Christians who had left the neighbouring communities of Ndu, Taku, Ntundip, Ngarum, Kakar, etc. for the Bible conference in Luh, found themselves amongst the multitude combing the grass on that plain for God's concrete blessings. Young boys and girls, men and women, amidst the buzzing of inedible insects and with dewy grass swishing against their legs, fondled through the green undergrowth, looking for grasshoppers, with containers and bottles of various sizes tied to their waist. And when someone caught the rare brown grasshopper, they would intone in triumph:

> *Me ko le ya ta nyonyo*
> *Ni pkaba nchep nwe oh yu la*

O mnsi ohh yu la ma ngvup ohhh
O mnsi!!

The brown grasshopper was a symbol of luck and a sign of a more fruitful catch ahead. It also had a rare and peculiar taste. On the third and last day of the conference, the grasshoppers continued to rain in the morning but the quantity dwindled during the day. That is when many could return to the conference venue at the GS Luh premises in time enough for the final prayer and farewell ceremony. Personally, after foraging for grasshopper amongst the already battered undergrowth, you finally went to the conference venue, motivated by the desire to see "Bastos" for the first time. Bastos was a famous Boys' Brigade Commander from Ndu, known throughout the Ndu area and beyond. He was to the Boys' Brigade what Colonel Jap was to the army, what Taylor Banga was to sewing and what Lawyer Njobara was to advocacy in Mbumland. Their names became synonymous with their professions. But you kept wondering, why would a servant of God bear as nickname, the name of a cigarette, a symbol of sin? Anyway, that is a different story. What is worth stating, however, is that the Luh 1993 Bible Conference is considered by many as the best Bible Conference of all times.

On your way, you were deeply absorbed by the flourishing farms. It was May and the Might of Nature was in full display. The beans were in full bloom while the maize stalks were already spreading their tassels, a moment of elation for kids that you were in those days. The nascent maize cobs had just started developing sleek and smooth brunette and blonde corn silks, which, as wanton boys, you plastered to your chin as beards to enact adult roles. You were welcomed by that priceless scent of life, by the fragrance that emerged from the luxuriant maize plants, fledgeling okra stems, bean leaves and the lush weeds that carpeted the furrows and ridges alike. You watched as the goldfinches, *rkansa*, flew from one maize or okra plant to the other, from one yam tendril to another, tweeting joyfully.

Those little birds could be caught by a tactful stretch of the hand, but no one could afford to disrupt the cosmic harmony. Moreover, even if you were tempted to catch them, they were no bigger than crickets when their feathers were plucked. You beheld the svelte petals of the huckleberry in the meadow and Wordsworth's "Table's Turn" sprang to your mind:

> And hark! how blithe the throstle sings!
> He, too, is no mean preacher:
> Come forth into the light of things,
> Let Nature be your teacher.
>
> She has a world of ready wealth,
> Our minds and hearts to bless—
> Spontaneous wisdom breathed by health,
> Truth breathed by cheerfulness...

That fragrance was only comparable to the smell of the soil after the first rains, that implacable aroma produced by the chemistry of the first raindrops and the home soil. This conjured in your affective memory that sense of homeliness, of being at peace with the earth. As a child, you would leave school and follow your mum straight to the farm, with your mind set on the clay pot of huckleberry leaves that awaited you under the meadow. Huckleberry leaves cooked on the farm tasted differently, to say the least. Sometimes, especially after the weeding season, you only visited the farm to check if the corn stalks were growing well and if the scarecrows had actually scared the crows. Sometimes they didn't, as testified by the chopped portions on the helpless fresh corn cobs. There you would stand on a small escarpment, amidst the verdant daffodils of maize plants, shouting *co coo co coo co coo, coo co co coo co coo* and uttering curses at the pied crows cruising the blue sky to Taku village.

You passed in front of Pa Alhadji's house. It was closed, but a faint smoke was swirling out of the thatched roof. The surrounding had not lost its smell produced by an alchemic mixture of incense, fresh tobacco, mixed with the scent of blossoming coffee seeds and fallen and rotting oranges. You were accompanied by the rustling leaves, trees creaking in the wind; the steady drip of rain from the nearby orange plants and the buzzing bees as they fluttered from one coffee plant to the other. Two *bakweri* banana plants beside the house were propped up by wedged poles to support the weight of fruits. As you got closer and closer to the farm, your mind focused on the imminent meeting with your mum and your sister-in-law. You had managed to face your dad, though none of you was able to fill in the silences that underlay your brief conversation. You were not sure of what emotional spark would result from your encounter with your mother. During your years abroad, she had been the most constant presence in your mind. As you travelled the world in the quest for knowledge, she was always with you. Now you were to look into her eyes, to feel the saddening warmth of her arms, to listen to her voice, to feel her breath. As you appeared at the northern tip of your farm, you beheld your mother and her daughter-in-law assembling the farming tools. Seemingly, they were already on the point of leaving.

As if by telepathy, your mother happened to cast her eyes in your direction as she was light-heartedly explaining something to her daughter-in-law. Under normal circumstances, you would have played hide-and-seek amongst the maize stalks before revealing yourself to them. But that was not the time. Immediately she saw you, she stood up and looked sharply at you as if to make sure it was not a mirage. As you were now closer, it became clear to her that it was her son. She informed her daughter-in-law that it was you.

"G, my son, is it you?"

"It is me, mum."

"You came right to the farm; you could still trace the road?"

"Of course, mum," you responded with an eerie smile.

You hastened your steps towards her, held her close to your chest as she burst into tears. It was not loud wailing, which made it all the more heart-rending for you. She was recounting in sobs the last days of your brother and the last time you talked to him on the phone in her presence. Then he was strong, he was alive, no sense of illness. You found it difficult to restrain her. Her words filled you with immeasurable anguish, made you realise the agonising fact that you were not going to see Barake anymore. At first, you had harboured an intimate hope that seeing your mother could lead to some miraculous reversal of fate, a re-awakening from a dream, an assurance that nothing had happened. Your sister-in-law stood helpless, withholding herself from crying, resolving to restrain your mother.

"Mum, it is ok. I know what you have gone through. I didn't know I would meet you alive. But here you are. Our God is alive. He will continue to give us the strength to forge ahead."

"My son, when it happened, my greatest concern was you. I imagined what would happen to you in a foreign land. I am glad you have come."

Your mum was right. The death of your elder brother shook you to the core. That evening, you sat in your room in cold Bavarian winter, imagining the commotion in your compound back home, visualizing the body of Barake being laid into the shaft amidst wailing. In that moment of agony, it was the voice of your mum that gave life a second chance in your existence. When you were able to talk to her on a shaky phone line a few hours after the burial, she told you: "Be strong, my son, God is in control." Though she was brief, her words consoled you thousands of kilometres away from home. You had not imagined she could summon the courage to talk to you in the first place.

After briefly shedding tears, your sister-in-law mustered the courage to stay strong. It was the first time you were meeting her face-to-face. You had only spoken on the phone. Ever since she got married to your brother, you had not come to the village. What could you say to console your mother and your sister-in-law whereas you could not console yourself? Your mother was the pillar of your life, the cornerstone of your moral upbringing. She taught you to show compassion for the underprivileged. She had borne the burden of responding to your earliest existential interrogations. She had always told you and your siblings: "My children, even in moments of hardship, I thank God, for none of you has ever fallen seriously ill or suffered from a terminal illness." That was her consolation. That was what sustained her faith. She uttered the above words not out of pride, but in sincere thanksgiving. You remembered the stories she told you about her first years of marriage, her first experiences of giving birth, the labour pains, the joy of seeing her first son grow into a smart and clever adolescent and a responsible adult. Yet, she had to relive the pains, to feel the full pangs of agony as the fruit of her labour perished in his prime.

You helped your mum and your sister-in-law pack their farm tools and you were set for home. You opted to carry the basket of vegetables they had harvested, giving a deaf ear to your sister-in-law's insistence to carry it by herself. As you climbed the hillock on your way home, your mum gradually regained her voice.

"My son, you have grown quite tall."

"Do you mean it, mum?"

"Yes, I always knew you would at some point regain your childhood stature. As a child, you always stood tall amongst your peers. But you have grown even taller than I could imagine."

She was your rightful weight measurer. She knew the tiniest scar on your body, the smallest pimple on your face. You recalled, when she visited you when you were still in the university, she discovered a pimple on your chin and pressed it with her hand until it popped. Though you were now a man, you were still her baby. Your sister-in-law inquired about life in Germany, your studies, when you would be going back or if you were in the country for good. You were a bit relieved that the discussion was gradually shifting onto lighter subjects. But it didn't make things easier. Your heart was still heavy. You were all coping, half a year after the sudden demise of your brother.

When you reached home, your dad had gone to the Baptist Church nearby. Meanwhile, your mum and your sister-in-law were carrying out chores in the kitchen, preparing a rather early dinner of fresh beans and Irish potatoes. After a brief stay with them in the kitchen, you decided to take a quick stroll right to the mission quarter, the heartbeat of the village, especially as you were not going to spend many days in the village.

You passed at the village palace. The memory you retained was that of a village dance group known as *njaman* (i.e., German). You wondered why it was called that way. But the memory went deep down to your childhood. There was a cultural event at the Fon's palace and the frenzy and dexterity of the *njaman* dance of Luh remained stuck in your memory. You wondered how many of the frenzied dancers who left their indelible imprints on your puerile memory now lay under the fertile soil of your native land:

> So many are asleep under the ground,
> When we dance at the festival
> Embracing the earth with our feet,
> Maybe the place on which we stand
> Is where they stood with their dreams
> They dreamed until they were tired
> And handed us the tail with which we shall dance,
> Even the weeds emerge in their praise,
> Yesterday there were vast villages
> We too shall follow their path,
> Our dust shall arise at the gathering place
> And the child will dance alone our grounds. ("Cycle I," Mazisi
> Kunene)

Like a solitary walker, you reached the Mission Quarter. It was where the market, the Catholic Church, the Catholic School and the village football pitch were all found. You were taken aback by the deserted nature of the market square. It was close to 6 PM, the time one would expect to find people in bars taking a sip of the local maize brew *sha*, palm wine or beer. Just two bars seemed to be open but the atmosphere was rather less funky. You lingered around, almost unrecognised by anyone who crossed your path. The field, constructed by Father John in the 1980s, was covered with undergrowth and seemed unused. One could not imagine that that rectangular space dictated the rhythm of life in the village in the 1990s, during the heated Inter-Quarter Football Games. Rambo F.C. vs Monaco F.C. was the veritable "El Classico" back then. You recalled that on 19th August 1994 these two teams played one of the most memorable finals. Both squads had reinforced their Galacticos with borrowed players from places as far as Lassin, Ndu, Tabenken, etc. Your dad was then head coach of Monaco FC and the family provision store cum bar was the club's headquarters.

The spectacular warm-up fits of the loaned players made spectators wait with bated breath for the game at hand. It was the match before the match. One of Monaco FC's loaned players, Piro (a defender from Tabenken village, with a black wig reminiscent of the ruthless Indomitable Lions defender, Jean-Claude Pagal), stood with his right leg on the ball and asked his teammate to hit his thigh with his rubber boots continuously. The enigmatic player stood his ground firmly as Nfoninwe applied all his energy on his unflinching muscular and rock-solid thigh. That was an inconceivable test of resistance and such warm-up stints gave fans all the assurance that the professional players were going to deliver a historic performance. The first few minutes were promising for Monaco, but as the game progressed, the cards seemed stacked against them. In the first half, the Rambo defence led by Jaspar and the midfield/attack line composed of Tigana, Njong James, Tantoh Edwin and Nyakoh

Petit Frère, made life difficult for the Monaco side, especially the defence manned by Mbuli Ngoh, Kongnyu Oliver and Piro (the loaned player). The dribbling feats and barbed shots of Monaco's no-nonsense number 10-shirt Ndi Charles were not enough to counter Monaco's outrageous fortune on that day.

Tigana and Nyakoh Petit Frère, Rambo's loaned players from Lassin left their marks on the sands of Luh football history in that final. Unlike their teammates who were in the fashionable rubber boots known as "Tigana", they wore leather boots. They were in Rambo T-shirts, but their shorts were unique and assorted: Petit Frère in particular wore a pair of black Adidas polyester nylon shorts, rather similar to that of a marathon runner. Whenever he flared up in his spectacular "ciseaux", the shorts seemed to suspend in the windy air, producing a rustling sound and before you realised it, he had wired the ball into the opponent's net. Petit-frère, like his name, was petit in size but gigantic in his moves. Tigana was no less spectacular. Like his namesake Jean Tigana, who, with Michel Platini, Luis Fernandez and Alain Giresse constituted the "Magic Square" (le carré magique) of the French national side in the 80s, the Tigana from Lassin was a veritable mid-field bulwark that frustrated all the efforts of Monaco's otherwise pervasive attack line. Even though a defensive mid-fielder, he was a fox in the box and nutmegged not less than three Monaco defenders in a single game. It was not Monaco's day and its loaned players did not add any real value. To be frank, they were a liability. Unlike Monaco's players who excelled in noisy football slang on the pitch, Tigana and Petit Frère did not talk much, apart from few laconic exchanges in their Noni mother-tongue. Whenever Rambo scored, Tigana would pick the ball and run with it to the centre circle, for Monaco's attackers to re-start the game as quickly as possible. Despite the euphoric and provocative ululations of Rambo fans, he maintained a melancholic countenance, as if unsatisfied with the goals of the game, and perhaps, the goals of life. Petit Frère celebrated his own goals with a series of back springs but returned promptly to action. They seemed to have been playing together for decades and their body language was telepathic.

On Monaco's side, it was a sad story. Piro, who had impressed with his melodramatic warm-up, took pleasure in kicking the ball into the bush rather than give constructive passes. Close to three decades after, two balls of FIFA Luh remain missing in the raffia bush to the western flank of the Catholic School Field constructed by Father John. Each time Piro sent the ball out of the field in a maladroit move, he kept complaining of "Na chaka", insinuating that his boots were the matter. Reserve players, one after the other, had to sacrifice their boots for the professional player, but the situation only worsened. The false Pagal was substituted by Nfoninwe, who helped him in his warm-up histrionics. In the end, Monaco was douched 4 goals to 1, with a last-minute flash-in-the-pan header by Ndi Charles after hitting the woodwork earlier into the game. Rambo was, indeed, your worst nightmare[12] in spite of Monaco's prior dominance of the league. Years later, you met Piro, the false Pagal in Yaoundé and when he heard you were from Luh, he reminded you of how he used to play professional football in Luh. You told him that he did not only make Monaco lose the finals, but also the balls.

In the days of the Inter-quarters football games, life bloomed in the village. It usually coincided with the beans harvesting period, when the colourful bean grains from fledgeling bean plants had been transformed into gorgeous Holland Wax and English wax fabrics in the Ndu Market and the village women shone brightly in new brands of fashionable sandals, shoes and sweaters. The beans harvesting and marketing season was the time of the year when men were most submissive to women, especially given the capricious nature of the coffee prices that had turned the coffee plants that surrounded many compounds into nothing more than an excessive ornamentation

12. In Rambo III, when the Russian colonel Zaysen asks Rambo who he is, the latter responds: "Your worst nightmare".

void of any market value. But when women were happy everyone was happy. The football competition created a propitious ambiance for other auxiliary activities: gambling grew considerably, in the form of cards, babyfoot and ballé ballé; the football clubs created self-help groups in the various quarters for 'chapearing' maize farms and for transporting harvested maize cobs from distant farms; the female members of the clubs created ballet groups that interpreted popular songs during half-time and the post-match gala evening: J.B. Mpiana, Bozi Boziana, Aurlus Mabele, Pépé Kallé, Papa Wemba, Koffi Olomide, General Defao, Loka Loketo, Diblo Dibala, Lokassa Ya M'Bongo, Rémy Sahlomon, Oliver N'goma, Meiway, Pierrette Adams, Papillon, Wenge Musica, Extra Musica, Werrason, Emile Kangue, Tshala Muana, M'bilia Bel, Yondo Sister, Charlotte Mbango, Monique Seka, Liza T, Rachel Mimbo, Nguea Laroute, etc.

Those were the days of the branché fashion, of the petticoat, of the waist purse, of Lacoste and MALCOLM X T-shirts, of wool trousers, of Levi's Jeans, of punk and of shalaman hairstyles. Youthful activities between the villages of Ntundip, Luh and Taku reached the peak during that time, especially during their respective market days, above all, thanks to the football competitions in the three villages. The degree of solidarity, conviviality and social intercourse between the three localities was so intense that at that time, any child born out of wedlock was most likely to be blessed with the genetic stamp of a triple heritage.

For anyone who had lived through that period in Luh, many things had changed. The deserted nature of the village square was a testimony of the degree of rural exodus in your area. But there was another phenomenon for which exodus was an understatement, a new form of exodus that snatched the likes of Nfor Augustine, Tantoh Edwin, Nfoninwe, Gamnje Nyawah, etc. Nyawah, a staunch Monaco fan, used to hide a bunch of sparrows under his black *lanton* cap and would release one into the air each time Monaco scored a goal. The more goals scored, the more sparrows he released. Even opposing fans yearned for that sensational spectacle!

When you left the mission quarter, it was dark. By the time you crossed the River Mbim, it was almost difficult to make out faces. You made haste to go home, knowing you did not have much time to spend with your parents since you needed to travel to Nkambe the following day. When you arrived home, after having dinner with your parents in the kitchen, you went straight to what used to be your deceased elder brother's room. Your kid sister Mamulih had insinuated that was where you were likely to find the book. There were two large boxes placed on a wall-length table. One of them, the smaller one, contained mainly his clothes while the second, the larger one, was full of books and hordes of papers. You rummaged anxiously through their contents but did not come any close to the object of your quest.

At the bottom of the box filled with clothes, you rather found a series of novels, including *The Rebel's Love.* Amongst the maze of papers and envelopes, you found two small-sized photographs, sheathed in what seemed like pieces of a disintegrated album. One was seriously corroded by rust, while the second still bore traces of its brightness, though rust seemed to have begun its irrevocable and malicious task on it too. You carefully dragged them out of the plastic sheaths, not without causing them few additional bruises in the process. In the first one, he was in a group of five mates with radiant faces, squatting on the lawn. You could make out the faces of some of his friends for he used to tell you many stories about them. You wondered where they could be at that moment. The second one was certainly taken years later given his air of relative maturity. He was standing alone, in front of the school signboard. By then it was still Government High School Nkambe. He looked rather composed to the point of melancholy. Under the photo was written: **Why think? Why worry? Be**.

You recognised both pictures because you used to take pleasure in going through the album of your elder brothers, enthralled by what seemed like secondary school bliss, dreaming of one day being in their shoes. Nfoninwe, Kong and Barake used to tag a caption on each of their photos, carefully inserted as a slender piece of paper into the transparent sheath. Some were biblical verses while others seemed to be severed excerpts from novels or poetry books. You used to take time and read them carefully, enjoying their poetic profundity and attempting to connect the text with the state of mind or the spirit of the photographed subjects.

As you stared at the second picture, you realised that you had never really known the face of your elder brother. Or you had not known it as it was on that picture. You felt overwhelmed and as you looked at his face, it seemed as if your memory had completely merged with your eyes, yielding a combination of density and weight that assailed your soul in that confusing moment. How can something be and then not be again? What is present or the present? Are we or are we not? Nay, are we and are we not? How does one trust presence and the present when sooner than later what had been is not anymore? Your eyes started to wet as you thought about these things. That was the brother in whose image you grew up. You used his clothes and shoes, you used his books, you used his school notes, you copied his handwriting. He pre-disposed you for the arts in your early secondary school days, through the archive of books that he bequeathed to the family library. You were bereft. As you relinquished the search, misty-eyed, the words of the letter reverberated stridently in your mind:

> ...I have contacts with the NHRC officials in Bamenda where I now have a desk in their office in Commercial Avenue. I have been promised sponsorship and subsequent production of my piece of work. You will do me a favour by sending me the number of that your friend from the British Council for prior editing before I proceed to present the novel to the organization. I am still waiting for their promised funding to make photocopies of

the original text and send you one for editing...
Yours brother,
Barake
09.02.

He had sent you this letter a few months before your trip to Germany. Before your homecoming, you discovered it among the maze of secondary school love letters that you carried along with you.

Where were you going to lay hands on the book he talked about? You had tried to contact the British Council official whose phone number you sent to him as requested in the letter but was not able to reach him. The NHRC[13] office in Bamenda was also coming under renewed pressure from the government. Once you talked to him on the phone when you were in Yaoundé and he told you the police had raided their office and confiscated a typed draft of the book. It was not uncommon for the police to raid the offices of the NHRC in Bamenda due to its caustic criticism of government actions. But, if you remembered well, he told you he still had a manuscript. What could the book be about? Was it autobiographical? Was it in any way related to the NHRC struggle?

Later in the evening, before bedtime, your father congratulated you for your academic achievements in a more formal tone. Your mother joined in. You were filled with gratitude for both of them. Their parental love, resolve and sacrifice in a rather difficult economic climate had paved the way for you. You realised just how indebted you were to them. On your laptop, you showed them pictures of your PhD defence and of the day you were awarded a Prize by the German Academic Exchange Service. They were all filled with pride for your achievements. Your elder brother died about five months before your PhD defence and you were afraid on that day you would be overpowered by the sad memory. But fortunately,

---

13. National Human Rights Congress.

you sailed through courageously.

You searched in your luggage and brought out a printed copy of your PhD thesis which you handed to your dad. He held it in his hands affectionately for some minutes and passed it onto your mum. Then he went to his room and brought a voluminous and slightly deteriorating book. You recognised the other book, a thick type-written text whose pages had turned yellowish brown by the passage of time, exuding with a strong scent of distilled dust and with edges partly chopped by rats. As your father stood there, teary-eyed, the entire story behind the other book unfolded in your memory.

To my Father, Konfor Kilo

The most decent of dads, so said my mom
Who never as once did raise his voice
Against his own, against the world
But lived his life beyond reproach

It is more than a quarter century since you left
Yea, more than a whole generation since you left
I, a son without a father, thus far I have crept
Living by the sweat of my brow,
I've lived the life of a tramp
Little to eat, little to wear, no place to sleep.

Do not lament, dear kindly dad
With myself and with the world
I turn the page inside out, and as I pore
I share my grief, I share my joy
I weep for me, I weep for you

Do not lament, dear kindly dad
As I think about you now, I bow
Atop the mount, dear kindly dad
I know your heart, do not lament
This is the mount you would've climbed
I've climbed for you, I've climbed for all.

With trembling hands and swollen eyes
I lay this on your tomb

It is your wreath, refreshing wreath
Will still be fresh till Kingdom come.

And to my mother Eleanor Mbaseng

The most decent of moms, I know myself
Who would praise my dad as exemplar
Who these years has brought me up
Fulfilling the dual functions of parental love.

Who never at once did raise her voice
But went to work that we might live
My sisters know, my brothers too
You lived your life beyond reproach.

Little did I know your time was near
Day and night as I sat to write
Hoping to show you this just very soon
So you could see in twilight years, dear tender mom
What I have done these many years
Alas! It wasn't to be, because you've left.

Dear precious mom, what a time to leave!
What a time to leave! With me abroad
Struggling by day, struggling by night
To die bereft of care, unloved, unclothed.

Do not lament, dear tender mom
I know your heart, a lion's heart
I sought the best for all the rest
As I think about you, I bow.

With trembling hands and swollen eyes
I lay this on your tomb, dear tender mom
It is your wreath, refreshing wreath
Will still be fresh till Kingdom come.

And to the African Continent

That through education and political democracy
You may wake up from your slumber and backwardness,
Rise above the ashes, and be a full partner
In the development of the modern world.

By Konfor Stephen Ngeh

THE DOCTOR

So runs my dream, but what am I?
An infant crying in the night
An infant crying for the light
And with no language but a cry.
("In Memoriam A. H. H.", Lord Alfred Tennyson)

Luh, August 1990. Nothing in the gentle flow of River Mbim had heralded an incident so bewildering that would bring to a halt life in Luh, a village hitherto shielded from the arrows of outrageous fortune by the natural radar of the Kaa and Nchindong mountains. Early on that day, you had gone to the farm at Njeng, about a kilometre away from your compound. It was the maize harvesting season. Not long after you and your mother arrived at the farm, you heard the unusual sound of the bell. It was not yet noon, the time the Catholic Church bell usually rang. It was still 10:30 AM. Moreover, the bell seemed to be coming from close quarters and its arrhythmic frequency did not come any close to the systematic time-keeping Catholic bell. Certainly, it was from the Baptist Church which was closer to the farm. As both of you stood wondering who was ill in the village, Bradog, your family dog, appeared at the northern edge of the farm. It ran towards you and began ruffling your trousers with its front claws. Bradog was your friend, but a better soulmate to your younger brother, Tabong. Though he had a habit of sniffing your traces and following you to distant places unexpectedly, you still felt something was amiss. Minutes later, Tabong appeared, panting like Bradog.

"Mum, mum, Pa Tanko sent me to call for you. Someone has died." He announced the news with the brutality of an innocent child.

"And who is that?"

"He said the Doctor who was in America."

On hearing this, the hoe slipped off your mother's hands and she stood still. She remained immobile like a scarecrow for what looked like eternity. Bradog's caressing of her legs and your confused voices could not bring her to the present. From the pensive look on her face, you knew the purported deceased must be someone dear to her. She was trying so hard to hide it from you and your brother, but you had known her all your life to understand when she was in pain. You looked at her face, entreating her to share whatever it was that put her in such a pensive mood.

"How did he get the information?" your mother queried Tabong, pretending fruitlessly to sound calm.

"It is the taxi driver, Sam Bob, who brought the news. He stopped at the Baptist Church before stopping again at Pa Tanko's compound," Tabong explained.

Unfortunately, his story began to make some sense.

"Could it be an accident?"

Tabong shrugged his shoulders. Probably, she did not mean it as a question to be answered by Tabong. She was merely wondering aloud.

"But what did Sam Bob say when he handed the letter?"

"Nothing."

Your mother did not query any further. You all knew Sam Bob as a taciturn, unbending and tight-lipped person. He was an enigmatic character, with a deeply sedate but slightly sullen face, and only uttered few words to his passengers, usually to bring order in his taxi and bid passengers not to damage any part of his car. He was the owner of his taxi and thus took good care of it. Usually, people preferred his taxi, not only because it was the cleanest but also because he was not used to overloading passengers like sardines in a can, as did other drivers such as Nya. More so, he was slow and steady and never bordered to speed up in order to scramble for passengers with his peers cum competitors.

Still not having come to terms with the news, your mum ordered you to go home. Your younger brother suggested you harvest some few cobs of maize for the evening roast before leaving. But your mother insisted that you leave immediately. As she spoke, you could hear the shakiness in her voice.

Tabong and Bradog led the way. As you walked back home, you heard your mother grumbling behind. At times, she would clap her hands and breathe heavily, then urged you to hurry. You tried on several occasions to ask her more about "the doctor," but the hastiness in which all of you were, made it impossible to turn and face her.

"It must be Dr Stephen. He was a soulmate to your father," she quipped. Though she was so loud, you did not know whether she wanted to engage you in a conversation or not. You hesitated for a moment and listened as the green grass along the footpath swept against your bodies. Though you still doubted whether mother wanted to get you involved, you, however, gave in after the long silence.

"Dad used to mention that name," you responded, asserting the power of your memory, with the hope that mother will offload some of the burdens on her mind and share with you. After all, was teacher Amos Takwa not used to saying that a problem shared is half solved?

On your way, you came across women harvesting maize on their farms.

"O' ya bi ooo' tapsi la' nii," (my people, courage in your work), your mum greeted.

"*Hawuleeeeee,*" they responded.

Both the utterance and the response were void of the usual elation that accompanied that communal exchange. It was a typical exchange between a passer-by and a group of women busy working on farmland. This was especially the case during *bofah*, a cultural arrangement based on peer solidarity whereby a group worked on the farm of each of its members in turns. This included cultivating, weeding, planting, harvesting corn, beans, groundnuts, the main food crops in your area. Moreover, if a member was bereaved, her peers would dedicate a day's farm work in her honour, as a gesture of condolence. This was often at the end of the period of bereavement when members of the bereaved family have shaved their hair as the ultimate sign of mourning.

She announced the news to the curious women who had certainly heard the bell and were left wondering. Although she did not sound conclusive, the magnitude of the situation was evident on the morose faces of the women. One woman, the wife of the Catholic church catechist, upon listening to your mum threw her hoe to the ground in desperation:

> *Hebeeeee, hebeeee*
> *hebeee hebbbeee*
> *Nyar a rkipti rdong*
> *Nyu ma Mbi,*
> *Nyu ni Kop Bvuri*
> *Lunga*
> *Lurchu*
> *Ji fa kir koni kah*
> *oooooo yerbeeee*
> *nyame ha yo heyyy*
> *bu ha bi yenda ni me le*
> *Tata nyu tehshi wir ni yo ngoro*[14]

---

14. *Lunga*, the Luh legend who went to heaven without dying; *Kop Bvuri*, the main natural forest of Luh; *Lurchu*, a legendary stone in Luh that is believed used to talk in ancient times; Mbim, the river that flows through Luh village.

The others looked equally mortified by a reality they were reluctant to admit. Instantly, they gathered their farm tools and the few maize cobs and left for their homes. Each time someone died, tradition proscribed any farm work in the entire village within three days of bereavement. The bereaved family could only resume work weeks afterwards, especially if the deceased was someone advanced in age. That was different from the customary public holidays in the village: Sunday, (for Christians), Friday (for Moslems) and most especially, *Ntala*, also known as *country Sunday*, one of the eight weekdays set aside by tradition for people to rest at home and allow the Gods to bless the farmlands. On *Ntala*, farm work was forbidden, except for general human investment or work on the fon's farm. Anyone who went against the Country Sunday rules risked being summoned to the palace with a *Nkeng*, the dracaena plant (aka peace plant) for which they would pay a heavy fine.

Upon arriving home, you and your mum went straight to Mr Tanko's compound. There, was the Baptist Church pastor, Rev. Nyong, surrounded by men and women clad in astonishment and disbelief, some with hands akimbo and others, especially the women, had their hands crossed over their chests and their heads. It was true. By every passing minute, any hope that it was the effect of collective daydreaming petered out: Dr Konfor, the illustrious son and the hope of Luh village was no more. Nothing could mollify that hard reality. According to the detailed information, the deceased was found dead in his apartment in America. Mr Tanko held a piece of white paper in his left hand as he spoke to the people. In his right hand was a black-and-white album from which he took a photo and brandished to the gathered men and women. You recognised the photo for your dad too had a copy of it in his archives. It was a photo of three able-bodied blokes in Afro haircut, white shirt and long trumpet-shaped trousers which canopied the shoes completely. Their shirts were unbuttoned at the neck level. They were certainly in their mid-20s and looked more like members of an acapella trio.

But their faces were rather grave, an effect of excessive disciplining of the body-self in front of the Canon camera in those days. The deceased was slightly taller than your dad, *chicha*, and Mr Tanko.

"From what *chicha* told me, the last time he wrote to him was in June last year. And from every indication, he was doing very well," he said, looking at your mum who nodded in confirmation.

"*Chicha,* has someone been sent to announce the news to his family in Ngaki- Mansa quarter?"

It was Mami Mulah, your neighbour from the compound across the road. Your dad, Mr Tanko and Mr Kong were simply referred to by the elderly people in your village as *chicha (teacher)* since they were amongst the few primary school teachers the village could boast of. But they usually pronounced it *chicha*.

"Yes, I have sent Ndukong to convey the news," Mr Tanko assured her.

"Oh, Pa Nkwinteh will surely collapse and die on hearing the news, especially as he has not been well in the past months."

"Yes, Ndukong will know how to convey the news to him. That is why I sent him and no one else."

Ndukong was your cousin. Though a teenager, he grew up amongst elders and almost came to share in their speech forms at a relatively young age. Thus Mr Tanko counted on his wisdom to convey the sad news to one who was the closest living relative of the deceased.

The news travelled like wildfire throughout the village. A member of the village elite Mr Machar came on his motorcycle to confirm the news with Mr Tanko. In the absence of your dad, Mr Tanko was the only trustworthy source for such information, given his relative closeness with the deceased. Mr Machar was the BBC of the village. He used to be a strong SDF militant in the 1990s and with his indispensable motorcycle, he could spread news both from and to the village at short notice especially on his way from Ndu.

That evening, your mum was restless, moving to one neighbour after the other to discuss the heart-rending news. It was your elder sister Mangwang who prepared dinner that evening. But your appetite was dampened by the gloomy atmosphere that characterised the day.

Your dad came home two days later. He had learnt the sad news through a radio announcement. He left the locality where he was teaching immediately on a hired motorcycle and arrived in Luh almost barehanded, not even bushmeat that he used to bring back from the village in Ako where he taught for years. He only came with a suitcase containing a few clothes and his JVC Radio.

In the days that followed, the villagers were informed that the body of the deceased was going to be brought to the village in a week. A series of preparatory meetings followed. Your dad was the contact point between the village committees and the host of people who intended to accompany the corpse from Yaoundé and Bamenda to Luh village. The Fon announced an all-inclusive human investment campaign given that the village was going to be in the spotlight, for a sad reason, though. People contributed foodstuffs and several wine tappers pledged to supply jugs of raffia palm wine at a reduced rate during the occasion. Since the announcement of the sad news, almost every car that came from Ndu Town brought a letter to your dad. Many dignitaries of Donga-Mantung Division and some personalities in the national capital in Yaoundé were involved in the preparations.

For an entire week, dark clouds hung over Luh and the rhythm of the hitherto peaceful village was conditioned by the impending event. Dr Konfor was by far the most educated person in Luh and the surrounding villages. In Luh village, in particular, he was a myth, even to his own family. Only your dad held the key to this myth. They had schooled together up to Form Three at Joseph Merrick Baptist College, Ndu. Your dad narrated to you how they used to trek to and from Ndu every week. Their dream was to further their education as far as they could. But your father was compelled to curtail his ambition by his sickly father. It was then that he decided to enter a Teacher Training College in Bello, in the neighbouring Boyo Division. He was the lastborn and one of the two males in a family of six. His elder brother, the firstborn, was a kola nut trader between Cameroon and Nigeria. He had earlier escaped from the village due to the harassment of tax collectors and only reappeared years later. In the days of Ahidjo, the first president of Cameroon, many families in rural communities lost members who ran away from tax collectors and never came back. After several fruitless years of waiting, funeral services were organised for the missing. In some cases, the disappeared member would later re-emerge after years and even decades just to learn with amusement or bewilderment about his funeral ceremony and the grave where he had been symbolically buried!

Your dad's elder brother would buy kola nuts from your locality and transport them to Nigeria. From Nigeria, he would buy products like coffee mills, radio sets, china plates, pans, etc. At one point, he smuggled in a counterfeiting machine and by the time the border police discovered it, he was already on the run. By then you didn't know that it was referred to as a counterfeiting machine. The family spent years without knowing his whereabouts. When he finally resurfaced and came back, he brought only a coffee-grinding mill. You wondered how your family situation would be had he succeeded to enter the country with the money machine. Your dad was therefore the more unsurprising of the siblings and he could not deny his ailing father the wish to have his Benjamin by his bedside in his last days. That is how your dad handed the flames of his dreams to his friend while he settled for a more practical option of a primary school teacher. Their destinies took different paths at that point. But the very few times your dad spoke of him in your family, you were left with the impression that there were deep affective ties between the two which time and distance could not vitiate. Some of their former classmates in the village used to talk about the brightness of the duo in highly superlative terms.

In the days preceding the burial, "the Doctor" was on every lip and youth discussed about him as they sipped palm wine in your family's provision store, which was often the place where popular sagas were shared in a convivial spirit. The true thirst of the stories lay not in their veracity but the telling. It was there that you learnt through the local BBC that India was banned from participating in the FIFA World Cup because in the previous editions they sustained a score sheet of ninety goals in ninety minutes in each game; that the Cameroonian goalkeeper Thomas N'Kono used to split into three different goalkeepers, thereby preventing attackers from scoring against him during the 1990 World Cup; that the ace attacking midfielder Cyrille Makanaky was fond of shooting far above the crossbar because he was 'pinned' by Roger Milla, the team's main goal scorer; that Paul Biya once converted into a bee to sting and kill Ni John Fru Ndi, the charismatic opposition leader, but that the latter discovered his tactics and escaped in the form of wind; that Paul Biya travelled abroad every year to drain his veins of old blood and refill them with youthful blood; that Super Makia, the intrepid Cameroonian heavyweight wrestler could let a Land Rover run over him, without damaging an ounce of his flesh; that the Cameroonian soldiers in the semi-arid northern regions sometimes used their boots to carry extra quantity of drinking water over long distances; that the soldiers at the warfront in Bakassi used to smoke their cigarettes at night in reverse direction, with the lit end in the mouth so as to avoid alerting the enemy Nigerian soldiers; that the brain of late Prof. Bernard Fonlon[15] contained more lobes than an average human brain, etc.

15. Bernard Nsokika Fonlon (1924-1986) was an eminent Cameroonian Professor of African Literatures and former minister. Commonly considered Cameroon's first bilingual citizen, he is generally acclaimed as a genuine intellectual and black Socrates. The African Literature Association (ALA) instituted a Fonlon-Nichols Prize in 1993 which is "awarded to an African writer for excellence in creative writing and contributions to the struggle for human rights and freedom of expression". Luh village of the Mbum ethnic group shares a boundary with his ethnic group, Nso.

Almost everyone in the village knew about Dr Konfor even when many of them had never seen him. He was your community's own Fonlon. Concerning his sudden death, some argued that if he had returned to the country, the lowest post he would have held would have been that of a provincial governor. Others argued that he was meant to be included in the new ministerial cabinet of President Biya but that he had denied the offer because he was allergic to corruption. And then some claimed he was a medical doctor, the only cancer specialist of Cameroonian origin. Some claimed he was killed by witchcraft; others said he was a victim of an American conspiracy because he was more intelligent than all of his American mates. And countless other postulations. No one understood the exact reason why he did not come home after his studies. Your father had addressed the issue in a letter to him, persuading him to come back home, find a job and settle down with a wife. He had promised to consider the suggestions.

Few days to the burial, you met *Chicha* in his sleeping room, the *mnu ndap* "inner room", as the sleeping room of parents is called in Limbum language. You came in to collect your Sunday clothes for ironing. As a matter of principle, your Sunday clothes were kept in your parent's room and you only collected them on Sunday morning. *Chicha* was going through a pile of pictures in a pensive and serene demeanour. You thought you should leave the room, so as not to behold him in such a dour and morose state. On the contrary, he seemed to need someone to talk to. Never had you seen him so frail and dejected. Since he was always far from home due to his demanding teaching career, you only saw him during the summer holidays. And you knew Discipline was back. You knew you had to sit up; to wake up every six o'clock in the morning to sweep the compound; to read even during holidays; to fetch water in time; to bathe in time, etc.

"Here are some of the photos I took with him," your father said as a way of invitation.

The "him" referred to the deceased.

The photos he showed you were not part of the family album. They were still very sparkling as though fresh from the studio. One was the photo his friend had enclosed in one of the letters they exchanged. He and a lady stood by the side of a seated elderly man. They were his female colleague and their lecturer, your dad explained to you. The background was a veritable book cave. Seeing him buried in books then reminded you of his big typewritten Book, a conspicuous and imposing sight in the trunk in the parental sleeping room. It was a PhD thesis in Political Sciences by Konfor Stephen Ngeh. You had tried a few times to open it but the English in which it was written appeared quite abstract, with long, undulating, snaky and unending sentences. So, you did not venture past the beautiful and touching poetry of the dedication page and acknowledgments, in which the name of your dad featured. As a child, you wondered how someone could write such a book without his head exploding!

On seeing the picture, you thought of asking your dad if one day someone like you could also study abroad. But a voice told you not to ask so many questions. You could ask him that on a brighter day. The second photo was taken in Cameroon. There, they were three persons: your dad, Dr Konfor and one other man who looked graciously old, with carefully trimmed white beards that gave him a certain air of wisdom.

"It was the last time we met. He had just come back from the University of Yaoundé after his first degree. We went to greet the Divisional Delegate of Education for Donga-Mantung Division."

"The man resembles Tarkfu," you quipped, referring to your maternal grandfather who lived in Taraba State, Nigeria.

"Oh, it is true. Even in his dressing," your father responded, almost in a disguised light-hearted mood. If you were a grown-up, you would have found some words to console him. But it was a role you were too young to play. As you were talking, your younger brother Tabong entered the room.

"Dad, Pa Kong and Pa Tanko are looking for you," Tabong announced.

They were the two other primary school teachers in your quarter. They were your father's seniors and taught in schools in and around Luh village. Your dad carefully inserted his pictures in-between his books and went to the parlour. The three were trying to come up with the plan for the burial and to propose ideas to the church, the bereaved family and the village chief concerning the entire funeral programme. Leaning against the corridor wall that separated your room from the parlour, you followed their entire discussion. You overheard them concerting as to whether the burial was going to be according to Christian faith or traditional rites.

"We need to discuss this with the chief," said Pa Tanko.

"Yes, but the pastor and the appointed deacon already held their meetings and are planning towards the event," responded Pa Kong, who was one of the deacons of the Baptist Church.

"All I know is that he was a Christian. We both got baptised when we were students in JMBC Ndu. However, he was also a man of culture. During the few days he lived in Yaoundé, he never used to miss any Mfuh seating. Stephen would rather forget his birthday than the day of the Mfuh seating."

"I think we need to consider the opinion of his family on this since he did not leave a will," Pa Kong suggested and your dad and Mr Tanko conceded.

At the end of the meeting, they developed a draft programme.

A few days later, when the final programme was ready, your dad asked your elder brother Barake to manually produce ten copies each of the two-page document. You usually envied your elder brothers for their handwritings that were very much similar to that of your dad. While Barake's letters were rather smaller in size, Kong's were slightly right-leaning. Klinsmann's, on the other hand, were much bigger and showed a greater disposition to letter 'carving'. But all of them retained the same calligraphic dexterity of your dad. You dreamt of the day when you would be big enough to be entrusted with that privilege. You were still in primary school and your handwriting already bore nascent features of the family tradition, though in its very rudimentary state.

Time passed faster than usual and the burial of Dr Konfor finally came. Even though news of his death preceded the burial by close to a month, it bore the full weight of a tragedy for which the entire village was ill-prepared. Something had come to an end. The collective mourning was overwhelming. An endless cortege of vehicles lined the village road in what seemed like the first experience of heavy traffic in Luh. There were vehicles of various shapes. You had never seen as many cars in your life. You were told the Governor, the Senior Divisional Officers and the top officials of your province were going to be present at the burial. Some people rumoured that the deceased was a classmate to the then Chief of Cabinet in the Prime Minister's office and that some ministers, his former classmates, would be in attendance.

On the fateful morning of 4th September 1990, as the sun rose at the fatal interstices of the Kaa and Nchindong mountains, the long-awaited hearse bearing the casket finally appeared around the curve just above the Baptist Church. Incredulous village folks stood by the road in utter moroseness. It was customary to tie palm fronds, reeds and other leafy branches to the vehicle's bonet as a symbol that it was carrying a corpse. The hearse made a brief stop at the Baptist Church. Members of the funeral committee had thought there would be a brief service at the church before burial, but that was not to be the case. Everything was going to take place in Ngaki-Mansa, the quarter of origin of the deceased. The entire village came out for the tragic homecoming of its illustrious son. Now, the tragedy was irreversibly real.

All roads led to Luh. While in Luh, all roads led to Ngaki-Mansa quarter. All the jugs of raffia palm wine and the baskets of *njamnsu* (huckleberry leaves) too. Several choirs were present and the ceremony began with a series of speeches by the representative of the bereaved family and other dignitaries of the village. This was followed by the sermon of Rev. Nyong, the pastor of the Baptist Church. He was a naturally slow and soft speaker but, on that day, God took total control over him and endowed his tongue with a potent and entrancing touch. He held the entire village spellbound with his lucid and unequivocal message: No one knows the final moment. So, beware, for the Kingdom of God is at hand.

The charge of his message was electric and you felt as if the Reverend had transcended his physical surrounding and was tapping directly from the transcendental realm. After the sermon, the English Choir of the Baptist Church followed with a special number. It was only after the sermon and the choral performance that the buckets of boiled corn and groundnuts were passed around amongst those squatted under the surrounding coffee plants. This was the customary foodstuff shared en masse during burial ceremonies. Only special guests had access to the stewed beef and goat meat. But for you, the taste of the corn beans was not the same after the message. You struggled with the insipid grains for a while and finally gave up, terrified by Pastor Nyong's sermon. Death was inevitable, even imminent, the Second Coming was at hand and you were ill-prepared for it. The message in the song of the Hallelujah Choir was foreboding to any sinner:

> *Jesus is coming back,*
> *Where will you be*
> *On the last day?*
>
> *Too late too late,*
> *Too late too late.*
>
> *I will run and take the Cross*
> *And go with Him,*

Where will you be?
I will run and take the Cross
And go with Him

Too late, too late
Too late, too late...

That song stuck in your memory indelibly.

The Master of Ceremony, the appointed deacon of the Baptist Church, then called on your dad to say a word about the deceased as his long-time friend and classmate. You wondered what he was going to say if he would have the emotional stamina to speak at all. He had been tremendously aggrieved from the moment he returned to the village upon learning about the sad news until the day of the burial. He gently moved forward from the section where members of the organising committee sat and came close to the casket. He removed his red traditional cap, as a sign of respect for the elders and especially the chief. He held a tiny piece of paper in his left hand and began speaking in English after brief words in Limbum.

"My dear fathers and mothers, brothers and sisters, I cannot believe that I am standing here to give this testimony. I have waited for someone to tell me that it is a dream, but time seems to be running out. Here I am. Stephen, is it true that you are no more? Is it you lying still with sealed lips in this wooden box?" His eyes were fixed on the coffin as he spoke. He went ahead to give a brief rundown of the life of the deceased amidst intermittent sobs. It was your first time seeing your dad cry. To make matters worse, he was weeping in public. You had never felt such affection, pity and sympathy for him before. After being restrained by Pa Tanko who gave him a handkerchief with which to wipe his tears, he continued with his eulogy.

"In his ultimate letter to me, accompanied by a copy of his PhD, he told me he had wanted to come home immediately after the completion of his postdoctoral programme but was retained by his university to develop a curriculum for African Legal Studies. He did not make mention of any health problems in a letter that touched on almost every detail of his life in the USA and the presidential campaign of President George H. W. Bush. He informed me that the US government had wanted to send him on mission to the Middle East but he rejected the offer due to the critical conditions in that part of the world. He opted for a job opportunity in California and to the best of my knowledge, it is this month that he had to assume duty in California. It is thus with a sense of disbelief that I followed the announcement of Stephen's death on the radio and later on received the letter from Mr Gwei, present here, to that effect. Perhaps, we will learn more about the actual circumstances in the days and weeks ahead, when we must have made adequate contacts with Wayne State University, where he was working. He dies a few months after his fortieth birthday. Stephen was not just a determined person, he was determination incarnate. Stephen was not just altruistic, he was altruism. He would go an extra mile to help others and even forgo his own things. He was kind to everybody. Those who have been to the US and back talk of the same Stephen I knew who would do everything possible to help others."

As your father spoke, in grief, your mind settled on a poem you had found in *The Sheldon Book of Verse*, one of the priceless books in your family library. You had felt the grief of that poem even when it expressed reality in a distant time and place. It was a tribute by William Wordsworth to the great English bard, John Milton:

London 1802

MILTON! thou shouldst be living at this hour:
England hath need of thee: she is a fen
Of stagnant waters: altar, sword, and pen,
Fireside, the heroic wealth of hall and bower,

> Have forfeited their ancient English dower
> Of inward happiness. We are selfish men;
> O raise us up, return to us again,
> And give us manners, virtue, freedom, power!
> Thy soul was like a Star, and dwelt apart;
> Thou hadst a voice whose sound was like the sea:
> Pure as the naked heavens, majestic, free,
> So didst thou travel on life's common way,
> In cheerful godliness; and yet thy heart
> The lowliest duties on herself did lay.

Listening to the words that percolated from the sobs of your father, it was difficult to have a clear picture of the trajectory of the deceased. The following morning, you found the tear-stained pleated paper he held in his hands during the emotional eulogy lying on his reading table. It read: Dr Stephen Konfor was born on 14th January 1950. He did his primary education in Luh, CBM Taku and Ndu, later proceeded to Joseph Merrick Baptist College in Ndu where he passed the GCE O Level in 1968. The following year, he was recruited by the Department of Customs, where he worked as an assessment clerk in the City of Victoria, Cameroon until when he succeeded in the GCE Advanced Level in 1971 and enrolled in the University of Yaoundé in 1972. He obtained an LLB in Law in 1977 and a BA in Languages (English and French) in 1979. While studying, he worked in the city of Yaoundé as Controller of Customs. Upon graduating from the University, he was posted to the City of Douala as Inspector of Customs at the airport. In 1981 he left for the United States of America where he graduated with an MA in Development Administration from Western Michigan University in 1982. He then moved to Wayne State University, Detroit, for his PhD in Political Sciences with specialization in Public Policy which he defended in 1989.

Your father's testimony cum eulogy was one of the last items on the programme after which the body of the deceased was laid into the grave. The Fon did not speak, contrary to what many had expected. However, he was amongst the first to throw the handful of soil into the grave as tradition required. The wailing reached an unprecedented pitch when the gravediggers introduced the coffin into the shaft. Amongst all the members of the bereaved family, the younger sister of the deceased was the most deplorable sight. It took the personal efforts of the Fon to restrain her. The chief himself looked dejected, seemingly affected by the gravity of the moment. Usually, he was a hilarious personality, with authoritative and yet contagious laughter. But the gravity of the moment left no one untouched.

After the first layer of soil was poured in, a group of six youth entered the shaft and began to tamper the ground under their feet. At the end of every seventh minute, they alternated with another standby group of six. While one group was in the shaft, the other members were sipping some palm wine as they prepared to take over. There was a certain beauty in the songs intoned by the village "chief burier" Nyamifo who equally led the choreography.

> *Yo nyu a keh we*
> *Du la yo-yo bong bong*
> *We du yo-yo nfih muchar*
> *Tee wir koni we.*

> *Yo nyu a keeh we*
> *Du la yo-yo bong bong*
> *We du yo-yo feh muchar*
> *Tee wir koni we.*

> *Yo nyu a keeh we*
> *Du la yo-yo bong bong*
> *We du yo-yo feh muchar*

Tee wir koni we.

After the burial, the masquerade made its appearance. It was the feathered masquerade with a wooden mask known as *mabuh*. It is amongst the very inoffensive and benevolent masquerades in Mbumland, specialised in various celebrations, rituals and funeral ceremonies. The charcoal-black face of the *mabuh*, with its popped chubby cheeks and bulbous eyes is a veritable image of musefied ancestral lamentation. While the facial masks of most masquerades inspire fear and awe, that of the mabuh is an open plea, a plea for sympathy and empathy. It is a somewhat 'effeminate' version of the sprightly, swift, sharp mouthed and spear-shooting masquerade known as the *wan*. But while the *mabuh* and the *nkoh* belong to the most important secret society, the *nwarong*, the *wan* belongs to the second most important secret society in Mbumland known as the *ngiri*. The *ngiri* also has a rare version of the *mabuh*: *mabuh ngiri*, which does not have the wooden mask and does not produce a whistling sound. In the place of the wooden mask, its head is covered by a cocoyam leaf.

The *mabuh* went straight to the grave and leaned its head on one of the bunches of reeds, producing a shrill whistling sound that aptly created a sense of pathos and empathy. It then went and sat at the feet of the village chief before proceeding to where the close relatives of the deceased were seated. It was an emotional display from a masquerade. It brought tears down the cheeks of many, including the Christians and the Moslems. The *mabuh* only required you to squat as it passed by and no one could dare oppose that basic rule, except they vehemently wanted to face the wrath of the three or four accompanying masquerades, *chumbuh*, which played the role of "disciplining" the crowd for the main masquerades. They were to the main masquerades what church ushers were to the church dignitaries but were usually more forceful and steadfast in disciplining any renegades. Bystanders shouted *"chong tasai chong tasai"*, to calm down the *chumbu* as the latter hit the sticks in their hands menacingly on the ground, compelling everyone to squat and give way for the *mabuh*. That was followed by fingersnapping to indicate to the *mabuh* that the coast was clear for its passage.

The display was brief and as soon as *mabuh* had consoled the most affected family members, it made its way back to the palace. But not without collecting its jug of raffia palm wine and a full-grown hen as tradition required. For *mabuh* to go out and come back to the palace without a hen was anathema. That is why its body is covered with hen feathers. The jug of palm wine was often carried by someone chosen by the *bellman* while the latter clapped the wings of the quacking hen under his armpits. He held the pitched bell in between his left hand and forehand while tapping on it rhythmically with a wooden stick. The *bellman* was the bondsman of the group and with the sound of his bell, he determined the rhythm and tempo of the display. It was when the gifts were handed in that the display took a frenzied dimension, depending on the agility and the energy of the masquerade and the dithyrambic praise chanted by any bystander or a member of the juju entourage in honour of *mabuh*:

> *Yu bo Nfor, yu bo Nfor,*

> *Ndung eh ndung,*
> *ndung eh ndung*

> *Mabuh eh ndung,*
> *ndung eh ndung*

> *Mendang mendang*

It started getting dark and the cars slowly began trooping out of the village. But others were still parked along the road. Many of the august guests and visitors were going to spend the night in the village— some spent the night at your family home.

That evening, as you went home, you were overwhelmed by the dramatic funeral scenario, especially the conscience-pricking message of the pastor and the song by the Baptist Church Choir. You asked your sister Mangwang how the body of the deceased looked like. She had sat close to your mum throughout the burial and as the latter joined the queue to catch a glimpse of the corpse, Mangwang followed her. Since you had followed your mum out of headiness, you stayed away from her during the ceremony. She had asked you to stay at home for Ngaki-Mansa was too far, but you and your peers later followed the mammoth crowd.

"It was covered with a veil. So, I did not see it well. But from what I saw, he was looking very fresh, just as if he was alive," Mangwang replied.

You looked at your sister with a mixture of envy and eeriness. You had always thought that if you ever saw a dead person's body, especially the face, it would haunt you throughout your life. But you were envious for she had seen the corpse of someone who would forever remain a myth to you. How does someone look like when they die? You had heard different accounts of dead bodies before. Some people said the eyes were closed, while others maintained that they remained open as though they could see. You were particularly afraid of the latter case. Mangwang later talked of a shining clock watch that hung on the wrist of the deceased. Were the hands of that watch functional? What would become of that watch in the grave? What kind of time did it mark?

You only met your parents the following morning, not realising when they had come home the previous evening. You had gone to bed quite early that evening because it was only the five of you kids at home. But that night, the image of the corpse being introduced into the grave amid the wailings left you with a creepy sense of existential solitude. You were haunted by the scent of the freshly dug earth, the tears of your dad and the sorrowful humming of Mami Kfukfu who sat close to you at the funeral. With her back leaning against the coffee plant, she was oblivious to the entire funeral ceremony. She inconsolably sang and hummed her dirge all along, punctuating it with a series of proverbial utterances and thoughtful silence. Unlike others who found time to chew something in between the wailing and sobbing, Mami Kufkfu refused to taste of the funeral corn and groundnuts. All you retained from her was the constant reference to 'Mbaseng', the name of Dr Konfor's late mother, whom she was addressing as if she was standing there before her.

Why do people die? What is the difference between sleep and death? How can someone be and then not be? Will you ever be righteous enough to go to Heaven when you die? As these questions jostled in your confused puerile mind, you regretted why God created you, why He created the world, why He could not 'uncreate' you to save your loved ones from any agony when your own End comes. You would like to be a doctor in the future too, like Dr Konfor, but you did not want to die! During the funeral, as the buckets and basins of boiled corn and beans circulated, news also spread that Dr Konfor had died of 'Sugar Sugar'. 'Sugar sugar'! The word echoed forebodingly in your mind, each time with an even greater pernicious connotation. That was a stern blow to your love for sugar. You were fond of swallowing cubes of sugar especially when left alone in the family provision store. Your mum had talked of sweet things like sugar as being the cause for worms in children's stomach and as a danger to their teeth. That did not deter you. 'Sugar sugar'! Now, the writing was on the wall. Like you, the Doctor had certainly consumed too much sugar when he was a kid. And may be as an adult too. His death was your death begun. 'Sugar sugar'! You were left with bitter memories of the sweetness of sugar on your taste buds.

At the age of seven, you began to look at life through different and ever-changing prisms depending on certain circumstances. There were moments when your vision was sharp enough to cut through any barriers, natural or man-made; when life spread its petals in warm embrace, beckoning you to take the next boat to boundless shores; when your body was at one with the spirit, endowed with an unstoppable kinetic thrust, turning your inner self into a drone that could deliver at any target. At such moments, life seemed to be a promise within your reach, with a coherent inner purpose. But on some days, like those following Dr Konfor's funeral, you felt like a wet albatross, rudderless, with wings clipped by malignant destiny, like a snail hemmed in its shell and forced to peep through its carapace onto a rather crepuscular horizon. You could not understand why life's trophies were always haunted by unfathomable catastrophes; why joy or happiness was tragically ephemeral and evanescent while pain and grief were palpable, real, tactile, concrete, corporeal and long-lasting. Such moments cast a shadow on what you wanted to become in life and where you wanted to be in the afterlife. Thus, the question of being or not-being visited you before you ever met Hamlet.

THE CHURCH

Those who bow down on the roofs to the host of the heavens, those who bow down and swear to the Lord and yet swear by Milcom. (Zephaniah 1:5)

The location of your new apartment at St. Georgen in the German city of Bayreuth was peculiar. The most distinctive feature of St. Georgen was the *Ordenskirche* that stood close to three hundred metres from your apartment and whose imposing belfry was visible from your window. A few hundred metres away, behind barbed wire spirals on top of an elevated concrete wall, stood the prison. No other signs augured the proximity of a correctional facility in that vicinity. To go to the central town or the university campus, you had to ride along the corridor that separated a vast graveyard from the long column of houses. You often met some three persons tirelessly working in the graveyard. A middle-aged man and a slightly older woman were usually meandering through a forest of carved headstones in marble, concrete and granite in hues of white, black and gray; well-tended lawns; decorative flower beds; dried flowers and wreaths left on tombstones; and bouquets and garden tools. The maintenance culture of the graveyard accorded it a rather clinical aura and imagery. The third person, on the other hand, was a grave-faced man, operating what seemed like a marble tombstone workshop at the mouth of the graveyard. He often received visitors who packed their cars right in front of his workshop. Certainly, they came to negotiate for tombstones for their departed loved ones and perhaps dictate the wordings of the epitaph to be engraved on their tombstones.

Each time you rode along the one-metre-wide corridor (of death), looking past the panoply of impressively styled tombstones above the parapet, you were constantly reminded of the ephemeral nature of life; that whenever the bell tolls, it tolls also for you. You had always wondered about the way the phenomenon of death was handled in your host society. During your long years in that city, you had never witnessed anything that seemed like a funeral ceremony. But, looking at the graveyard, you were haunted by the thought that, under one of those tombstones or any other graveyard in that city, probably lay some persons you knew. Your thoughts settled on two persons quite symbolic to Bayreuth who had journeyed beyond – Eckhard Breitinger and the librarian.

Breitinger was one of the pioneer German researchers on African literatures and one of those who converted Bayreuth into the hub of African Studies. Not only did he teach in several African universities from the 80s to the 2000s, but he also invited many African colleagues and students to Bayreuth, for conferences and doctoral studies. One of them was Ngugi wa Thiong'o, who spent three months in Bayreuth as a guest scholar, living in St. Johannis neighbourhood, not far from your apartment. It is there that that eminent literati wrote the decisive chapters of what became one of the most influential texts in postcolonial studies - *Decolonising the Mind*. The last time you met Eckhard was during the defence of your Kenyan colleague for whom he was a co-supervisor. He had been ill and even at the last minute your friend was not sure he would be able to attend the defence. You had gone to the defence a bit early to help in arranging the seats in the hall. As you climbed the stairs to the second floor, you found Eckhard sitting on the bench outside the defence hall. He came almost an hour before the start of the defence. You could hardly recognise him. Illness had taken a heavy toll on him. The brief discussion with him was telling:

"I am down for some time now but it has been particularly tough on me in the past months…"

He somewhat entailed, in that chat that followed, that his sunset was rather near. You were rather astonished at his openness concerning his illness. At the end of the defence, when the time came for him to address his gratitude to the members of jury and the audience, your friend burst into tears. He had barely expected that Eckhard would be there for him. At that very moment of vulnerability and recognition, the tears he shed expressed the feelings of many people in different parts of Africa who were part of the Bayreuth family. Eckhard died a few months after.

The second person that came to your mind was the librarian. It was in 2012 and you had just returned from holidays in Cameroon. After frequenting the Bayreuth university central library for close to three weeks upon your return, you noticed someone was missing in that space. The person usually occupied the front seat of the central library, registering in-coming and out-going books, while remaining very attentive to the inquiries and requests of library users. One fateful day, after having a horde of books registered by one of the librarians, you were about to leave the library when memory held you back.

"*Entschuldigen Sie bitte, ich hätte da eine Frage.*" (Excuse me please, I have a question for you.)

She looked at you, indicating she was all ears.

"*Ich habe Ihren Kollegen, der hier immer gearbeitet hat, schon lange nicht mehr gesehen. Den Mann mit Bart.*" (For some time now, I have not seen your colleague who used to work here. The man with the beards.)

You said, almost sounding childish in your description, but it was the most legitimate distinctive factor about the man that you could find in the immediacy of the moment.

"*Vielleicht meinen Sie den Herrn Detlev Gassong,*" (Maybe you are referring to Mr Detlev Gassong), she surmised.

You weren't sure. You didn't know his name. You thought your description was 'precise' enough. She quietly scrolled down some Google pages. You felt almost guilty for wasting her time, for there were some students behind you, in a queue. Then she tilted the computer for you to see an enlarged picture.

"*Ja ja den meine ich.*" (Oh yes, he is the one).

You recognised the face.

"*Bedauerlicherweise muss ich Ihnen mitteilen, dass er vor ein paar Monaten verstorben ist.*" (Unfortunately, I must tell you that he passed away some months ago).

Thus came the solemn and remorseful voice in response.

The man died. The boatman had visited the coast. Perhaps you had been away for too long. You felt the loss in your soul. You felt guilty for not having noticed and acknowledged his absence early enough. He was not just the hand that registered or sorted out the books for you. He was a very dutiful and likeable person. During break time, he would stand at the library entrance under the red-painted library signpost, smoking a stick of cigarette, with a calm and welcoming countenance. He was your connection to the library since you came to Bayreuth in 2010. In the false starts characteristic of a newcomer in a new system, you usually made recourse to him for rescue. And he was always on point to assist. He would ask you to follow him amidst the shelves to the location of the book you wanted, and with quantum precision and astonishing ease, fish out the fugitive text from its cranny in the labyrinth.

You came to associate his luxuriant beards with the effervescent forest of texts in a library that contained almost every book ever published anywhere on Africa. Several years later, when you were leaving Bayreuth for a much longer period in South America, you went to the library and carefully bade farewell to the front-desk workers and took proper note of their names, including the lady who had broken the news to you. In a brief exchange with her, she revealed to you that when she started work in the university library in 1985 as a freshwoman from the library school, Detlev was already in service and was always steadfast in answering any library-related question from his colleagues with commendable patience and lucidity.

In August 2019, you had another memorable encounter with another librarian. Given that it was the heart of *Urlaub* (holiday), you were about the only person in the Geography Department library where you used to read, due to its quiet nature. One afternoon, you were informed per WhatsApp from Cameroon about the shocking news of your aunt's untimely demise. Distraught, you packed your things and got ready to go home. You had nearly closed the library door behind you when you stepped back to briefly explain to the librarian why you were leaving the library earlier than usual on that day. You murmured to her but she bade you speak aloud for there was no one else in the library. The library had become a home for two. On hearing the sad news, she left her desk, came around and gave you a compassionate embrace as she uttered her words of condolence. When she asked you how old the deceased was, you told her sixty. "That is my age," she said, with a forlorn countenance. She was there not just for the books, the barren leaves, dixit William Wordsworth. Rather, the books enabled you to connect. Frau Wittmann was there for you. When all is said and done, during your years in Bayreuth, you had spent much more time with her in the library than you had spent with the deceased or any other member of your biological family.

The graveyard near your abode belonged to the St. Georgen Church, situated just a hundred metres from your apartment. It was a solid and thick grey stonewalled structure. From your window on the second floor, the church tower seemed incredibly near and the visible arrows of the giant clock on the church tower pointed menacingly to your window. The snowflakes that covered the rooftop granted the clock a marked presence. The exterior of the church looked rather abandoned, less well catered for than the graveyard. But you had been in Germany long enough not to be fooled by surfaces. On Sundays, you found more people carrying flowers to the graveyard than those carrying Bibles to the churchyard. You had the illusion or rather the hope that the proximity of the church might enable you to visit it more frequently and possibly revamp your faith. You began to imagine how much your life had been influenced by the proximity of your family house to the village Baptist Church. On the other hand, not far from your house, close to five hundred metres down the road, was the village palace, the seat of the local authority and the secret societies that harboured the masquerades. As a kid, your imagination was caught in-between these two worlds in a very uncanny way. The Baptist Church was one of the oldest religious institutions in your village. Sundays carried with them specific sounds, fragrance and colours. It was a day on which time found an anchor.

Living near the church provided you with the vantage prism through which to gauge the rhythm of life in your church beyond Sundays and to watch the deacons and deaconesses on call as they laboured tirelessly in the churchyard. During choir practices on Saturday, the chimes and hymns of Melody Choir, King Solomon Choir, Calvary Choir and English Choir penetrated right into the parlour of your family home. One of the most interesting of the choirs was the Melody Choir. Melody was not always melodious but it was the animation, the conviction and the joy on the faces and in the voices of the singing women that gave that choir a transcendental touch. One of their Limbum songs has stuck in your memory for decades: "A voice is crying from the wilderness, O Lord, send me, send me to the wilderness, O my God send me, send me to go and preach your Word". Since the wilderness translates into Limbum as *ngong nsarung (land of sand)* one could not help but relate it to Nsarung, a quarter in the neighbouring Taku village. Although you had never visited Nsarung quarter, you invested that place with biblical myths.

Amongst other things, it was a stronghold of the Baptist Mission in the Ndu Field. That song was certainly a rendition of John 1:23: "I am the voice of one shouting in the wilderness. Make straight the way for the Lord, as Isaiah the prophet said." The divine atmosphere of the church was reinforced by the presence of faithful servants and local homonyms of biblical characters such as Ezekiel, Martha, Rebecca, Judith, Esther, Hannah, Miriam, Deborah, Rachel, Amos, Lydia, Shadrack, Abednego, Exodus, Timothy, Stephen, Gabriel (Gaberia), Paul and Peter.

You used to wonder where the motivation of these faithful labourers in the House of God came from. Did dedicating so much time to church or God's service become a self-sustaining routine or did it spring from an unflinching belief in (the existence of) God? However, you were deeply troubled by the fact that some of the deacons, like many other Christians, did not practise what was preached in church. Some were smokers and would often come to your family kitchen to light their cigarettes using the incandescent wood from the fireside. Other times, they came to ask for cups for the local maize brew, *sha* or palm wine. Didn't the Bible forbid smoking? As for alcohol, it was not clear if the Bible forbade it completely or only condemned it when taken in excess. That was often a topic of heated debate during the two-week annual Short-Term Bible School in the Baptist Association, with a panoply of biblical translations (from King James to NIV) brought in by opposing sides to justify their positions.

At times, you were the one behind the counter of the family provision store that belonged to your father's second building close to the road and the church. Then you saw the worldliness of even those who were so pious during church service. The metal wire net of the store counter became the moral prism through which you sifted the spiritual authenticity of the church goers. The distance between the provision store and the Baptist Church was a space of transition and translation, where the Word interacted with the

World, veering off the radar of church censorship. Sometimes, when people whom you thought were hardcore Christians got tipsy in the evening after sipping a *jung* (in full 'junguru, i.e. two-litre bottle) of palm wine, they revised the gospel verses and songs to their thirst. One of such songs was:

> *My soul is searching for you Lord*
> *When shall I see you face to face?*
> *My soul is searching for you Lord*
> *When shall I see you face to face?*
> *Show me your garments, oh my Lord oh*
> *If I see your garments, I will be saved.*

In this song that is fashioned out of Matthew 9:21 and Psalms 42:2, the 'Lord' got replaced by a different noun and a less holy and ludic dimension was added to the chorus. 'Wo' was also added to 'man' in Genesis 32:26: "Then the man said, 'Let me go, for it is daybreak.' But Jacob replied, 'I will not let you go unless you bless me.'" But the most memorable song, a veritable epoch-marker in your area and era was the song about the "good Christian woman": "A good woman is one that has washed herself clean…is conscious of her character and gets herself ready for the Lord's work…" *Njingwe mbong-mbong yu njinwe shi ambo suhsi ji nyor...* The zeal with which the Baptist church women sang that song was rivalled by the way it was sung out of context in the provision store cum bar. That song was the Hillsong of your community in the mid-1990s. In many cases, the officious versions of church songs became even more popular than their official version: "In my cup, in my cup, I want to see mimbo (wine) in my cup, in my cup" safely implanted itself in place of: In my life, in my life, I want to see Jesus in my life, in my life.

With their spell-binding English-Limbum interpretations of the NIV Bible during pastoral sermons, Mr Amos Takwa and Rev. Nyong transplanted Apostle Paul's Great Commission as well as his warnings, rebukes, admonitions, pleas, entreatments, counsels, reassurance, consolation, promises and encouragements to the Thessalonians, Corinthians, Philippians, Galatians, Romans, Colossians and Ephesians so impeccably that they seemed to address none other than the various quarter groups that made up the Luh Baptist Church membership: Mission, Njinsa, Njimbo, Mbohbar and Ngaki-Mansa. And the ever-committed Christians of Ngaki-Mansa were the most abiding and often came first during Harvest Thanksgiving contest. Blessed with rich soil, their offerings were mostly in kind, a veritable mini agro-pastoral show in honour of the Lord: clusters of plantains still dripping with sap; healthy fingers of yams and cassava; tins of multi-coloured beans known as 'Mideno beans'; sheaves of sugarcane, the sweetest type that, when taken in excess, made one drunk; a rooster in a *nkeng* (bamboo cage) that crowed along with its cheerful giver as they danced along the aisle to the alter; baskets of vegetables such as huckleberry and bitter leaves pressed down, shaken together and running over. Ngaki-Mansa Christians followed the Word both in letter and spirit: "He who supplies seed to the sower and bread for food will supply and multiply your seed for sowing and increase the harvest of your righteousness" (2 Corinthians 9:10).

You used to wonder what made these Christians so unconditionally steadfast in the Lord in a world where circumstances tempted many to be doubtful of God's existence, even if just occasionally. Though you lived close to the church, you often trailed Christians from Ngaki-Mansa and Njimbo who were the first to open the Church door on Sunday mornings. During those years, you maintained, in your imagination, a list of Christians who would go to heaven if God were to come on the ever-imminent Judgement Day. Needless to say, the list was almost entirely made up of women (most of them from Ngaki-Mansa), for even your own name hovered helplessly on the edges of that list, too conscious and mindful of your little sins, as young as you were. According to the gospel as you knew it, you had only one slippery chance: to live your life fully as a youth and only repent of all your sins as an old man on your sickbed and then make it to heaven in flying colours. But what about those who died in an accident when they had not made their path straight with the Lord? There's the rub. Life, what an inextricable web! But modern-day Christianity seems to have extricated itself from that web, having shoved off, for better or for worse, the excruciating anxiety of Rapture that characterised Christian life in the 1990s. The emphasis seems to have shifted to prosperity here-and-now and imminent miracles and visas.

During the regular Sunday morning service, you used to wait impatiently for the usually long Baptist sermon to draw to an end. Freedom came when the church door, closed during the sermon, finally opened. Then the breeze awakened some of those good Christians who were enjoying bouts of sleep as the pastor preached. Your aunt Celina, in particular, was a case in point, even though on Sunday evenings she was always the first to tell your mum how wonderful the day's preaching in the Baptist church was. Auntie Celina usually had very harsh judgment for the Second-Coming preachers and preferred the ones with softer messages that even the committed sleepers could easily summarise to the absent. Perhaps even more long-drawn than the sermon was the pastoral prayer that followed the morning procession. It was a mother-tongue challenge for every pastor. In a marathon feat that could take more than forty-five minutes, the pastor prayed about almost everything in the world, touching on all the continents and committing every aspect of life into God's hands. Done in Limbum, it was a veritable exercise of translating the entire world for the local context. The pastoral prayer was not for the weak, but the strong in flesh and spirit. It was a true test of faith. During the forty-five minute long pastoral prayer, you would close your eyes, re-open them, sleep, dream and wake up, while the pastor was still in the Middle East or Asia Minor, on his way to East Asia!

Offering time was always a tricky moment in the Baptist Church. Normally, the offering basket was passed around for people to drop in their offering. But, whenever there was an important occasion in the church, offering time gained more pomp and pageantry, becoming the moment for showcasing the true joy of salvation. Members were required to form a queue along the aisle according to their seats and then move or dance to the front of the church to put their offering in the offertory basket. Though full of style, this set-up usually proved awkward if you did not have offering on that day. It was unsettling to remain seated while the benches around you were empty as God's children were giving back to Him a portion of what He had blessed them with. The only option was to rush out of the church just before offerings time, pretending you wanted to change money and just linger there till offering time was over. You knew of one woman who had the habit of changing one hundred francs into plenty of five francs and sharing them with her five kids. So, each one of them gave offering in two or three rounds, to showcase the blessings of the Almighty and their generosity in thanksgiving.

For some reason, you never used to go beyond the threshold of twenty-five francs as offering, a childhood habit that has risked accompanying you throughout your adult Christian life. Offertory money had to be kept as a secret, known only to you and your God. But there was usually the risk of settling on one hundred francs instead of twenty-five francs coin. The two were nearly the same size, followed by ten francs, while fifty francs was almost the same size as five francs. During that time, you would rub the coins against the walls of your pocket until you were convinced that what you intercepted between your index and thumb was unmistakably a twenty-five francs coin. That was generous enough. God knew you were just a kid and the late eighties and early nineties were hard times, and the devaluation of the currency affected the young more than the old. Mistaking one hundred francs instead of twenty-five francs coin during offering could deprive you of the delicious after-church *akra*[16], cassava, puff-puff, groundnuts, pancakes, etc. Any

---

16. It is a dish made from peeled beans formed into a ball and then deep-fried in palm or groundnut oil. It is found in most West African and Brazilian cuisines.

delicacy bought with money that was meant for offertory had the bittersweet savour of forbidden things. For you, the church was after-church.

Apart from being the biggest church in your village, the Baptist Church was always the last to close due to its long sermons. Being a Baptist Christian was a mixed experience. Mixed, because of the long sermons that lasted as long as the pastor was inspired. And sermons about hellfire and repentance were very present. And the ushers closed the door during the sermon, meaning your soul could be pounded incessantly with memories of your sin with no way for you to sneak out. You used to envy Catholic Christians who, after a series of repeated prayers, gained their freedom. More so, the priests merely murmured their homilies and the church responded in chorus.

But the sweet part of the Baptist Church Sunday service was the after-church activity. So, you often waited anxiously for the rustling sound of the congregation rising simultaneously for the last prayer that preceded the choral procession out of the church. The church-yard became a bustling space after church service due to the auction sales of some of the offerings that were made in kind. Christians from other churches used to come to the Baptist Church to buy foodstuffs through auction sales. Thinking about the auction sales reminded you of Nyamifo (literally "animal in the bush"), the son of the village chief who was a choir conductor and an usher. He was the best auction seller your church ever had. He brought a Midas touch to the art. His humorous but tactful utterances, accompanied by commensurate body language, always ended up drawing money from even the most lukewarm buyer. Many people admired his sense of humour.

Nyamifo was a multifaceted and deeply syncretic person. He had spent his early childhood in Nigeria with one of his uncles and only came back to the village in his late adolescence. He excelled in everything he put his mouth, hands or feet on. You insist on the feet because he was the professional burial conductor in your village and the neighbouring villages. He was a great football goalkeeper but also a gifted referee. Whenever the football suffered a puncture on the eve of an important game, he would collect the money from the Inter-quarters' Football Committee and jog right to Ndu to get a new ball, sometimes arriving back in the village before a vehicle that had undertaken the same journey at the same time with him. But apart from his passion for grave digging, marathoning etc., many people also remember him as an exceptional referee. He usually carried a whistle which he used in refereeing football matches in maintaining order during meetings as a chief whip; in performing the role of Boys' Brigade commander; in the funeral choreography; and as a village security agent.

You especially recall how, as a referee, he would use his sanctioning powers whenever a team was late for kick-off. With the ball in his hands, in his trademark cross-gartered yellow stockings and long energetic strides, he would march from the touchline close to the Technical Bench to the centre of the pitch; and in a fervent tone, recite the FIFA regulations. Then he would sound the final whistle and, in a complex display of referee body language, declare the team that showed up on time as the winner BY FORFEITURE. His decision was final and unimpeachable. And whenever it was contested, he would further recite the latest amendments of the FIFA regulations on that specific infringement in impeccable FIFA English. Nyamifo only focused on refereeing in the late 1990s after a great career as a goalkeeper and when circumstances warranted, a defender. If he happened to be the linesman, the eloquence of his flag often superseded the loudness of the central referee's whistle. He was very adept at sanctioning bad throw-ins, by using the occasion to imitate the fault, folding his body into an arch to show how a throw-in is executed and then handing the ball to a player from the opposing team. How you wish FIFA knew that, in the far north-west region of Cameroon, there was such a great referee in the person of

Richard Nyamifo, one with such charisma, authority, precision and firmness, comparable only to Pierluigi Colina.

At some point, his syncretism raised eyebrows and many a Christian found his toing and froing between church(es) and tradition troubling, to say the least. That was in the early 1990s when a streak of a young, firebrand and newly minted evangelists from the Cameroon Baptist Theological Seminary (CBTS) Ndu turned the Baptist Church into a "born-again" church. But Nyamifo remained true to himself. Above all his other roles, his popularity was due to his dexterity in directing burial ceremonies. He did to the solemn act of burial what Ronaldinho did to football or Usain Bolt to sprint. He brought life to it. Same as in football, he was both the referee and the player. Anytime he intoned the "masham"[17] song as a group of young men took turns into the grave, the morose atmosphere of the funeral nearly disappeared and many a mourner became enlivened.

> *Tata we kwi ha le rlah ni nda*
> *Hehe hehe hehe*

> *Tata we kwi ha le rlah ni nda*
> *Hehe hehe hehe*

> *Tata we kwi ha le rlah ni nda*
> *Hehe hehe hehe*

> *Sini ha la nda, sini ha la nda*

The row of six young men in the grave intensified the trampling on the ground in rhythmic choreography. Whenever one of the young men in the grave showed signs of fatigue or was out of tune, he would show him a yellow card. If that persisted, the punishment was

---

17. Pidgin rendition of "to stamp the ground under one's feet", in this context, to make the ground compact.

a red card and the concerned would be replaced by a reserve "player". Most often, the conductor himself would jump in as reinforcement, accelerating the tempo and galvanizing the crew almost instantly. Through his animation, he brought relief to the hearts of orphans, widows, widowers and the bereaved families in your community. Thus, when people gathered for burial, the pangs of loss were not only soothed by the gulps of palm-wine or by the sweet savour of "funeral corn" (a mixture of corn and groundnuts or beans usually served in large buckets during burials), but also by the animation that Nyamifo and his team brought to burial ceremonies. Amid elegy, they brought energy and relief. He could sing the *Mfuh, Ngiri* and *Nwarong*[18] with dexterity, sometimes lacing his chants with verses in Lamnso and Noni, the languages of the neighbouring ethnic groups.

The *Nwarong* remains the most dreaded secret society in *Mbum-land* and its outings were purely nocturnal. Even though the ululating or singing voice could betray the identity of its bearer, he belonged to a different world. Whenever the *Nwarong* group passed at the road in the night and noticed a lit hurricane lamp from a nearby household, a voice would sound the warning:

> *O njingwe ha ye ohhh*
> *Oh njinwe ha ye ohhh*
> *Nka ha mkwi rbenni ohhh*
> *Rereng gwi makop a yuh nga ple*
> *Aki yer mbu ghor lo jo bar*
> *Nya rkwi iki yuh mbi kah*

A woman has seen!

18. Secret traditional societies in the Mbum community of the North-West Region of Cameroon. Mfuh, a defence society, is the least secret of them and it meets during the day. Though it is a men's society, it does not make any issue of initiation. The *Ngiri* and *Nwarong* are very secret but the latter is the final adjudicator in the village for it can override the powers of the village Chief or Fon. The two societies have two different sets of masquerades that display on specific cultural occasions. Members can belong to both of them simultaneously.

A woman has seen!
Curiosity killed the cat[19]
A word to a wise is sufficient
When you wipe your anus too much
You end up touching excrement with your hands
An animal meant to die does not hear the sound of the bell

Most often, such utterances were followed by the menacing and deafening sound of *nkoh*, the charcoal-dark and large-headed masquerade, the most frightful member of the *Nwarong* society. And so, the lamps were either put out or their glow significantly tuned down amidst murmurs. For non-initiates and (especially) women to 'see' the secret society was abomination. Those who saw it were cursed and it was rumoured by the village BBC that one woman in Binka village ventured to catch a glimpse of the *Nwarong* had given birth to a strange creature, half-human, half-beast! The *Nwarong* remained the most dreaded secret society in Mbumland. A crying baby could be frightened into silence by the threat of masquerades like *mndengtu*[20], *psoh, ntantasong, kintang* some of which were merely figmental and only existed in the collective unconscious of the Mbum people. But not the *Nwarong*. It was not a name to evoke haphazardly. The passing of the *Nwarong* was usually speedy and transient, leaving you with an eerie trail of beautiful ritual music to which tone you dare not dance.

Usually, after the auction sales in the Baptist Churchyard, you would go straight home and begin the long wait for your mother to close from the Presbyterian Church. It usually took her a couple of minutes to walk back to the house. More so, she was the Church Elder and always had some matters to handle after church before returning home. You would lean on the wall of the veranda, observing the

19. Although the figure used in the original Limbum proverb is the "monkey", literally – A monkey died due to peeping."
20. *Mndengtu* in Mbum culture can be likened to folkloric representations of the elf or the duende in some European cultures.

movement of the people, tantalised by the array of foodstuffs sold on the churchyard nearby, waiting impatiently for your mother to return. You paid attention to the least hint of her voice amongst the multitude that went up and down the main road. Your mum was the founder of the village Presbyterian Church. When she got married to your dad, she continued worshipping in the Baptist Church but was not allowed to take communion given that she was not baptised by immersion as the Baptist faith required.

Feeling rejected, she started attending the Presbyterian Church in the neighbouring Ntundip which was dominantly Presbyterian. That was a bold step and many tongues in the village criticised her. After a few years, a Presbyterian Prayer Cell was accorded to your village by the main church in Ntundip. She was the founding Elder. Some accused her of opening a 'born-again' church. But she had the blessing of her husband. Your dad, a Baptist Christian, had a carefree attitude towards matters of religious choice. Gradually, more members joined, especially women from Ntundip, who, like your mum, had gotten married to men from your village. The Prayer Cell grew in strength and numbers and was upgraded to a full-fledged church. Some formerly Baptist and Catholic Christians started joining it. Though the pastor occasionally came from Ntundip, your mum was usually the main preacher. In the evening, she used to revise her biblical lessons with you as you did your class assignments. You always wondered what would have become of her had she been given the chance to study beyond standard four in her youth. She was a fast learner and had a great talent in pronunciation and oratory. She would tell you how disappointed she was with her dad when he migrated to Nigeria and there was no one to pay her school fees. She had no choice but to drop out in Standard Five.

If Sunday provided the rhythm for the week, Christmas marked a turning point in the year's calendar. Not only did it anchor annual time, but it also gave meaning to life. Unlike some of those Sundays with troubling messages of repentance and the imminent Second

Coming, Christmas was a clean slate of celebration and merry-making. At Christmas, Rice and Christ seeped into your puerile conscience and consciousness with the same redeeming and redemptive force. While Christ was being born, Rice was being boiled. The birth of Christ the saviour could not be dissociated from the savour of the special Christmas rice. Christmas was a long-awaited moment, with the promise of new clothes, like the khaki up-and-down. In good times, your parents bought you separate new clothes/shoes for Christmas and New Year. But Christmas clothes were often more sophisticated. Christmas Eve was the merriest part of the celebration. Life was endowed with a joyful purpose and divine coherence. Earthly existence appeared as a preparatory ground for everlasting bliss in Heaven. After weeks of practice under the moonlight in the various quarters, there were several theatre performances, sketches, memory verses and choral singing on the Christmas Eve church programme.

Most often, those who took part in the theatre were the rough boys who, in the entire year, saw the frame of the church door only on Christmas Day. The penumbra of the candlelight meant that "all cats were grey at night". Young boys and girls usually paired up to chime the latest melodies in the gospel music repertoire, giving the evening a particular joyful and holy ambiance. The recital of biblical verses was also great fun and those kids who got stuck in the middle of the 'mumury verses' (memory verses) earned even more applause from the jolly audience than those who completed their:

> For unto us a Child is born, unto us a Son is given; And the government will be upon His shoulder. And His name will be called Wonderful, Counsellor, Mighty God, Everlasting Father, Prince of Peace. (Isaiah 9:6)
> Now after Jesus was born in Bethlehem of Judea in the days of Herod the king, behold, wise men from the east came to Jerusalem, (2) saying, "Where is he who has been born king of

the Jews? For we saw his star when it rose and have come to
worship him." (Matthew 2:1-2)
And she gave birth to her firstborn son; and she wrapped Him
in cloths, and laid Him in a manger because there was no room
for them in the inn. (Luke 2:7)

If the choral singing programme took place on Christmas morning, the focus was more on the singers' clothes than on the song.
Christmas carried with it a specific colour and scent, the scent and
colour of new clothes, not forgetting the puppets which some kids
displayed around the churchyard to the envy of those from less
privileged families.

Gradually, the sense, sensation, colour, texture and sounds of
Christmas faded into the night. 26th December signified empty
bottles of Fanta, leftover rice, dregs of *sha* (the local corn beer) and
a certain sense of constipation. There was also the listless feeling
of nothingness, of loss of meaning incarnated by the now bygone
Christmas. You wondered why Christmas Day was so short and
the other days so long. The one week separating Christmas and
New Year was characterised by a mixture of languor, boredom and
expectation. New Year was not the same as Christmas. New Year
clothes smelt differently from Christmas clothes. More so, you were
painfully aware that a day after the New Year, i.e., 2nd January, the
day you watched your overambitious New Year Resolutions collapse
irremediably before your eyes, you would wait for another three
hundred and fifty-seven days (three hundred and fifty-eight in the
case of Leap Year) for another Christmas. From the 2nd of January,
Christmas clothes gradually became Sunday wears and subsequently
turned into every-day attire. January (apart from the first day) was
to the year what Monday was to the week: catastrophe.

But for the grown-up and youthful population of Luh, Ntundip
and Taku, Christmas was after Christmas. For these three communities bonded not just by geography but also by strong ties of kinship,

the period between Christmas and New Year was divided into party days to mark the end-of-year. The holy atmosphere of Christmas Day quickly gave way to youthful exuberance and more mundane merrymaking and revelry. Sometimes, young people would return from one gala night in the morning just to catch some sleep, bathe, tidy up and continue to the next gala in a different village. The DJs used the long-distance loudspeakers (popularly known as 'horn') that enabled the first echoes of the disco evening to strike the waves of the neighbouring village, giving a foretaste of the frenzy that was gathering steam. It was a literal clarion call for everyone to put on their dancing shoes and follow the direction of the sound.

In your early youth, inasmuch as you yearned for Christ and salvation, the village masquerades also aroused your curiosity. The marvel at the taste of communion was equalled by the mystery behind the masquerades. During the dry season, some youth used to assist the village Fon in harvesting sugar cane in his large farm as a way of courting his favours in view of the initiation into the *Nwarong* secret society. The initiation was going to unlock the mysteries that lingered in your mind about the masquerades. However, when it finally occurred, it did not carry the dramatic turn that other young initiates had made you to believe. Unfortunately, you did not visit the secret society many times afterwards because you left for secondary school later that year. Henceforth, you spent only limited time in the village during the holidays.

That year, you bade farewell to primary school education, not after a funky graduation ceremony which your Headmaster organised for you as the first batch of the school. You received several sealed prizes as the best pupil in English, History and General Knowledge. They were three books, all related to Christianity. One of them was to accompany you at every track and turn of your life long after that: *The Second Coming of Christ*. Based on the imminence of Rapture, it documented the testimonies of famous people who underwent a complete transformation in their faith. They were

Johnny Cash (The Man in Black), CS Lewis and Jimmy Carter. These were models of the dramatic, down-the-road-to-Damascus conversions that proved that one was truly born again. That particular book accompanied you for many years, from your secondary school in Nkambe to your University in Yaoundé 1. It was a relic of your battle with Christ. It meant hope for you at some moments and terror on other occasions. The urgency of its language meant you lived in permanent expectation of newness and self-transformation that sometimes seemed quite possible but at others, not only far-fetched but impossible and worthless. There were moments when you wished that Jesus should come as soon as possible before you fall back into sin. But at other moments, you knew if Christ came, you would be a sure candidate for hell. Hell, for you did not come as a result of any deadly sin. Rather, it was the equivalent of scoring nine out of the Ten Commandments, simply because once in a while you sinned in your thoughts, that vexing form of sin!

When you later got baptised while on second term holidays in Form One, you waited for that instant moment of transition, that crossover from the realm of the world to the redemptive realm of Christ. But during baptism, even when you thought you had surrendered all to Christ, you still felt a sense of lack, nothing of that deep inward peace promised in the Bible and the book *The Second Coming*. You had envisioned the spirit of God landing on your head like a white dove or like thongs of fire that landed on Christ's disciples in the Upper Room on the day of the Pentecost. Even though your inquirers' class teacher said some transformations were less dramatic, you still hoped for the more disjunctive, assuring and irreversible version. The delay of such a change troubled you intimately and made it impossible for you to respond with certainty, to the question "are you born again?" in the years to come. In your heart, you thought you were, but again a little doubt lingered on. On the day of baptism, you had clutched in total submission onto the firm hands of Rev. Nyong who thrust you into the cold grey water of the Mbim River with all your body, all your heart, all your soul, all your spirit, for the Lord to remake you. The choir sang and ululated in celebration as you emerged from the water gasping for breath while the Reverend wiped your face with a white towel. You were born again. Along with the leaves of Nkolip[21] plants, your sins were washed away, carried over the long and meandering course of the Mbim River that disappeared into Lassin in Noni land and subsequently emptied into the vast Atlantic Ocean, thousands of miles away. But *how can one be BORN AGAIN when he is young?*

The doubt often thrust you into a terrific dilemma each time there was an altar call after a sermon. Were you really born again? Those days were full of confusion, not only in the soul but also in the city. While to be born again was a condition sine qua non for redemption, being referred to as born again raised some sort of an alarm. It meant that one belonged to the firebrand wing of Pentecostalism. While it was a catchphrase amongst Pentecostal Christians, the mainstream churches only used the phrase "born again" in its strictly biblical context. The Baptists used the expression more often than the Presbyterians and more so than the Catholics. In the early nineties, one of the girls in your village had joined Deeper Life Church while studying in Bamenda and that became a scandal. When on holidays in the village, she would argue with the more moderate Christians at the junction close to your family's provision store over biblical interpretations. She stopped using the wig, lipstick, pencil eye, perfume. No other body lotion apart from Vaseline or Glycerine. While she completely depreciated physically in the eyes of man, she believed in her regained spiritual beauty in Christ.

Though you and your elder sister Mangwang got baptised at the same time, she suspected you of going a bit too far in your devotion. One day, during the summer holidays in the village, you started to talk to her as if you were preaching. Mangwang made a sneer at you

---

21. A plant that grows on riverbanks in tropical areas

in a way that watered-down your initial missionary zeal. "Heeeeyyy, now you want to start preaching like the born-again people." You went on the defensive, explaining to her that you merely wanted to implement what you were taught in the inquirers' class. You told her you were determined to be close to your Bible and your faith, for no one knows the time of His Coming. Mangwang was not alone in noticing the change in you. Your family started to worry about your gradual transformation. You confessed to your mum that sometimes you felt pity for almost everyone around you. To that, she told you it was a negative attitude and that you needed to pray against it. One evening, you entered the kitchen after taking time off your reading and found the whole family seated around the fireside. As you stepped on the threshold, you felt a sense of unease in the air. Your mum was focused on the fufu pot on the fire, tilting it open to see if the water had started bubbling. Nshie and Mangwang were picking huckleberry leaves on a tray. Tabong was caressing the furs of Bradog as if in a plaiting exercise while Takwe, your youngest brother, was roasting maize cobs by the fireside.

"Joseph, which one are you reading again?" your elder sister Nshie asked, in a sarcastic tone.

"Joseph" was the name of a distant uncle after whom you were named. Though it became your pet name, only your mum and some elderly members of your extended family who had known Pa Joseph in his lifetime called you by that name. But you felt that Nshie was referring, in bad faith, to the biblical Joseph, the dreamer.

"I wasn't reading." You responded calmly.

"What were you doing alone in your room"? your mother joined in the inquisition.

"I was just reflecting over certain things." They did not bother you with further interrogation.

Reflecting. Maybe you had raised more eyebrows than you intended to avoid. Reflecting. Over what? What did a child of your age have to reflect on? You felt you were out of place in your family.

Perhaps that was the beginning of your persecution. Did not the Bible say that even your family will forsake you when you decide to follow Christ? But again, you felt you were taking it too far. Perhaps that was not persecution per se. More so, you were still struggling with your faith. If anybody were to persecute you, it would not be your family, not your mother. You found solace in numbers, for the Baptist Church itself was undergoing an evangelical revival.

A voice of one calling: "In the wilderness prepare the way for the LORD; make straight in the desert a highway for our God. (Isaiah 40:3)

During the Short-Term Bible School, guest pastors reinvigorated the Christians with two weeks of intense Bible teachings. The daily programme involved a sermon, thanksgiving offerings and a question-and-answer session on biblical themes, leading to very heated debates on biblical interpretations. The pastor posted to your church in 1996 was a student-pastor from the Baptist Seminary in Ndu. He had the incandescent zeal of a student pastor and greatly transformed your church with his Second Coming sermons. While a few conservatives were slightly discomforted by the "born again" pastor, many saw him as a godsend to inscribe their names for good in the Book of Life. Christianity, which was hitherto a Sunday event, became a practice of the everyday life; The Churchyard was thronged daily by Christians clearing and sweeping every nook and cranny of God's vineyard; some choir songs whose biblical origins were doubtful or whose original meanings could easily be derailed, were banned; traditional title holders started coming to church, removing their red-feathered caps of traditional authority during prayers as a sign of submission to a higher authority.

Evangelisation was yielding fruits as God was turning Baptist Church Christians into veritable fishers of men from every hidden corner of the village. People who had never been to church in their lifetime became the earliest birds to the daily church service, with

Bibles of various sizes and shapes clutched to their armpits. In those final days, certain expressions changed: from "Are you born again?" to "Where will you spend eternity?" and "What is your salvation testimony"; from the near-romantic and nostalgic "Second Coming" to the more foreboding "Rapture". The word "Rapture", though signifying the rising into Heaven of the righteous with Christ, also expressed the tragic connotation of the encounter with Christ, especially for those not spiritually prepared. Rapture was most especially used at the approach of the Year 2000, which was believed by many to be the End of the World. When the mysterious Year of Rapture came and passed, some kept their faith while others lost steam and went back to their old ways. Elsewhere, things were even more dramatic. At the dawn of 1st January 2000, news came that there was a shortage of beer and *sha* (corn beer) in Nkambe and Ndu, as makeshift converts in the Word woke up in total disbelief to the bittersweet experience of post-rapturous life, to the tragedies and redemption of everyday life.

The new pastor's sermons posed a great challenge to your faith and you started reading the Bible more regularly than ever. During those days, you would bathe earlier than usual in the evening and lock yourself in your room, feeding on the Word. You became slightly introverted. Noticing your change of mood, those around you tried to dig into the depths of your innermost self. When that happened, you would doggedly resist and keep to yourself. Letting that part of you go was not a concession you were prepared to make. It was the 'you' which nobody had to access. Not even yourself, only God. Sometimes you felt that you had two selves, one that was urging you persistently to live the way your family and friends expected you to sail along the waves of the world. But you would not give it a chance. At times the impulse was really strong and you felt you were putting too much strain on your life. Maybe life was just the bare face of the earth. Nothing more. Maybe life was just the mere passage of time and nothing more. But the other part of you refused to concede, making you believe in an ideal, and that ideal was Christ. That part invited you to follow the biblical chapters, the verses and the world they depicted, beyond the daily concerns of life. You sought to go into the fabric of things to discover their religious essence, to scrutinise their transcendental purpose and plot them as part of a divine design. You grew up frustrated with the humdrum succession of days, weeks, months and years. That for you was not Life enough. There must be more to Life.

Earlier in your childhood, you had thought there was going to be a world feast in which all men would meet, embrace each other and grasp the essence of Life; and celebrate in pure Love and Freedom. You thought Life was an event that was yet to come. The human condition seemed insufficient, not to say hopeless. But why was the road to Christ itself so full of angst and uncertainty? Why was it so short of the ultimate assurance of the existence of God? That infantile longing for a crystal-clear assurance of a divinely ordained future was maybe never to come. The Baptist Church itself, the foundation of your faith, went through a series of trials but the undaunting spirit of its Christians prevailed. The pioneer 'born-again' pastor of that Church survived a ghastly accident years later that nearly cost his life. During the renovation of a cracked wall, part of the Church building crumbled, injuring three of the bricklayers. Your dad, who was at the construction site to give a helping hand to the bricklayers as one of the Church deacons, missed the accident by a hair's breadth. He had left the scene of the accident some minutes before for the provision store to collect a *junguru* (two-litre bottle) of palm wine and some kola nuts for the workers to quench their thirst after lunch. One of the deacons, the most seriously injured of the three, was rushed to Ndu where he was hospitalised for close to three weeks before his vertebral fractures could heal. But three years after that incident, he fell ill from an unrelated ailment and died shortly afterwards. As one who was witness right from childhood to his commitment to God's work as he toiled on daily basis in the churchyard, you were very touched by his fate. He had fought a good fight, he had finished the race, he had kept the faith.

THE FRINGES

A man passes with bread under his arm.
Will I write afterwards of my double...?
A cripple passes, lending his arm to a child
Will I afterwards, read André Breton?
(Untitled, César Vallejo)

Your village had a sizeable Fulani community. They were called the Mbororos. They were mostly pastoralists who lived on the fringes of the village, on the *Kaa* mountain chains where they had enough pasture for their cattle. Besides their language, many of them spoke Limbum. But they mixed everything. In tone and lexicon, Fulfulde, Limbum, Pidgin English, Hausa languages intermingled in their utterances. As kids, whenever you saw a Mbororo horseman on the main road, you would leave the veranda and rush to the back of the house to alert your siblings. Together you would move closer to the road, curiously observing the spectacle of the melancholic horseman and his neighing horse. If you were unfortunately not at home, the imprints of the hoofs or punctuations of dung on the main road would testify that a Mbororo horseman had passed on the main road.

Many youngsters in your village mastered some expressions of greetings which they uttered enthusiastically but fearfully to the

passing horseman. They included *Sanuh,*[22] *Adili hatoy,*[23] *Jam mandu,*
Jam warina, Oseku.[24] The horseman would respond with a smile
and even come down from his horse to ask for water and *goro,* kola
nuts. Once, you fetched water from the kitchen and brought it to a
hussar while maintaining your distance, gazing curiously at him as
he gulped down the water. As for the kola nuts, the horseman used to
give you some coins in exchange. But sometimes, some provocative
boys greeted the horseman with expressions such as *dan durunwa*[25]
that were derogatory and he would chase them on his horse into
the nearby coffee farms. Other times, the expression came from the
horsemen themselves. But most of the Mbororo horsemen were kind
and built great friendship with some elderly persons in the village,
especially those who were Moslems and who spoke the Mbororo
language with fluency.

Most Mbororo families lived in scattered settlements on the
flanks of the Kaa Mountain on the eastern border of your village
with Kuvlu, which belongs to the Nso ethnic group. They would
lease small portions of cow dung-filled land to the village women for
the cultivation of fresh huckleberry. The huckleberry cultivated on
such lands had a peculiar taste. It was commonly called *njap wadde,*
huckleberry cultivated on cow dung manure. Your mum also had
her small portion, offered to her by Mami Fanta. Fanta was a cute
Mbororo girl and most of the young boys from your village died
of admiration for her. Like most Mbororo girls, she was always in
seamlessly fitting English Wax wrappers, blouse and headscarf of the
same fabric and colour. Her wrists were full of jingling bangles and
her slender fingers profusely tattooed. Her adroitly knotted headscarf
was usually perched on top of her head, making her geometrically
concise braids form sleek horizontal ridges on the sides. She was a

22. "How are you?"
23. "Where are you going to?"
24. "How are you?" The Mbororo, it was generally known, would inquire about everything
    in the house when they greet someone: from kids, cows, chickens, sheep to vessels.
25. In Hausa, it means "son of a monkey"!

bit portlier and plumper than the usually svelte Mbororo girls and was always part of the Mbororo dance group that would animate wherever there was an important ceremony at the village chief's palace or the market square. However, unlike many of her fellow dancers who almost broke their back and sprained their waist to the frenzied tunes of the "Maimouna" dance, she always danced with a certain majestic hesitation, as if to preserve the golden springs in her body and as if she was conscious of the metabolic effects that her measured swerves had on some of the young boys in the audience.

> See her caught in the throb of a drum
> Tippling from hide-brimmed stem
> Down lineal veins to ancestral core
> Opening out in her supple tan
> Limbs like fresh foliage in the sun
>
> Tremulous beats wake trenchant
> In the heart a descant
> Tingling quick to her fingertips
> And toes virginal habits long
> Too atrophied for pen or tongue
> ("Agbor Dancer", John Pepper Clark)

Many of the boys did not master the tactic of approaching Mbororo girls for the latter always moved in very close and inextricable groups, certainly as a security measure. So, many young boys who yearned for Fanta were stuck in fantasy. Her periodic descents from yonder mountains high where she lived to the expectant vales raised hopes in many hearts, but those hopes were always short-lived. There was also the risk of inadvertently attracting the wrath of any of her male relatives given the myth that an average Mbororo man never lacked a knife as a means of defence anywhere he went. Even Damari, the Mbororo boy who played football with you had a knife stuck in his stockings, or so it was believed by many. Thus, you were always careful not to step on his toes. The only Mbororo person whom you knew as an exception to this myth was Adamu, your Class Three classmate and friend in the Catholic School. He was very kind, smart and would bring you *muling* (milk) and meat especially during the Feast of the Ram.

One day, you accompanied your mother to the farmland offered to her by Mami Fanta to harvest huckleberry leaves. You always insisted on going with your mum because it was an opportunity for you to see a donkey at a close range. You arrived at the farm just to discover that someone had recently harvested the vegetables. The sap was still dripping from the thick huckleberry stems typical of gardens and farms manured with cow dung. You saw the frustration on your mother's face but she struggled to maintain her equanimity. You knew your mother was upset. You persuaded her to harvest at least the garlic by the malignant reaper but she maintained that it was better to return straight home. What happened to the huckleberry garden was not different from the corn and potato farms. Sometimes, the same Mbororo family that gave you cow-dung manure for your farmland would be the same to let its cattle raze down your maize and potato farms around their grazing lands. Sometimes, they simply helped you in harvesting part of the fresh maize, in good faith.

You and your mum passed in front of the compound and saw kids playing with a meek lamb. Your mum asked them if their mum was at home and all they did was shake their head in denial. You were not even sure if they understood your question. You asked in Limbum and Pidgin English to be sure they got at least one of them. Unfortunately, she was not there, they claimed. Perhaps if Fanta was there, she could have understood the question better. But you knew the kids might not be telling the truth because just a few minutes before, as you and your mum left the place, you had heard the voice of Mami Fanta echoing out of their small dome-shaped hut, the *butere*, which served as kitchen, parlour, dining room, sleeping room, etc. So, you simply returned home. In order not to get back home with empty baskets, you passed through one of your family's farms closer home, near the River Mbim, where you harvested fresh maize cobs and pumpkin leaves.

One of the Mbororo women, Mami John, was a good friend of your mum. She used to rear chicks and developed an informal but vibrant chicken market with the villagers. She would come to meet your mum very early in the morning for their transactions. At times, she came so early that you would wake up and find both of them in the kitchen, finalising their transactions. Mami John would come with one or two small chicks enveloped in her wrapper for "Mami Barake", as she called your mum, always in a funny accent that made you giggle. Each time your mum happened to leave any of you in the kitchen with Mami John to bring the gallon of palm oil from the parlour, you were often scared of being left alone with the Mbororo woman in the kitchen.

One of the things that scared you was the charms she wore as a necklace. That was common with many Mbororos. They even tied some around the wrists of their kids. The knotted seams of Mami John's wrapper were usually very big and you used to wonder if it was full of money or rather of protective charms. The curiosities about Mbororos were endless. They were both rich and poor and they alone knew how they used the proceeds from the sale of their numerous livestock. The village co-operative union attempted to entice them to join its savings scheme without much success. Though some villagers were fond of cheating Mbororo women, usually thought of as both malleable and sly, you did not think your mother ever did such a thing. Instead, she always added an extra quantity of oil to Mami John as *dash* (bonus). In the same way, many customers of the family provision store passed through her kitchen to negotiate for credit. It was such gestures of generosity that accounted for your mum's business losses. She always put sympathy before business, to the discontent of your dad who never saw any possibility of gain in any business venture. He would factor in the transport, time, energy, stress, packaging, bargaining, unforeseeable circumstances and come out with a deficit for any commercial endeavour. However grudgingly, he always ended up bailing out your mum's social welfare scheme cum business whenever she ran out of fiduciary currency.

Another woman whose dealings with your mum raised a lot of questions in your mind as a child was Mami Munchep. She was short and fair and had a goitre. She lived near your family farm, about one and a half kilometres from your home. She was married to Pa Alhadji. He was dark, short, slightly sturdy, eccentric and a highly temperamental old man with curved legs. He was called Alhadji even though he had never been to Mecca. You were not even sure he was a practising Moslem. He lived in a world of his own. He was one of the few old people in your village who had facial piercings. Apart from his biblical sandals, one thing you remember about him was his pipe. When he spoke, with his pipe protruding from his mouth, he produced a mumbling sound, making it very difficult to understand him. His compound, surrounded by coffee plants, banana stems and orange trees, smelt of a mixture of cigar smoke and fresh tobacco stems that grew on his mud veranda. The scent of the smoke from his pipe welcomed one several metres away from his compound. Mami Munchep and Pa Alhadji had just one child called Mary who was in her early twenties. Unlike her parents, she was quite tall. They all lived in a single thatched house, close to your mother's farm, near your village's western boundary with Taku village.

As children, as you approached the farm, you would dance in sync with distant tones of xylophone from the clustered settlements located across the border with Taku. They were produced by the rehearsal sessions of a dance masquerade known as *Mkung*. Unlike the many awe-inspiring masquerades in your ethnic group, the *Mkung* is some of the friendliest masquerades known for their well-choreographed acrobatic dance feats. Though it wears a mask, calling *Mkung* a masquerade is a near misnomer. The *Mkung nip*

Mbeng quarter of Taku village, owned by Pa Samari was one of the most popular in the entire Mbumland due to its widely recounted performances. Others included *Mkung njip Tfu* (Tabeken), *Mkung ma Botoh* (Luh), *Mkung mi Yer* (Taku), *Mkung mi Tamba* (Taku) and *Mkung Mangie* (Njap). Though Mkung is mostly masculine, the female version can be said to be the *Toh*, a dance of majestic and graceful movements, with the *Toh* dressed in the most expensive vestimentary tapestry. In addition to the rattle usually tied to the ankle of the *Mkung* or *Toh*, both (like Baptist church female choristers) use the tufty decorative horse tail as part of their colourful choreography.

In what was mostly farmland, Pa Alhadji's was one of the few compounds, safe for that of *Pa Soja*, your paternal grand uncle who lived virtually on the frontier. The latter had fought as a soldier in the Second World War. For the few times you visited him, he used to describe to you the battles he fought alongside the British army in *Buruma* (Burma). But you used to ask yourself why, after the war, he came back so empty-handed, spending the ensuing years depending on the latitude of your dad and dying in his late eighties in desperate circumstances. But that is another story.

Mami Munchep used to collect litres of palm oil from your mum on condition that she would till or weed a portion of your farm close to her house. Though that arrangement did not include the items that your mother used to give her for free, such as sugar, salt and maggi cube. Sometimes she worked with her daughter, Mary, though she often complained of the latter's laziness. But in the same way as Mami Fanta, you and your siblings suspected that she used to harvest vegetables (pumpkin leaves, huckleberry leaves, green, etc.) from your farm behind your mum's back. But your mum always turned a blind eye to that.

Since you spent most of your time with your mum in the kitchen, you were privy to her conversations with Mami Munchep. You were very intrigued by her living condition and lifestyle. It was Mami

Munchep, with the meagre means that trickled out of her 'businesses' with your mum, who catered for the family in every aspect. One day she came to your house very early in the morning telling your mother that Pa Alhadji had driven her and Mary out of the house. He complained that Mary was sleeping around with men and Mami Munchep was an accomplice so as to get the proceeds from her daughter's 'prostitution'. Your mum always had the right words to console them. She would even let Mami Munchep and her daughter spend the night in your family house during such turbulent moments when they were chased away by Pa Alhadji.

You wondered why some people were so poor; why living was such pain and burden for them; what happiness meant for them; how much your mother could do to change their lives. Why couldn't Mami Munchep leave the old man for good? But to go to where? That was the question. Your mum told you that one of Mami Munchep's brothers was in Europe, but you wondered how someone could abandon their sister so totally. As a child, you prayed to God to enable you and your siblings to sustain the love for one another when you grow old. Even though you fought amongst yourselves, you never dreamt of life without each other. You used to wonder how siblings could grow up to become enemies or so unconcerned about each other's fate.

Sometimes your mum resorted to the Word of God to inspire hope in Mami Munchep and Mary. Mami Munchep was a Baptist Church Christian and Pa Alhadji blamed her and Mary for spending all their time in "their damned church". Your mother became an enemy to Pa Alhadji who blamed her for enrolling his family into a religious sect, although Mami Munchep and Mary were not even members of the Presbyterian Church where your mum was an Elder. He went to the extent of banning them from visiting your mum. That was an utter bluff for there was nowhere he was going to follow up on his interdiction since he confined himself to his thatched house and scarcely went out.

The dramatic twist came when Mary became pregnant. That turned out to be a village saga for everyone was curious to know who was responsible. Mary was meek and timid, and people thought her pregnancy might have been through Immaculate Conception. It was difficult to guess which knight in shining armour noticed the charm in Mary's meekness and innocence and burst the nest of her solitude. But village rustics did not abstain from pointing fingers at each other to find out who was the culprit amongst them. Many rumorous tongues claimed it was Mallam, a Moslem guy who was brought in as a prayer guide from Ngarum village by Pa Tantoh, one of the few Moslems in your quarter. When Pa Tantoh died, many thought Mallam would go back to his village but he persisted, apparently to the dislike of his host family who devised every method to drive him away, to no avail. The duck-feet Mallam was foul-mouthed, unkempt and there was hardly anything in him that represented the faith he claimed to uphold.

In a short time, he became well socialised in your quarter and was versed with the nitty-gritty of other people's family lives even though no one knew anything about his past. Thus, many suspected that Pa Shey Tantoh had only used the Islamic rationale as camouflage and that Mallam was nothing more than an undercover charlatan. However, rumours of his involvement in Mary's fate were more out of his disrepute than facts. As for Mami Munchep, all she said was that Mary started leaving the house during evening hours and whenever she asked her where she was heading to, she would reply in Pidgin English, *"na for dey sef sef"* (to that same place). Mami Munchep did not understand given her illiteracy in English. The end justified the means. Pa Alhadji felt vindicated and brought hell upon Mami Munchep and Mary. Your mum was their sole anchorage. She became a constant judge of countless conflicts between Mary and Mami Munchep but more especially between these two on the one hand and Pa Alhadji on the other.

You remembered when, at one dawn, between sleep and wake,

you and your sister Mangwang heard voices coming out of the kitchen, close to the window of your room. It was Mangwang who shook you with her characteristic left hand. While you were the deep sleeper, she was a lark and the one who used to wake you up early so you could go out and pick kola nuts and avocados from the orchards around your compound. As you listened carefully and fearfully, you discovered the voices were those of your parents. You moved close to the window, tilted it open and asked in a murmuring voice:

"Mum, is anything the matter?"

"Mary has given birth. I mean Mami Munchep's daughter. We just came back from there now," responded your mother.

Mami Munchep had come very early to the house to inform your mum that Mary was in labour. Your parents accompanied her to their home, passing through the thick orchards of coffee plants and kola nut trees. You always wondered how Mami Munchep walked across that fearful orchard alone at such hours of the night.

Your parents arrived just in time for your mum to midwife Mary's baby boy. Your mum was a midwife by necessity. Once, she had assisted a certain woman who gave birth on her way to the village Health Centre. On leaving for Mami Munchep's home, she had taken along some baby clothing for the new-born. Back then, it was common practice in the village for a woman to offer her less privileged friend or neighbour some baby clothing, especially when the baby arrived earlier than the expected delivery time.

Not long after her grandson was born, Pa Alhadji died under circumstances difficult to establish. From what you gathered from your mum, he complained to his wife one evening of headache and the latter prepared for him boiled lemongrass, commonly known as fever grass. He did not wake up the following morning. Perhaps his trademark cough, the kind of cough similar to that of Paul Biya, also contributed to his death. His burial was carried out with the swiftness typical of Islamic burials, even though there was no religious authority present. Not even a masquerade display. He was a member of none of the palace secret societies. He left as he lived. Only a few relatives of the bereaved family from the neighbouring villages and some grey-haired notables, including the village chief, attended the burial. When you inquired from your mum about the late Pa Alhadji's family, she told you that Mary died shortly after her father. Mami Munchep and her lone grandson are the only two living members of that family.

THE MURTALA

But each person is tempted when he is lured and enticed by his own desire. Then desire when it has conceived gives birth to sin, and sin, when it is fully-grown, brings forth death. (James 1:14-15)

It was one of those boring days when your parents and siblings leave for the farm and you wonder what on earth to do alone in a large family house; when time seems to crawl at a snail's pace; when you loiter on the veranda, subjected to the listless tune of what sounds at once like a humming bee, a distant engine saw or a motorcycle; when the dusty main road seems to offer nothing but empty and bidirectional infinitude; when your soul simply yearns for newness, for something to stir the world of stagnant water around you, to give meaning to life, even if just in the meantime; when the half-open door of the living room creaks to the whims of the zephyr. You left the veranda, moved by desire. As you walked on the corridor that led to your parents' room, your heart started thumping, but you could not resist the prospect. You got into the room, which was always open. You looked in your mother's box, turned her clothes upside down, in search of the white powder, to no avail. But when you searched under the table on which the box lay, you found the object of your quest: the Murtala.

You pulled it out. Formerly, the Murtala used to be kept in the parlour. With the economic crisis of the early nineties, things completely changed. Your father could not sustain the extended family, his salary having been slashed. The morning tea, which used to be a family habit, became an event. The Ovaltine, sugar and milk, hitherto basic necessities became goods of ostentation and had to be safekept. Not because your mother distrusted any of you, rather as a mere precautionary measure. There were two equal-sized tins and a packet of sugar wrapped in black polythene. In one tin was the brownish Ovaltine powder, half full. In the other was the whitish milk, the object of your desire, half empty. It always used to get finished before the Ovaltine. Its pleasure was direct, both raw and refined, and it stuck to the gums of your teeth even after consumption, procuring you an delectable after-taste. Ovaltine, on the hand, only made sense when combined with milk and when soaked in boiled water. It could not afford the same instant pleasure. Though you would swallow a cube of sugar from time to time, its taste was nothing compared to the white powder.

You stood there, helpless, baited irresistibly by the milk and the promise of pleasure it would bring to your enzymes. There was no one around. It was drizzling outside. You quickly gulped three handfuls and made way to your room. As you lay in bed, the after-pleasure procured by the pilfered milk was marred by a nagging sense of guilt. You were taught in church that God was omniscient and had eyes that accompanied you even in the darkest corner, to protect but also to keep watch over His children. You felt remorseful and repentant for the sin you had just committed. You also feared that your fingers had scooped far more than you had intended, but your enzymes did not complain. You were perplexed and pleaded silently for His forgiveness but, importantly, for His understanding. You were taught He had a soft spot for the little ones. So, He knew very well about their soft spot for sweet things. Slowly, you fell asleep, encouraged by the intensified drizzle that soon degenerated into hailstorms.

You later woke up when the rain had subsided, but continued to lie helplessly in your bed. It was getting dark. Your parents and your siblings had returned from the farm and were in the kitchen, roasting fresh corn by the fireside. Your mum prepared dinner relatively earlier on that day. It was cabbage, your favourite dish. Your younger brother came to your room to wake you up for dinner. You followed him minutes after, caught in the fear that your sins would be discovered sooner than later. It was as though your mum sensed you were not in the right mood. She kept asking you if everything was fine and you responded in the affirmative. The more sense of concern your mum showed towards you, the guiltier you felt. Cabbage did not procure its usual savour in your mouth. That night you had little sleep and again pleaded to the Almighty to forgive you.

The following morning, you woke up and brushed your teeth, waiting for the tea to be served. It was Sunday, the day you took tea with milk and Ovaltine. Your mum sent Mameng to bring the Murtala. Your adrenaline started rising exponentially as Mameng hurried to your parents' room to bring the precious paraphernalia for tea.

When your mum opened the milk, her face instantly took on an expression of astonishment that quickly transformed into frustration and then anger.

"What am I seeing?"

"What is wrong, mum?," all of you asked as if in a chorus.

She merely tilted the milk tin for everyone to see how far it had been drained.

"Meanwhile, it was bought just last week."

Everyone expressed astonishment. You maintained a calm innocent face, expressing your utter surprise and bewilderment. As a child, you were rather quiet, with a rather pious and innocent demeanour that often made you the least suspect whenever anything was amiss. More so, you never lied. Rather, whenever you thought you were lying, it ended up becoming the truth. Which means any lie you authored was nothing but anticipated truth. You sincerely and constantly sought Christ and your dedication to studies also endeared you to your parents.

Your mum's rage was unprecedented. It fell on Mameng, the one who was sent to bring the milk in the first place. She was hastily judged for spending more time in the room than necessary in bringing the Murtala. She explained that she had difficulties removing the lid of the Murtala that had got stuck. That did not save the situation. Maternal hands amidst insults pulled her jaws while she sobbed helplessly. During that time, two voices battled within you, one calling on you to own up while the other beckoned you to stand your grounds. Your mother was not one to raise her hand against her child. You sat there, helpless, pious, religious. An innocent sinner. Before that instant, your imagination of The Second Coming was a picture of you and your mother (in her white Presbyterian Elder's gown), the most righteous of her kids, gliding in white wings above the Kaa Mountain onto the Heavens amidst tunes of "Hosanna in the Highest". While you had intermittent doubts about yourself, you had no such doubts about your mother.

You were witness to her goodness. Apart from her service to the church, her infinite kindness to her kids, her empathy for Mami Fanta, Mami John and Mami Munchep, were attestations of her goodness. Now she got your sister unjustly punished. She sinned because of you and that compounded your own sins. You were disappointed with the biblical claim that a single sin cancelled out all the good things one has ever done. You prayed to God to forgive your mother. But on your part, you were not yet willing or able to confess. You dithered on the mouth of Hell, that bottomless pit, that ravaging crater lake of fire mixed with brimstone that burnt without definitely killing its victims, sustaining their breath for further suffering.

THE WALLS

The walls of your family parlour, through its array of posters, contributed immensely to the frame of your imagination, enabling
you to interrogate your background and imagine the future. Each
edition of the African Nations Cup and the FIFA World Cup settled
in your parlour through the colourful posters which your dad often
bought from Ndu, Nkambe or Bamenda. The posters brought colour
and rhythm to the walls. At first, they usually shone with lustre.
But with time, they waned due to the dust from the nearby main
road and the constant fingerprints of the kids in their attempts to
identify favourite players, jerseys and teams. Your father also used to
buy successive posters with the portraits of African Heads of State.
The faces on them pointed to the world beyond the walls of your
home, the world that came to you through the radio. Such posters
helped you immensely in your general knowledge lessons in primary
school. Other prominent posters included those of the Baptist and
the Presbyterian Church leadership, with their annual calendars of
events. The twin posters reflected the ecumenical nature of your
home: your dad was Baptist while your mum was Presbyterian. There
were also framed portraits. While older posters were often replaced
by current ones, the framed portraits remained permanent. The
portraits represented three key people in your life: your grandad,
your grandma, President Paul Biya. Added to these, was the poster
of Samuel Okwaraji. Those portraits and wall posters, combined with

specific happenings, created several impressions on your fledgeling imagination that only revealed their true nature long afterwards.

Grandpa

Tarkfu died before you were born. Amongst your siblings, only the first two were privileged to meet him alive, but even they were too young to remember anything substantial about him. So, you usually stood in the parlour, especially when everyone was away, looking deep into those eyes, scrutinizing them, trying to find the hidden signs of your provenance, to conjecture what kind of life you might have led. You wondered why you bore such an uncommon name in your ethnic group. Perhaps your father or grandfather came from Nso? Later on, most people came to take you for a Nso or Chinese whenever they heard your name. When you arrived in Germany for graduate studies, one of the administrative assistants of your doctoral institute quipped that she was waiting to meet a black Chinese for the first time in her life! You once met a Chinese man with your name in a bus in Bayreuth and told him he was your lost and found cousin. At first, he doubted but later accepted your offer.

You had always thought of asking your father if that photo of your grandfather was taken when he was alive or when he had already died. His eyes were caught somewhat in-between stillness and liveliness, a fact that reminded you of the *momento mori* portrait photography in Victorian England where the family album was a means to pay the last respects to the deceased. Given that the daguerreotype camera was a luxury to many families, it was when a family member died that the need to take a family photo became urgent. BBC journalist Bethany Bell stated in one of her reports on the subject that "On some occasions eyes would be painted onto the photograph after it was developed, which was meant to make the deceased more lifelike." Looking at some Victorian family photos, one would thus see a horde of siblings gathered around their parents, looking perfectly alive whereas one of them, perhaps the one (seemingly) most imbued with life, was not actually alive, merely propped up for the family photo.

Grandma

*M*akfu died in 1995 when you were in the final year of primary school. She used to pronounce your name in a very peculiar way: as 'Jurber'. You remember her for the special dark brown bananas known as *pyuh ngarong*, the delicious reddish-purple bananas, *musa acuminata*. Hers tasted differently. Perhaps due to the patience with which she allowed them to get ripe unlike you, her grandchildren, who bullied and bludgeoned the bananas into ripening. She had suffered from chronic cough in the previous days but no one could imagine it was her death rattle. She lived in an adjoined kitchen attached to your mother's. But your dad had built that kitchen just to grant her the private space which old people often need for their various idiosyncrasies. She ate from the same pot as the rest of the family. Whenever your mum cooked any delicacies, you the kids scrambled on who would take her share to her. Then you sat back and listened as she called for the chosen one to collect the plates. Grandma knew your trick and sometimes the one she called for turned out not to be the one who brought the food to her in the first place. Like her son, your father, she was not used to eating much. One day, you were awakened by your mother who announced to you that grandma was no more.

You remember how you and two of your cousins, Ndukong and Kanjo, had trekked for three and half hours, under the dreadful moonlit dawn, to the neighbouring village of Mbinon (Noni ethnic group) to inform your aunt, her daughter, about the sad news. You have always considered that trip as one of the uncanniest you have ever made. As you and your cousins trekked across the veldt of grazing land of Mbowyah and Rbutih, you were haunted both by the bitter reality of *Makfu's* demise and the possibility of encountering any unruly herds of cows on the way. Amidst the whinnying of horses, the snorting of cows and the bleating of sheep, one of you would occasionally soak his foot in a mound of fresh dung and wipe it off on dewy grass by the roadside. It was at that time of the night when the sight of one's own shadow could leave one with hallucinations of a ghostly apparition; when a mileage post nearly lost in the weeds could appear as the forked head of a lurking beast and when the chorus of insects from the moated woodland could bring back memories of some frightening fairy tale. As was often the case with borderlands in your area, the open space between Mbowyah and Mbinon was full of legendary tales and local lore that defied the boundary between fiction and reality. If you met a duende or a ghost on that path you won't know in which language they would speak as the boundary between Luh and Mbinon villages was as porous as the borders between their two languages.

Your aunt, who had taken the news with courage as if she saw it coming, preferred to travel the following day. She knew she would be away for at least a month and needed to prepare for it. But the three of you were bent on returning the same day, so as not to miss any stage of *Makfu's* burial. On the return trip, you were accompanied all along by a heavy downpour. To make matters worse, Ndukong, who had been to Mbinon more often than the two of you claimed to know a short cut that would lighten the trek back home. That is how you ended up losing your bearings in a vast stretch of badlands, in the middle of nowhere. Amidst the crackle of lightning, the mooing of cows, the rick-racking of cattle egrets, the screaming of kingfisher birds and hailstorms smacking against your cheeks, the three of you trudged through bumpy passages of sandy trails, rock walls and deep wet ravines. Sometimes you were sure you had found your way out just to encounter a cul-de-sac in the form of a barbed wire cattle fence. Unsure of the escape route from the quagmire in which Ndukong had led the trio, you struggled through thin rock spires, jumping across watering troughs, even smashing animal skulls and skeletons picked clean by scavengers. You crossed canyons straits surrounded by stunted shrubs and finally found yourselves close to the main road under the foot of the Nchindong Mountain – a sign that the way home was still long. You arrived at the family compound drenched to the marrow, having to meander through the mammoth crowd to your rooms to change your clothes, before joining in the dance:

> *Mama hey du amba*
> *Mama hey du amba*
>
> *We du ha te mi ngo bi*
> *Wir ha la wir ne do hamba*
>
> *We du ha te mi ngo bi*
> *Wir ha la wir ne do hamba*
>
> (Grandma, farewell
> Grandma farewell
>
> When you go, be in good company
> We say go well
>
> When you go, be in good company
> We say go well)

Paul Biya

06.06.1992. It was Ndu Market day. The first vehicles that came from Ndu told of mayhem. The population of Ndu disappeared into the surrounding villages and beyond. Your entire maternal family had trekked to your village, Luh. Still too young to fathom out the actual dimensions of happenings around you, you were happy to see grandma and other members of your maternal family. Why didn't they bring the special Ndu *ching-ching* and *blockade*? That was quite unusual. But their mere presence meant you and your siblings were going to listen to the euphonious /s/ and /z/ sounds of the beautiful Ndu dialect of the Limbum language. The Ndu dialect was a marker of style, class and modernity. It was music to your ears and you had always mockingly reproached your mum for adapting too fast to the dialect of her husband's village. It was when your family guests began narrating their ordeal that the flair of the Ndu dialect was superseded by the awful nature of the barbarity which they recounted. They were not your family guests; they were refugees. They talked of people being indiscriminately massacred in broad daylight by gendarmes and bottles inserted into women's private parts. How was that possible? Who ordered the killings? In the days that followed, your relationship with Ndu and the portrait of Paul Biya which hung on the wall of the family parlour underwent a crisis.

Before then, Ndu irrevocably stood for modernity and development and your mum used to reward any good behaviour from any of her younger kids by promising to take them to Ndu. The image of boarding a car always procured a certain joyous foretaste coupled with that fabulous sensation that everything around you was gyrating in a widening gyre. Unfortunately, these promises never materialised until when you turned six. Ndu stood for the promise of newness, of a new pair of school shoes, of new toys, of a new football, and above all, new Christmas clothes. Sometimes, you held your breath the whole day, counting the hours, the minutes, the seconds and then that final moment at dusk when the taxi driven by the loquacious Nya or the taciturn Sam Bob would make a redemptive stop in front of your compound for your mum to step out. But the fulfilment of the gifts depended on the fluctuating price of beans, at a time when salaries ceased to mark the actual beginning of the month. But that is another story.

As for Paul Biya, you had always thanked God for giving the country such a handsome man as president. With the impeccable smile and blue suit, you had wished him to be your second father. You only wondered why he could not cure the cough that made his voice so raspy and wheezy like a permanent death rattle. Nevertheless, he was still your choice for a second father and was the most handsome in the calendar of African presidents on the walls of the parlour. With Kenya's Daniel Arap Moi, of course, as the ugliest. That is why you did not bother why some countries changed their own Paul Biyas, as can be seen from the changing posters on the wall, while your own Paul Biya was there forever. But how could your father's soldiers have committed such crimes? More than a quarter of a century later, two names were still stuck in your mind amongst the tens that were killed: Mary Bina (alias Iron Lady) and Nfor Ignatius (alias Promised Land).[26] Promised Land symbolised the end-of-month salary for he was the one who would drive your dad from Ndu at dawn to Bamenda for his salary. He was the Promise.

---

26 The list of those who died afterwards from injuries, like Promised Land, is a long one. Those who died during the strike include Ngeh Glory, Njieta Hilary, Tonga Ferdinand, Shey Yongla, Tarla George and Regina Nkosi. (Source Ndi Michael Ndi, *The Truth about the Ndu Genocide*. Onitsha: Riena Arts, 1995).

Sam Okwaraji

Samuel Sochukwuma Okwaraji, Nigerian football star and lawyer (M. Sc. Law) collapsed and died on the football pitch during a World Cup qualifier match against Angola in the Lagos National Stadium on the 12th August 1989. Since your father only bought a TV set on the eve of the 1990 FIFA World Cup, one of your greatest sources of information was the wall poster. Amongst all the World Cup and African Cup of Nations posters on the walls of the parlour, the poster of Samuel Okwaraji stood the test of time. That poster, which was quite popular, captured the final moment of Samuel Okwaraji, lying face-up and a guardian angel flapping his white wings over the corpse of the fallen green Eagle to ferry him onto heavenly glory and lasting peace. World events were brought to you through such posters. At the same time, they underlined the influence of Nigeria in the popular culture of hometown, Ndu, especially in the late 1980s and 1990s. Though full of spelling errors, sensationalism and religious idealism, they animated life and were great decorations on the walls of parlours, bars, shops, barbershops, etc. On some of the posters, the strictly calendar section at the base of the main image even contained dates such as 30th February!

THE NANGA HILLS

Ay, for doubtless I am old, and think gray thoughts, for I am gray:

After all the stormy changes shall we find a changeless May?

("Locksley Hall Sixty Years After", Lord Alfred Tennyson)

1

You came back to this town on the morning of 20th May, about twenty years after you first stepped foot on its precincts. Visibly, it had not changed much. Even the bustling of the National Day celebrations could not placate that fact. Some new modern buildings had cropped up here and there. Internet cafés also popped up in strategic parts of the main street, a rather rare feature when you studied here as a secondary school student. But that was all. After witnessing the National Day festivities upon arrival, you woke up the following morning prematurely, interrupted at daybreak by the thumping drums of the Mbororo dance groups. Your hotel room was a stone throw from the grandstand, in a structure owned by late Pa Lufthansa. You later learnt that he was given that nickname due to his trade deals in several German products that launched him onto the path of wealth.

You doubted in what ways those songs by the Mbororo, always about a certain "Maimouna Ndolo", were related to the National

Day. Sometimes they extended the national feast for three days, depending on how much was left in their pockets from cattle sales. It often took the Fon of Nkambe or council authorities to request them to go back to their settlements. You wondered if the country's owners in Yaoundé who made patriotism their business could go to such extremes in celebrating the National Day with the enthusiasm of this nomadic group at once within and without the imagined community of the nation. You had chosen the hotel in order to feel the pulse of the city. However, the noise was more than you could bear, coupled with the vibrations from Matignon, the nearby nightclub. It felt a bit strange for someone coming from Germany, a country where sound was regulated by elaborate legislation with regard to specific hours of the day, even when it had to do with the National Day.

Nevertheless, at about 7:30 AM, you took your bath and dressed up, resolved to visit your alma mater. It was what brought you to Nkambe in the first place. That you came here on a National Day was mere coincidence. The day itself was a historical misnomer. Nor did you come to meet any specific person in that town. You vaguely remembered some acquaintances and your initial impulse was to seek their contacts and announce your trip to them. Your maternal aunt, known as *Mami pepper soup* who used to sell pepper soup near the grandstand, had died few a years after you left High School. So, you decided to come as a solitary wanderer, to thrust yourself onto the flow of memory, to let memory be your only companion, to watch and observe, to recollect in tranquillity. This place, its buildings, its inhabitants, dead and living, contained fragments of your life's archive, your anxieties, your hopes, your fears and your dreams. Where you needed to pick the pieces of the broken cisterns and piece together the shards, so be it. Where you needed to raise your head high like the Achebian toad, so be it. Looking at the townscape, one thing was crystal clear: the traces of a titanic political battle. Apart from the overtones of conflict that surfaced during the National Day parade of the previous day, the central townscape was replete with opposing political banners of the two major political parties: the ruling CPDM and the opposition SDF. Each banner did not only state party ideology but also extended a hand of provocation to the other. During the march-past, a militant of the ruling party bore a banner whose message was rather caustic against a specific opposition politician. One of the gendarmes at the grandstand immediately marched towards the provocative militant, scrapped the banner and confiscated his identity card. It was drama. The entire crowd greeted that prompt gesture with applause. The message on the militant's banner was contrary to the discourse of reconciliation under which the National Day was commemorated in Nkambe Town. For once, that was a true force of law and order. You sometimes thought that the fight between politicians was more a tussle of egos than real disagreements over development agenda. Coming to this town, you were shocked by the state of the road. You wondered if the politicians were not ashamed when travelling by the same road to disturb the peace of the local folks with their partisan propaganda.

Cars, motorcycles and pedestrians jostled for space on the narrow main road. The streets were bustling with people attending to various activities. You felt like a stranger in your hometown. Once in a while, you came across a face you recognised or thought you did. Your memory zoomed some faces closer but eventually, their traces simmered and then faded irretrievably. Perhaps, you had been away for too long, like Okonkwo. The passage of time had left its marks on many faces here, on yours too. At least, you tried to 'capture' some faces, but no one seemed to recognise you in return. During the previous day's celebration, you discovered that the lady standing by your side was a former schoolmate. She did not notice your presence and you also kept to yourself. In your school days, she was about three classes ahead of you. Looking at her face, you were struck by the violence of time. It drew your attention to the undeniable fact of life - the ephemerality of human bodies. You concluded that, deep under the epidermis of the body, reigns an incorruptible Big Ben, controverting the laborious work of cosmetics, wig, powder and other forms of veneer people use to procure or recover the bygone glaze. It occurred to you that, once past, Youth can be performed but never re-lived. As the hands of time tick, one takes their leave slowly but irrevocably. Time was sketched, drawn and inscribed in the furrows of that face.

2

The grandstand was now empty, making the recently painted parts interlock with the dirt left behind by the previous day's festivities. Perhaps, the grandstand, like the nation itself, would have to wait for a whole year for another facelift, the kind that lasted just for the two hours of the parade, for the nation to sink back into the old habits of the New Deal. There was a sense of sad beauty about the thick veneer of green/red/yellow paint sprayed on innocent electric poles at the grandstand on the eve of the National Day. Nevertheless, the scent of fresh paint made you think of the period of Plaster and Paint. Plaster and Paint was the nickname of a Senior Divisional Officer posted to that locality during your school days. He wanted to clean the Augean stables by implementing a town-wide human investment and clean-up campaigns in which he himself led the way. He wanted to give the town a facelift and if anyone doubted his resolve, they had to look at him straight in the face to understand he meant business. He decreed that everyone had to plaster and paint their house, especially those by the roadside. This edict led to an atmosphere of fury in town for even though the idea was good, house owners had other priorities. It didn't take long for nearly half the houses in town, especially those who lived close to the main road, to be marked with the red "X" sign. This entailed a hefty fine and the threat of outright demolition by the authorities. But most victims were students, for some would come back from school to find their modest walls sprayed with the awful Passover sign. Some landlords raised the rent and compelled students to pay several months upfront. It was a challenging time. That era accounted for a generation of houses that were painted before plastering, for some could afford the paint before the cement. A paste of paint on a bare brick wall (since paint was sometimes easier to improvise than cement) could procure some breathing space in the new dispensation. In another dimension, anyone who lived in Nkambe in those days would bear with the fact that plaster and paint did not only apply to buildings. Plaster and Paint coincided with the era of de facto facelift obtained with the help of 'Immediate Clair' lotion and 'Top Gel' soap. The result was the so-called 'Fanta face, Coca-Cola legs'. In reality, someone could be black today evening and turn yellow tomorrow morning. Even in this dimension of the facelift, the Senior Divisional Officer still seemed to lead the way. Several years later, you were to meet Plaster and Paint in the Ministry of Territorial Administration in Yaoundé, and his yellow face with black stripes reminded you of time past. In any case, both forms of facelift left behind enduring traces of an abortive aesthetic quest.

The empty grandstand made you recall an insane woman called Kihla who was fond of roaming around the premises in the mid-1990s. She used to sing and clap her hands rhythmically, calling her own name in the song, as if responding to implacable inner mirth and peace of mind only comparable to Wordsworth's solitary reaper. Strangely, you became convinced that memories of mad people were indispensable in conceptions of place-making in public spaces, market squares, public junctions, local borderlands, etc. You recalled a flurry of mad persons that peopled the community when you were growing up and wondered how many of them were still alive and what efforts society made to give them just the basic minimal care: Wakube, Amouros, Ntasi, Japanese,

Maria Nye, Peter Yimngar, Nyakoh Mbohdai, Mamuloh, etc. You began to consider mad people as indispensable in communal memories. Mad people defy local borders. They are trans-local and, in most cases, trans-lingual. They are known by different (nick)names from one village to the other. Nyakoh was known in Ngarum as "Nyakoh Mbohdai", whereas in Luh, he was "Nyakoh Attention", for he often walked in attention posture as if in response to some metaphysical national anthem to which he and he alone was privy. As errant and nomadic characters, mad people are usually both subjects and vectors of rumours and sagas. Some are rumoured to be dead just for them to reappear, like ghosts, in different communities. With the spatial practice of the mad in public spaces, a certain ethic of disorder, a certain subversion of sanity is at work. They carry with them a degree of affect that conveys the spirit of the time and in the public space, they often engage in practices that are purely of the private order, blurring the distinction between the "pubic" and the "public" in sheer disregard of reigning moral norms.

Lost in thought, you conjectured how much your idea of madness had evolved over the years. Only time, you thought, would tell who is insane and who is not, for what is considered as insanity and illness depends to an extent on the social mentality and the availability of hospitals to cater for the limitless gamut of illness and madness in every society. The category of people with the highest rate of madness, it occurred to you, were politicians of that country. While the nakedness of the body of the madman and madwoman reminds the sane ones of their own bodies, the equality of their bodies in nature, before the Law and before God, the fopperies that cover the politician's body seek to conceal this equality. The politician's body sustains itself by preying on other bodies, by basically eating other bodies. 'Eating', because, for the body of the politician to secure access to state resources, to state protection, to state elephant meat, other bodies, the bodies of the wretched of the earth, the bodies of the nobodies, must suffer, must be subjected to death. In other words, some politicians are madmen backed by guns. Both madmen and politicians are adepts of the public space and are incensed by crowd response to their performance. The difference is, while the former is vulnerable and cares, the latter is (over)protected. While the body of the mad is carnivalesque, that of the politician is cannibalistic.

The grandstand had been renamed after the Fon of Nkambe. That was perhaps a befitting tribute to the role of the traditional authority in that town but you wondered if it might not be a divisive gesture given that the Fon was much associated with the ruling party. It was here, at this grandstand that in the mid-1990s Ni John Fru Ndi, the charismatic leader of the main opposition party, Social Democratic Front used to arouse the crowd with his entrancing speeches, making you dream of something new to come, of a better country. Whenever the rally fell during school hours, the school campus speedily vacated and there was nothing the principal could do. Fru Ndi had a rather hypnotic effect on the crowd. It was believed he had magical powers. During the rally, he was usually introduced by Martin Yembe, a young firebrand militant from Ndu. Yembe symbolised youthful leadership. The climax always came when Fru Ndi, rolling his sleeves, raised his left hand in the air and rumbled:

"ESSSSSSSSDI EFFFFFFFF"

Crowd: "PAWAAAAAA".

Fru Ndi: "ESSSSSSSSSDI EF"

Crowd: "PAWAAAAAA."

The third round of responses always required a full sentence. "Power to the People and Equal Opportunities to all." That was when many merely hummed and rumbled along, like during the Lord's Prayer and the National Anthem. The SDF party was better known in pidgin as "Sofa Don Finish" (Suffering has ended). For many people who cared less about socialism, but more about the end of suffering, the second stood as the one and only meaning of the abbreviation. Like Armah's Maanan, the voice of Ni John Fru

Ndi always sought you out from the entire crowd and addressed you personally.

> Ah man, let me wet it
> Let it soak itself in love,
> Today things have gone inside me
> And they have brought out what I have hidden in me
> He brought them up. They were not new to me
> Only I have never seen anything to go and fish them up like that
> He was reading me, I know he was speaking to me, to you too
> But did you hear him? How can a man born of a woman tell me my thoughts
> Even before I myself know them? I ask you. (*The Beautyful Ones*, Ayi Kwei Armah)

Walking on these grounds, you could not bear to think that the SDF was still in the rain, not even granted the chance to disappoint, more than two decades after its victory was stolen in the presidential elections of 1992. Two days before your trip to Nkambe, you could not resist the questioning gaze of your mum while in your village. You could not tell her, as you always did before now, "I will marry when I want." You had entered your thirties and so had Paul Biya's "New Deal" regime.

3

You walked past the Deeper Life Mission, on the way to the New Market. The Deeper Life Church was an enigmatic building in your secondary school days when Pentecostal churches stimulated myriads of conspiracy theories. For many, the Deeper Life was not a church but rather a sect. Some claimed that at night lights were put off and doors sealed. Putative passers-by purported to have heard strident screams coming out of the building during late night hours and even early in the morning. Some considered them mere prayer rituals while others supposed that in moments of religious ecstasy, as they prayed in tongues, better (and deeper) things were happening. Proponents of this thesis used it to explain why many of the born-again Christians had broken marriages. Others claimed the born-again converts used to perform esoteric rituals behind closed doors.

You needed a haircut and went into a barbershop just a few metres from the Deeper Life Church, on the way to the Old Market. There used to be a video club around that area, managed by a man named 'Toukouleur' whose mannerisms constituted a film in their own right. Most students would dodge from school in order to catch up with 'Toukouleur's film schedules. That was when action films and Indian love films dictated the rhythm of life amongst teenagers and youths in Nkambe. That hegemony was only displaced in the final years of the Second Millennium by the advent of Nigerian films. "Glamour Girls" and "True Confession" were the latest by then and their soundtracks had followed you ever since and you sometimes hummed them almost unconsciously.

It was going to be your second haircut in two weeks since you arrived Cameroon. Back home was unlike in Germany where you could turn into a rastaman or punk without answering questions to anyone. Once, your siblings were unable to recognise you at the airport upon your arrival due to your overgrown hair. Your chin was stubby now, whereas when you left you left for Germany, it was as bear as that of the Ethiopian eunuch. German society's liberalism meant that physical outlook was a matter of personal choice, not much to do with social acceptability. As you sat waiting for your turn in the barbershop, your memory roamed. You did not know if you needed a cut or it was just a pretext to relive the space of the barbershop that so much shaped your secondary school life. A social history of Nkambe town could not be written without reference to the barbershop that sprouted in the 1990s. Located at spaces of transition in the urban landscape, barbershops were spaces of the circulation of fashion and new trends in pop culture. Most of them were owned by non-student youth but most often, out of friendship or kinship, they offered some students the opportunity to subsidise their income by acting as part-time barbers. As well as commercial outposts, these shops were spaces of peer in/formation, dissemination of communal idioms, and the showcasing of a 'sappeur' culture amongst students. Out of the school premises, most of them were spaces of continuum for juvenile peri/scholar practices.

Within the minuscular perimeter of the barbershops, students exchanged notebooks and CDs as well as MADS, a lyrics manual for the latest RnB/Soul Top of the Chats, accounting for the mastery of pop lyrics by many students. The shop was a place for social commentary about the latest girl in town. As a form of publicity, most of the barbershops carried on their facade the painted portraits of the haircuts of Usher, Joe, Shaggy, Craig David, Puff Daddy, Boyz II Men, K-Ci & Jojo, not excluding the non-conventional hairstyles of Sisqó, Snoop Doggy Dog and DMX. In another dimension, the barbershop was where news was shared both about the local football championship and the main European Leagues. You remembered the players of Nasara FC, one of the most successful football clubs in Nkambe Town. Its star players such as Eric Cantona, Jean-Pierre Papin (aka JPP), Kala and Kevin used to congregate around specific barbershop and cafeteria at the Old Market, in colourful European Champions League team jerseys at a time when these rare and costly outfits gained currency in the Nkambe fashion landscape. The frontage of barbershop was a space of desire, longing, self-ostentation and if the secondary school love/lust stories of those who had the unique privilege of studying in Nkambe in the 1990s were to be documented, the barbershop would figure highly in most of them.

4

After you were given a perfect and rejuvenating haircut, you then moved up to the Old Market, better known as Njari Market. Few places had that natural magnetic and convivial character typical of Nkambe Old Market. Located close to the minarets of the Nkambe Fon's palace and surrounded by some of the best *sha* (the local maize brew) bars, the Old Market was a must-visit in Nkambe. It hosted a weekly market for products such as spices, cereals, vegetables, fruits, palm oil, etc. from the Ako area, one of the most fertile localities in Cameroon. It was as if the umbilical cord of Nkambe was buried under the grey soil of the Old Market, making it central to the identity of the town. But the main reason why the Njari market was narrowly tied to student life in Nkambe was the presence of palm-kernel, commonly known in Pidgin as 'mbanga' (not to be confused with 'banga', which also means marijuana in Pidgin English). Many students used to look forth to the Njari Market day with impatience and when it finally came, the list of students who left school before closing time (dodgers) was longer than usual. 'Mbanga' perfectly combined with parched corn.

In reality, the popularity of parched corn with 'mbanga' or groundnuts was only rival to soaked garri (aka garrium sulphate), a student 'delicacy' derived from the granular flour of crushed cassava. Given its relative affordability, parched corn with 'mbanga' was a basic resource and recourse for students during arid days. However, on some days, the 25 or 50 frs needed to buy a portion of 'mbanga' to combine with corn was not a given. On such days, a student would engage in a thorough archaeology of his/her pockets to search for any providential coin that might have been forgotten during greener days. Others, the more sharp-witted ones, simply engaged in a tasting spree and after tasting the 'mbanga' of close to five generous sellers, they would be left with a handful, fit to change the fate of a reasonable quantity of parched corn. Such a character would put a grain of kernel in the mouth, chew it ruminatively as if testing the chemical proportion of magnesium, iron and zinc in its pulp, just to come out with a complaint that "dis mbanga over strong", while carefully pocketing the remains. Most often, when the seller complained, the student would confuse him/her with big grammar so as to justify their not-buying and continue with the fruitful tasting. Whatever the case, the end justified the means. The consumption of parched corn with 'mbanga' was never a solitary practice. Rather, it was often a joint enterprise. Most often, in student quarters, some would contribute coins to buy 'mbanga' while others contributed corn. Or some would contribute 'garri', while others would bring sugar, and perhaps groundnuts, avocado and/or milk. If 'banga' (marijuana) often led its consumers into solipsistic delirium, 'mbanga' (palm kernel) mixed with corn was a community builder. In the eating, there was the telling.

In relishing the parched corn and 'mbanga', students exchanged stories from school or from their various localities. At times a bowl of soaked garri or parched corn and mbanga was what one could afford for the entire day. You went through such days when one would handle a slice of tomatoes in a soup with the same gentleness and protocol due to a proper slice of meat or fish. Such a slice was often reserved as a complement for the last handful of *fufu*, when the necessary enzymes were properly summoned to give the combination its full savour. You had a small vegetable garden close to your dad's compound in Nkambe on which you had planted some carrots, cabbage and huckleberry. However, conditions did not often grant you the patience to witness the true colours of its petals; you simply nipped them in the bud!

Thus, the Njari Market day represented a temporal anchorage, a day of redemption. It was the day you would expect a letter from your dad who at the time was teaching in a village in Ako known as Ndaka. Sometimes, he would come to Nkambe on the market day but most often, he would rather send you money, bush meat and other foodstuffs. This was always accompanied by a letter. It was a day of smiles. Your father had a very assertive and enviable handwriting. Each time you read his letter you felt he was standing right there talking to you. Your handwritings constituted a sort of family heritage, and your father, the originator of that heritage, was the master at his craft. You and your older siblings ended up writing like him, but no one could copy the assertiveness with which he carved out each letter of the alphabet. During the holidays, whenever he gave his lesson notes to you, then still a primary school pupil, to copy, it was your initiation into a family tradition. You wondered how the advent of the computer keyboard had almost levelled every idea of a distinct handwriting!

When he was transferred from Ndaka to Gvung (also known as Bongom) Village, you missed the delicious bush meat, but you did not regret it. This was because, every first weekend of the month, you trekked to Gvung to carry foodstuffs that would sustain you for the entire month. Going to Gvung meant passing at Ngie, a special and even mythical place in Mbumland. When people die, it is said that, they pass at Ngie before going to the world beyond. In other words, Ngie is a form of purgatory or transit point for the human spirit as it crosses the bar. Also, when someone comes too early to an event, it is said that they have come as early as the Mkung (a traditional dance) of Ngie, certainly an anecdotal reference to an occasion to which the Mkung of Ngie came earlier than anyone else and that became an idiomatic expression in Limbum for exaggerated punctuality. Certainly not *as early as a njaman*! Topographically, Ngie is a place where the lush mountain chains wrap like a stereo cassette tape, in the vicinity of Tang-mboh division and the rest of Njap village, leaving Ngie in suspension on a creeky landmass difficult to describe even by experts of physical geography. The names of the localities southwards to Ngie lend credence to its image as a place of transit for the dead: Sirnga (kitchen counter), Sirpko (barn), Njipti (below, the world below) quarters and Gvung (witch bird) village. Further afield from Gvung, towards Lassin, (Noni ethnic group) is Masi, that land of infinitude where reality meets myth.

In your memory, Ngie was connected to the uncanny sweetness and the earthy inscrutable flavour of its yams (*mreh*), cassava (*ngashinga*), and aerial potatoes (*mthuh sahmbing*). The last time you relished these delicacies in Ngie, was sometimes in 1999 (you were then in Form Four) on your way from Gvung. After a long trip from Gvung, you settled down in a *sha* (corn beer) house at the Ngie Market Square and ordered a combination of *sha, mreh* and well-ripened avocado, *pia*. The effect was transcendental and you found yourself later in Nkambe without feeling the least pain in the otherwise tedious journey across the hills. That combination was magical. In Limbum the taste would be described as *rvuhti* or *gehti* which go beyond flavour, aroma, sweetness, or pleasure. The only term that comes close to *gehti* might be the French *jouissance*. Could it be that these delicacies help in purifying the soul of the dead who transit through Ngie territory?

5

While your father came to Nkambe at least every month during your secondary school days, it was not the case with your mother. She had stopped following your dad around to his place of work in the early eighties, after they left Subum, around the Lake Nyos area. She remained in Luh village, quite a distance from Nkambe. So, you could only see her during the holidays. Nevertheless, your life was papered on the rhythm of her life and she came to represent the bitter price you had to pay for your secondary education.

In the first years of secondary school, you were gripped by terrible pangs of filial separation. Whenever you came back to Nkambe after the holidays in the village, you were tormented by a deep sense of longing for your mum. Most often you would lie on your bed and sob silently and helplessly. At times your cousin, Klinsmann would surprise you in your doleful mood and you would rapidly switch on and pretend you were fine. But you knew Klinsmann sometimes noticed such moments of gloom though he might not have addressed it with you head-on.

During the first term, the longest term, from September to December, you could not bear the thought of spending about four months without seeing your mum. The first term was to the school year what Monday was to the school week. You were on the tenterhooks of homesickness. This caused great pain in you. You recalled an instance in your early childhood when your mum occurred to you as Epiphany. There was a Baptist Bible Conference in your village and you were looking for her in the multitude. By then she was still a Baptist Christian. You saw one woman from afar and mistakenly thought it was her. When you discovered your mistake, you felt absolute disappointment. When you finally found her, you felt Life. You hung on her wrapper, existentially secure and anchored in her presence. Each time you left the village for Nkambe at the beginning of each term, even when she knew your dad would cater for your needs, your mother would slide some coins or a banknote into your pocket. It varied between two hundred francs and five hundred francs.

While in Nkambe, you never used to spend the money except when you were really hard up. You kept it in the safest corner of your school box. It was a symbol of remembrance. You saw, smelt and touched your mum through it. It was your fetish and whenever you ended up spending it, you often felt the pain of loss. It was like severing part of yourself. For many students in that school, the most persistent temptation that could make you exhaust your last penny was Mami Julie's puff-puff. During break, its fine aroma would invade the entire Cheap Side irresistibly. The charisma of her character went hand in hand with the aroma of her puff-puff. Mami Julie spiced her services with an enticing commercial smile that bonded any customer with her puff-puff forever. With the temptings of her puff-puff, your attempt at frugality in those Cheap Side days was dead on arrival. She was ever ready to sell to her most trusted customers (i.e., the entire school) on credit.

In the very first days of Form One, you began regretting your choice of Government High School, Nkambe for your secondary school. Nkambe had ripped your soul away from its maternal cast. In fact, after passing the Common Entrance Exam, you had done your oral exams in Government Secondary School (GSS) Ndu, closer to home. However, when it came to submitting choices in order of preference, you went in for Government High School, Nkambe as the first choice. You were motivated by your cousin, Klinsmann and the stories he and your elder sister Nshie used to tell you about GHS Nkambe. As a result, when the list of successful candidates came out, your name was not on the list published by GSS Ndu. You felt downcast, certain that your dreams of secondary school education had crashed. When your father inquired from the school authori-ties, he was told that since GHS Nkambe was your first choice, they had forwarded your oral exam results to that school. A week later, he confirmed through a colleague in Nkambe that your name was on the admission list of GHS Nkambe. That brought peace to your heart. GSS Ndu was relatively young and was still building its own myth and framing its image. Thus, its stories could not match the luring force of GHS Nkambe. You now had to face the consequences of your choice.

After the haircut, you crossed the palace and then went down to your father's compound to greet the tenants. It was a large com-pound, close to fourteen rooms. When you arrived there, very few of the tenants were around and you explained to them that you were their landlord's son. You tried to be as unassuming as possible but at the same time, you could not avoid feeling a sense of pride that goes with "my father's property". While some greeted you with affective zeal when they heard this, others instead adopted a more distant composure. Perhaps they owed rents and thought you were there for the accounts. The apartment where you lived twelve years back was locked. You were told it was inhabited by a police officer with his wife and two kids. During your time, your dad could accept only students as tenants. Soldiers, in particular, were known for reneging vehemently on their rents and sometimes cowering down on landlords. Surely, the situation had changed. The student population had dropped due to newly created secondary schools in neighbouring villages, at a time when opening schools without the necessary infrastructure was part of an absurd political strategy by the government to court party appurtenance.

You met the tenant who occupied the apartment that was traditionally reserved for your family members who studied there, or for your dad, whenever he travelled to Nkambe for one reason or the other. Your dad had decided to rent out that apartment because none of his children schooled in Nkambe anymore. Neither did he have the energy to visit Nkambe as often as before.

The tenant, a customs officer, seemingly in his mid-forties, took you to the storage room to take a look at its contents and decide if anything was worth saving. Certainly, he wanted to get rid of the stuff and make better use of the space. Apart from the books piled on the bookshelf that bore the names of previous occupants, most of the things were furnitures: side cupboards, wardrobes, stools, tables, beds, etc. Most often, the student tenants abandoned their furniture in compensation for unpaid rents. Some merely disappeared, and never came back. That mostly happened with those who failed the GCE and never re-summoned the patience for studies anymore. So, you had to break the door. Many of the cover pages of the books had peeled off. As you scampered through them, you found a picture of yourself. You situated it in the year 2000 when you were in the throes of GCE O Level preps. You resurrected it, squeezed as it was between an equally deteriorating cover page of Jean Racine's *Britannicus* and the hard plank of the bookshelf. Beside it was a slightly damp parchment of pages and it is by carefully tilting open the leaves and encountering 'Samba Diallo' and 'Diallobé' that you discovered it was Cheikh Hamidou Kane's *Ambiguous Adventure*. Then there was a bunch of pleated paper containing a series of poems in French, the language of most of your high school poetry. You felt bemused perusing them, for many were written in the throes of a romantic feat. The leaves were damaged by dampness at the edges.

The other discoveries were three love letters: the first by a girl telling a boy that she wanted them to just be friends and not what he was asking for; the second by another girl on a flowery paper telling her love that her body lotion was finished; the third by a girl (who had moved to Yaoundé) to her love (back in Nkambe) telling him she loved him dearly. She promised to send him her photo which he had been asking for in her next letter. This last letter, beginning with a "Ditto", was full of biblical quotes on the margins of the pages and ended with "Je t'aime". Some of the letters were calligraphed on decorated love letter pads which, during your days, were bought from the Summertime shop at the Nkambe New Market. After assembling a few of your younger sister's books that you could comfortably take to your family library in the village, you gave the tenant the go-ahead to dispose of the flotsam and jetsam in the storage room. You bade farewell to the tenant and then began the long walk to your alma mater, more than a kilometre away from the main settlements.

6

Two streams separated your father's compound from the school campus: the Magha and the Chua-Chua. At times, you used to be filled with fear when crossing the forest after the Magha at a lonely hour. The thick eucalyptus forest harboured a quixotic mad man, known as Mallam Chumbuh, who purportedly had a hut under those trees. He was known for his dry, thunderous but transient laughter that was often followed by pure gibberish. Whenever students dodged from school, their main fear was to come into collision with Mallam. He was considered a bit aggressive although you now doubted how many people had ever been victimised by him. He often spoke Hausa and a language that was far from the Limbum mother-tongue. Perhaps he was a Moslem, from his name or title 'Mallam'. There were rumours and extrapolations about his identity, his habits, the kinds of things he ate, how his hut looked like, etc. Most of the students would not dare pass at the forest alone, especially during evening hours.

You descended towards the second stream, Chua-Chua. The stream seemed quite dry. You could not believe that it was the month of May. You guessed the town must have been facing acute water problems since the two streams were the main sources of water. You continued your sojourn and got closer to the campus. The farmlands covered with thick undergrowth including spear grass reminded you of the legendary stories you were told about a former principal - Dr Vuga. Anyone who entered Form One in the mid-1990s had the impression that they had come after the golden age of that institution. Is it that the past is always more dramatic than the present? Or does the drama lie in the telling itself? As Form One foxes (as fresh students were called), one had the feeling of coming to the world when epic years had already gone by.

Amongst the narratives you heard, none was as intriguing and fascinating as those of Dr Vuga and Mr Mbehnkum, the charismatic principal and vice-principal whom you did not have the luck or ill-luck of meeting. You heard that Dr Vuga used to chase latecomers right into the farms with his dog; that he used to 'follow' female defaulters right into the girls' dormitory. He certainly must have been quite different from the principals from your time: the gentle Mr Sunjo George with his trademark keys that jingled euphoniously as he descended to the General Assembly ground; Njikta, the pragmatic principal and the drama he caused each time he declared the verdict of the much-feared Disciplinary Council (DC); the vice-principal Dr Ngala who used to begin all announcements with "I want to draw your attention...", drawing a grumbling reaction from the gathered students.

On the road junction at the mouth of the school stood the signboard: "Government Bilingual High School, Nkambe", above its French version *Lycée Bilingue de Nkambe*. The signboard had lost its lustre and the inscriptions looked terribly faded. Each letter was invaded by rust. It was certainly far from the vision Mr Nguh Scots, the Biology teacher-artist-referee-guitarist-politician-entre-preneur-MC-coach-ping-pong player-painter had when painting it. The entire frame stood virtually on one leg, the other limping leg having been twisted terribly by a contrary force. In any case, you were in your alma mater. Tennyson's verses spoke to you with incredible potency:

> Comrades, leave me here a little, while as yet 't is early morn:
> Leave me here, and when you want me, sound upon the bugle-horn.
>
> 'T is the place, and all around it, as of old, the curlews call,

Dreary gleams about the moorland flying over Locksley Hall;
(Locksley Hall)

The entire entrance seemed deserted. It was perhaps to be expected because it was a day after the National Day celebration, almost the end of the third term. That time was usually known as 'rasta week', a time when discipline was lax and many students came in assorted attire. Some put up rasta and dreadlocks which were otherwise proscribed on campus.

7

As you entered the campus, your mind began to recapitulate your very first days at secondary school, nineteen years back in 1995. You came to Nkambe with dreams but also with fears, the fear of failure. In 1995, you had left Luh village for secondary school in Nkambe. Due to the economic crises facing the country at the time, you did not take the main road through Ndu to Nkambe. Rather, your dad, your cousin Klinsmann and you had to trek through Tabenken village and from there boarded a short distance transport car to Nkambe. On your head, you carried a heavy *Ghana- Must*-Go bag filled with clothes, books and food. It was a tedious trip. That was far from the college experience you had dreamt of, but you were still grateful to your dad for sending you to secondary school in the first place. Out of the twenty-one of you in your final primary school class, you were the only one who continued to secondary school. The rest opted for different life choices. Those were hard times.

You bore the dream not only of your parents but also of your primary school, Government School, Luh. Only two of you had written the Common Entrance from your school, and even though she also passed in list A, your classmate finally chose to learn tailoring. Your elder sister, Mangwang had also chosen to go into hairdressing and did not write the entrance at all. Thus, you bore her dreams as well. In hindsight, you came to believe that had your father's financial situation been better by then, he would have insisted that Mangwang sit for the Common Entrance and continue to Secondary School. But it was difficult to make a judgment on the past. All you knew was that the early and mid-1990s was a difficult turning point. After civil servants' salaries were considerably slashed, your dad was left with few options given the weight of responsibility on him.

To add insult to injury, your Class Six studies were interrupted by a series of strikes by government workers that brought you to the verge of returning to the Catholic School which you had left for the Government School two years before. The legitimacy of the school year hung on a thin thread. In the end, it survived and you were able to sit in for exams and move to Class Seven, the final year of primary school. But many dreams were killed and the prestige of education, right down to secondary schools, suffered amidst general despair and acute unemployment amongst youth. If not for your outstanding results, perhaps you would have faced a different destiny. There was a faint proposal for you to learn car mechanics under the tutelage of one of your cousins in Douala. You shivered at the thought of it, but everything was possible in those precarious days. What saved the situation was the fact that your dad had a house in Nkambe. So, the rental problem was solved.

8

Your first days at school marked the beginning of a new experience. Before that, your only knowledge of school life in Nkambe was from your elderly siblings, Klinsmann and Nshie. During the summer holidays, they recounted to you the main sagas en vogue and anecdotes about student life and the idiosyncrasies of certain staff members. One of the most entrancing stories that Klinsmann told you was about the exploits of Belmondo, a notorious armed robber in Nkambe.

Mbe Manya alias Belmondo was a larger-than-life character and his deeds remain the source of wonder and bewilderment in Nkambe till today. Belmondo was tall and dark, with a thick hitlerite moustache and always in his trademark blue jeans. Many people had never seen his real face which was constantly buried under dark sunglasses and blurred by the curly smoke from his Marlboro cigarette stick. He was not only physically clean but also clinical in his operations. In the eighties and early nineties, Belmondo and his gang sowed terror in Nkambe through high-level burglaries and other misdeeds but always succeeded in evading the dragnets of the police, often through mysterious means. At one point he and his accomplices, Ngi and Mundi Eboa (a physically lame man) were apprehended and detained just for the prison warders to discover the cell empty the following day, with no sign that the window or the door was forced open. The inmates had set forth at dawn.

Belmondo was a nightmare even to the police for, whenever they pursued him, he would metamorphose into a feline creature and pursue his terrified pursuers. Whenever he planned to break into any quarter, the way-out for its residents was to gather whatever valuable goods in their possession and offer to him in peace, to avoid double jeopardy. If shopkeepers at the Nkambe New Market knew he was around the corner, they instantly gathered money and handed to him to prevent him from mystically emptying their counters and shelves of their contents. For a girl to reject his advances was to expose herself to rape and one of the murkiest memories of Belmondo in Nkambe is linked to an infamous rape case in that town. There was, however, another face of Belmondo. Each time there was any incident of burglary of which he was not the author, one could always count on him to track down the culprits and recover the lost items with Scotland Yard precision. He was also a great lover and player of soccer and preferred to play barefooted. Belmondo died the way he lived and when he was buried in Nkambe, his uncle who resided in Mambila Plateau, Taraba State of Nigeria, received a surprise visit from his nephew, looking hale and hearty. It is only after he spoke with someone back home that he realised that the Belmondo who visited him was a double.

Klinsmann baited your anxiety for things to come through fictional stories, such as the story of Mbamu, the pubescent protagonist of *The Good Foot* who was locked in a room with a girl as an attempt by his peers to deflower him and cure him of his prudishness. That Mbamu did not do anything to the girl left you with mixed feelings of pity and admiration for the boy. However, the most beautiful harbinger of secondary school paradise Nshie brought home to you was the story of Okonkwo. Apart from the Oxford Advanced Learners' Dictionary and the World Atlas which you used to explore constantly, 'Okonkwo' became your bedside text. You used to take Nshie's copy of 'Okonkwo' and read quietly in your room. Nothing was as blissful as lying in your bed and reading 'Okonkwo' to the tune of raindrops on the zinc roof. The atmosphere of the world painted in that text was strangely similar to yours. The palm wine, the kola nuts, the proverbs of *Things Fall Apart* pertained to your culture. Ikemefuna drew pure pity and anguish from your innermost self. At the time when your knowledge of the Igbo people was nothing beyond the red cap, your dad seemed like your own Okonkwo. He had a red cap that became part of his personality and authority. Whenever he came back home for holidays, the telling signs were the red cap and the radio. At that time, whenever you came back home and found these signs, you knew you had to adjust your ways.

Secondary school life augured a sense of transformation and that was incarnated in Nshie. Whenever she came back for holidays, she put on a punk hairstyle, distinct from your cursory and scissors-shaved hair. As she carried out her household chores, she never ceased to hum the latest hit songs at the time. Sometimes, the pans she was washing became secondary to her solo singing.

Chaka Demus' 'Waka Bam-Bam'; Meiway's 'Zoblazo'; Monique Seka's 'Missounwa' were regular clips on her disco list. There was a popular *makossa* song in pidgin English she loved singing. It was adapted to subvert a certain staff member who dated one of his students and it became the biggest scandal in school:

> *I no fit marry ... Hey hey, hey hey*
> *I no fit marry... Hey hey, hey hey*
>
> *I no fit marry ... Hey hey, hey hey*
> *Pa... di vex oh hey ya hey*
> *Pa... di vex oh hey ya hey*
>
> (I cannot get married to .... Hey hey, hey hey
> I cannot get married to...Hey hey, hey hey
>
> I cannot get married to ... Hey hey, hey hey
>
> Pa... will get angry oh hey ya hey
> Pa... will get angry oh hey ya hey)

But Nshie also became headstrong towards your mum. She began answering back at the least rebuke from her, signs of secondary school assertiveness. By the year you were admitted into Form One in Nkambe, Nshie had transferred to Bamenda and came only occasionally for holidays. Your cousin, Klinsmann was thus your secondary school mentor.

In your Form One class, you came to discover that even though most of you spoke Limbum as mother tongue, the level of intelligibility amongst some of your dialects was considerably low. Many poked fun at the way some mates would tell stories in a version of Limbum that sounded like a foreign language to speakers of other dialects of the same language. Nearly all the main dialects of Limbum were represented in your class. On the one hand, there were those from Binju and Kungi. The Kungi dialect in particular was influenced by the Mbembe language, making it an extreme form of the dialect of Nkambe, Binshua and Tabenken. On the other hand, there were those from Ndu with their tendency to convert affricate sounds/ʧ/ and /dʒ/into sibilant sounds /s/ and /z/. When someone from Ndu spoke, you always thought they were acting and that sooner or later, they would revert to their 'normal speech'. They sounded cheeky and sassy. However, there was the special case of the dialect from Ntumbaw, which though close to Ndu, was inflected by words and interjections of Hausa and Fulfulde languages spoken by the Moslem communities in that area, not forgetting Lamnso, for its closeness to the border with the Nso ethnic group.

As a buffer zone between these extreme variants of the Limbum language, were those like yours from Luh, Wat, Ntundip and Taku area. When someone spoke in either the Ndu or Kungi dialect, it was both an event and a spectacle. In the very first week, during self-introduction, getting to know that one of your classmates was from a neighbouring village was always a cause for tacit celebration. But some mates, mostly but not exclusively female ones, were often hesitant to identify with their original villages, preferring to be considered as coming from Ndu or Nkambe, the centres of modernity. They were likely to respond in pidgin English if you engaged them in Limbum. Or when some spoke in Limbum, they made intentional mistakes to give the impression that they had little or no mastery and that they had grown up in the city. Later on, when you travelled out of your linguistic community, you discovered that such characters were likely to respond to you in the Ndu dialect even if they came from other dialect communities. The Ndu dialect had a high snob appeal!

9

Coming from a village school and a bit cowered by the swag of your town-raised peers, you were not at first sure if your previous academic record would thrive in your new environment. To make matters worse, you were in Form One C. Though you were not sure of the criteria used in partitioning students into A, B and C, there was a silent belief by many a student that Form One C might have been reserved for the weaklings. Nevertheless, you were determined to give your best. You had so many joint periods whereby the three classes would move into one classroom, usually in Form One B. That was the time when most students sought for notice, just like during free periods. Some three boys were particularly naughty and would always steal the show during free periods. One of them, blessed with an incredible talent for malice, was nicknamed Jawan the robber, the character from *Strange Tales from the Arabian Nights*. Another troublesome case was a repeater, nicknamed Tybalt, from *Romeo and Juliet*, for his bullying attitude. He was fond of mocking at his mates, newcomers, through the song "foxes can dance without music". As foxes, i.e., freshmen, your tails needed to be trimmed as a sign of initiation into secondary school life. The third was referred to as Touchstone, from Shakespeare's *As You Like It* and was adept at parroting everything a teacher had taught, giving it a perverted dimension.

It was during free periods that films like "Snake Girl", "Cynthia" and "No Retreat, No Surrender", were told and retold by mates, triggering all sorts of arguments and counter-narrations. You had some classmates who came to school purposefully to narrate specific Indian or Nigerian films and later on pack their bags for the Video

Club at the Old Market. One such mate was nicknamed "scientist," because right in Form One he had decided that he would be a scientist and had nothing to do with arts subjects. Scientist could narrate a film right down to its soundtrack, reproducing moments of tension through a glib twist of the pitch in his humorous idiolect. His rugged Hannibal shoes have not left your memory. They were a truck-shaped pair of dockside shoes that bore the colour of dust, not by design but by endurance. Free periods were times for the accumulation of social capital beyond academic performance and were cherished by those who earned an audience from the rest of the class through their power of narration. There was pride in demonstrating how many films one had mastered. Most of the re-narrations were done in Pidgin-English and in Limbum.

Some of the best stories during free periods were told by your mates from Binka, a village close to Nkambe Town. When you say village, you mean to be provocative, for the inhabitants silently shunned the appellation of their locality as a village. Deep in the mind of every Binka mate was the belief that their place of origin was, in reality, a city. They referred to their home as 'Sirlah' meaning (a horizontally located) home, supposing the common reference to an easily identifiable communal text/spirit and their familiarity with a specific space of provenance. Most of their stories centred on the great football trio: the three R - Rahim, Rogers and Roland as well as one Pa Ali Ngahbir, a veritable trickster. During inter-quarters football competition, Pa Ali Ngahbir would give the same type of performance-enhancing amulets to competing football teams, accounting for the tough finals that used to transfix the entire Binka in those days. As the games prolonged into extra time and penalty shootouts, outside the pitch, Pa Ali would be engaged in supplementary negotiations with covert officials of both teams and only the higher bidder would finally carry the day. The more interesting one was the claim that Pa Ali Ngahbir had invited the *Nwarong*[27] of

27. A secret society

Binka to his home and gave them a treat. However, as the *Nwarong* left his compound, full of gratitude, Pa Ali sang his incantations in a farewell to the august secret society, revealing that the sumptuous meal they had just eaten was made of the flesh of a pied crow, a *'kankoh'*, an otherwise inedible bird with black feathers and white silk lapel, similar to the uniform of most Baptist Women's choir groups in your area.

Complemented by stories shared by your mates from Binka and others, Literature was the subject that provided you with much material for fun time. It was taught by Pa Want'd and Mr Sammy Jato as your elder sister Nshie had predicted. The most difficult of all was *Thirty-Nine Steps*. It was about Scotland Yard and a character called Black Stone, but the plot was just too difficult for most Form One students to grasp. You always planned to re-read that text, which you haven't yet. But one tortuous quote from the book stuck in your mind: "The men who knew that he knew what he knew had found him". Even when the text was still being treated in class, certain classmates decided to sell their copies at the old market at knock-down rates. That is, if they were not yet 'pilfered' (to use Pa Forti's word) by the gang of biblioklepts in Cheap Side. The book dealers knew how to kill a man's spirit through their shylock dexterity in bargaining. They mastered the conditions that led students to sell books and gave them just enough to stave off the munchies for a day. Suffice to say the title Thirty-Nine Steps was so popular that it became the name of a popular local corn beer (*sha*) parlour in the Old Market, mostly frequented by students!

In early secondary school, no subject tantalised you more than the French language. French was not taught in your primary school that still had an acute shortage of teachers. Mates who had studied in urban primary schools were the fortunate ones. After the first term in Form One, you began to make sense of the French books you had taken along to Nkambe. You accorded more time to French than any other subject. In addition to the coursebook, *Transafrique*

1, you constantly read *New Practical French, Pierre et Seydou, The Second, Third and Fourth French Book,* books that were already out of the programme but which tremendously enhanced your knowledge of the language. You rehearsed these books fervently at home, relishing most of the stories that were usually excerpts from African novels by Olympe Bhêly-Quénum, Mongo Beti, Jean Pliya, Birago Diop, Paul Hazoumé, Camara Laye, Ferdinand Léopold Oyono, Abdoulaye Sadji, Bernard Dadié, etc. Even when you liquidated texts like *Pierre et Seydou* to make ends meet, usually at a price typical of books that were no more on the prospectus, those texts with literary passages remained close to your bed and to your heart. When you scored 20/20 in French, the first-ever secondary school evaluation in any subject, you felt on top of the world, and could not wait to break the news to your cousin and mentor, Klinsmann. You flew home like Aliocha[28], the immigrant Russian teenager, pushing his way impatiently through the bustling streets of inter-war Paris to announce the results of his French test to his immigrant parents.

In Form Two, you started devouring entire literary texts in French. You wept with Agrippina, Junie and Britannicus and cursed Nero in Jean Racine's *Britannicus*; sympathised with Agnes and Arnolphe in Molière's *Ecole des Femmes* (The School for Wives) and felt pity for Banda in Mongo Beti's *Ville Cruelle* (Cruel Town). You would memorise entire pages from these texts. These private readings gave you a considerable edge in that subject. Coupled with your interest in history that was undoubtedly due to your father's radio, you began defining yourself as a student of letters, even though you had a better score sheet in science subjects. You had begun grappling with questions of existence and the meaning of life at a young age and were sure that arts subjects offered you more possibilities in addressing those questions that constantly invaded your mind. In Form Three, you had to choose between the arts and sciences.

---

28. Eponymous character of a 1991 autobiographical novel by Russian-born French writer and historian Henri Troyat.

However, the school had already made the choice for the best students in each class, putting you on the science list! You protested to the principal and finally were brought back to Form Four A (arts). This brought you into serious conflicts with your Chemistry, Mathematics and Biology teachers. On the contrary, your French teacher and mentor, Mr Cedis aka 'Français' was rather delighted with your choice. Your dad also felt a bit disappointed when you informed him you chose to study arts and went ahead to assure you that all depended on you and the perception of your relative strengths in whatever domain you chose. There was no repeal to your decision and you were happy your dad respected your choice.

10

Stepping your feet on these grounds as an alumnus, the first part of the campus you visited was the Cheap Side. Passing in front of the Form Two C building of the Cheap Side, you recalled that it was where you assumed your first leadership role. It was the class in which you moved from the timid boy in Form One to a class prefect due to the new rule that made students who took the first position of merit in end-of-year exams automatically class prefects of their respective classes in the following academic year. You gained confidence in your performance and were ready to assume class leadership for the first time in your life. But you were also a backbencher, one of those who used to add double meaning to words like Shakespeare's court jester Fest, in *Twelfth Night*. Being the class prefect and backbencher made you privy to the different and seemingly contradictory trends at play in your class. During break time, a group of students would sit back to conduct prayer meetings. On the other hand, especially during the free period, another group used to stage the newest hit songs in class, to the applause of the class. Sometimes, some girls belonged to both camps. Occasionally, the two groups clashed for space and the sisters-in-Christ would ask God to forgive those who were still in the world.

By then, the Baptist Church was caught in a strong wave of Pentecostal evangelization. Some believed it was because some of the pastors were trained or retrained in Nigeria, where the born-again syndrome had gone viral. Times had changed. In these times of prosperity gospel, it is sexy to be born again. One needed a down-the-road-to-Damascus experience as a certificate of adherence, a salvation testimony. To the question: "are you born again?" the answer was either 'Yes' or 'No' and in the case of the former, the one preaching to you even interrogated you further in order to test the veracity of your testimony. Being born again was to live with the traumatic/redemptive imminence of Rapture. Prayer groups sprouted here and there, in classes, schools, quarters, etc. and a pin fall on the ground could as well be given a heralding and prophetic interpretation as the sign of End Time. You were on the precincts of the year 2000, the Year of Rapture. It was possible for a girl whom you had been yearning for and of whose love you were sick, to ask you if you were 'born again' and to go ahead to tell you that she wanted you as a 'brother in Christ' or a 'normal friend' and not as a 'lover'. However sincere that was, the end justified the means, and when the worse came to the worse, even the moments of affective pushing of hands, of affirmative denials and of angry smiles sometimes began and ended with biblical verses. Nevertheless, whatever was done could not be undone even with the recital of the entire Bible.

On the whole, with the utterance of the expression 'born again', something stopped and something else began. As a born again, you could not use any kind of body lotion, no skin bleaching lotion, nor put on any kind of wig if any at all. The Religious Club of your school and that of the nearby Government Technical High School were made up of young boys and girls who had abandoned the world for Christ. They organised religious crusades to pray for the school. For some students, many born again students often looked worried and melancholic and it was almost possible to identify them on campus. It was the time when the zipped Bible was *en vogue* and when the Baptist Church in your hometown was turned into a 'born again' church and people started praying in tongues as had already been prevalent in the Full Gospel or Deeper Life churches.

You have used the expression "Cheap Side" and this deserves an explanation. The entire campus was divided into two geographical sections. The part of the campus which hosted Forms One to Three B was called Cheap Side. On the other side of the campus, there was Dear Side, including mostly storey buildings that hosted classes from Form Three C to Upper Sixth, and the administrative block. Cheap Side was a bit aloof but strategic because it provided several avenues of dodging for its students. In terms of uniforms, the difference was clear. Cheap Side students wore blue armbands at the rim of the short sleeve jacket while the Dear Side dons wore white. One had to fight hard to merit the white armband. There were several patterns of transaction during break time between the two sides. The Dear Side dudes came to Cheap Side to take their girlfriends to the shed for lunch break. Vice versa, some Cheap Side mates had the guts to date Dear Side girls and would stroll down with them to Cheap Side in a gesture of ostentation and bravado, to the envy of the 'foxes'. Such daring boys were commonly called 'bao'.[29] Such students were usually not the best in classwork.

Then there was another group of students who brought news of life in the Dear Side to the Cheap Side foxes. These were the *flâneurs* from Dear Side who loitered in Cheap Side during break, perhaps unable to waylay some Cheap Side chick after prowling from one corridor to another with predatory intent. Cheap Side was not necessarily cheap and not every Tom and Dick from Dear Side could successfully wheedle a girl from Cheap Side. So, these *flâneurs* turned ambulant lecturers, schooled the impressionable foxes on the

---

29. Short form of the "baobab", a tree that grows in most African societies. In this context, it symbolises a student who stands out amongst his peers.

differences between studies in Dear Side and Cheap Side. Cheap Side was akin to the Chinese Parliament, while one could cross to Dear side only after Darwinian natural selection. They warned that while Cheap Side depended on 'cram work', Form Four was the beginning of real academics with the General Certificate of Education syllabus. Exams in Form Four were based on CRITICAL ANALYSIS. These professional scaremongers filled the minds of some Cheap Side peers with a sense of diffidence in the face of imminent academic storms ahead. But, on the other hand, they also made you yearn to meet the world pre-announced to you through euphonious and romantic titles such as *I Will Marry When I want, Jane Eyre* and *The Beautyful Ones Are not yet Born*. For those Cheap Side foxes who burnt with unreciprocated love for their mates but lacked the courage to approach them, these titles had an almost psychoanalytic effect. They promised better things ahead for the patient ones: I will marry when I want because the beautyful ones are not yet born.

Liaison

Souvent la Providence inconnue dépose comme voulu
Sur nos chemins, des êtres de divers contenus
Mais rares sont les êtres de pures âmes
Sous ce ciel d'âmes infâmes

Fille de Zeus, espèce rare, juste pour toi j'existe
La Nature, ton habile et unique styliste
Tu me remplis d'idées idylliques
Amy, nom par nature Musique

Fille au sourire de princesse, regard de tendresse
Visage radieux, innocence imbue de sagesse
Sourire, encore sourire, ton état d'âme
La bile bannie de ton cœur de dame

Les mots me trahissent par leur faiblesse
Car pour t'écrire il faut la souplesse
Devant toi la langue perd le sens
Et s'évanouit dans l'essence

Tu es l'oasis frais sur le sable fin du temps
La douce rosée de Printemps
Ta Flamme chaque seconde me rajeunit
A tes cotés, je redore mon avenir.

De ton amour, je me vante
Avec toi, je me réinvente
G.

11

As you continued walking down towards the assembly ground, you recalled the scent of cypress trees which separated Cheap Side from the rest of the campus in your days. Many of those trees had been chopped down. In those days, one recurrent form of punishment for those found guilty of minor crimes by the Disciplinary Council was the digging of cypress stumps. It was tedious work and after some few terms, the horde of cypress trees that canopied the campus had been felled, leaving only those that paved the main pathways. You recalled the scent of those cypress trees, dripping with raindrops, as you left the General Assembly in the morning hours of 5th September 1995, engulfed in the crisp and fluffy daffodils of newly sewn blue jeans and skirts and sky-blue jackets, with newly printed ledger books in your hands, heading to Cheap Side for the first class in secondary school, anxious to discover the mystery and magic behind nice sounding secondary school subjects like Literature, Chemistry, Biology and Physics but also the personalities behind the enigmatic names of "Pa Want'd", "Mr Jato Sammy", "Pa Ngarkah", "Pa Kuhni", "Mr Fonta", etc.

As often in your days in Nkambe, rumours often took precedence over reality. Behind the cypress trees that fenced the rear of the Assembly Ground, close to the school farm, was a small concrete structure that was rumoured to host the larger-than-life school generator. But the generator generated more alacrity than electricity. In other words, it generated more lies than light. In fact, during your seven years in that institution, never did you hear its sound nor see its light. And Nkambe in those days was not spared the tribulations of power blackouts, or *delestage* as it was known in the Francophone parts of the country. Stories abounded. Some claimed the generator was a German product just to attest to its power and durability. Others corroborated it was a gift from the German government, while some argued it was rather a gift from an American Peace Corps that had once taught in that school and sent it when he had gone back to the USA. Others claimed it was strong enough to light the entire campus, the whole town and beyond.

Looking at that concrete structure as you walked across the General Assembly you could not say for sure if the generator was still there or if it ever existed at all. At Cheap Side, stories were like palliatives with which students killed time during free periods and break time, especially when your pocket archaeology did not produce enough coins to 'make smiles meet' with regard to Mami Julie's puff-puff. When the Senior Divisional Officer aka Plaster and Paint sought to arrest the principal for the confiscation of school property at the centre of which was the school generator, amidst other travesties, it sounded to you like science fiction. In the end, the principal proved he could pull more strings within the ruling party than Plaster and Paint, the representative of the Head of State in the locality.

The Assembly Ground reminded you of Heartbeats, an all-male acapella group from the University of Yaoundé 1 that visited GBHS Nkambe in the late 1990s. The seven-man group created a sensation with their breath-taking performances that rippled across many other secondary schools of your area and left behind unforgettable impressions on many a student. They were young, dynamic and talented. Each one had a unique stature and personality but they all combined into undeniably beautiful synchrony on stage. Handsome youth in their prime, they merged a certain seductive and almost worldly snare with an evangelical attitude and way of life, brought out both in their songs and in the salvation testimonies which they shared with the audience at the beginning of their performances. They gave that name "Jesus" a certain flair, a certain euphonic touch and punch. Amongst their songs, "Sometimes I wonder why…", "I'm aware", "Rock with the Lord", "If we try" were undoubtedly the most popular. But beyond the beauty of their songs, they gave you a foretaste of university life.

They were nothing less than role models and ambassadors for the University of Yaoundé 1, at a time when UB (University of Buea), the newly created Anglo-Saxon university in the country dubbed affectively as "the place to be", had captured the hearts and minds of most high school students poised for university. When the Heartbeats singers introduced themselves as students of *English Modern Letters, Anthropology, Sociology,* etc., those names sounded so romantic and promising. Years later, many of you who carried your bags and hopes to Yaoundé 1 were to come face to face with the unequivocal reality of that institution. Few could have predicted that life in Yaoundé 1 was going to be an acapella of a totally different type, a veritable purgatory.

On a more personal level, the Assembly Ground was a place to remember, for that was for you, a space of triumph and distinction. During the end-of-term declaration of class results, you would march up, amidst applause, to shake the hand of the principal. It was customary to call the names of the first and the last three of each class. For you, such moments were always full of anxiety and tension. Your heart would thump to the rhythm of the class master's steps as he climbed the elevated rostrum to read out the results. This was in spite of the fact that all your peers were often sure of your position, for the competitive spirit pushed many students to indulge in the habit of calculating their marks and those of their peers to determine the end-of-term ranking. Yet, you always feared the class master could commit an error that would make you lose your stronghold. It never happened. You were always depressed after each test or exams because you were never satisfied with how you answered the questions. Nonetheless, the results most often proved you wrong and your mates thought that you were pretentious. "That is what he always says, but when the results come out...", your mates would say about you, mockingly. In fact, for all the twenty-one end-of-term results of your secondary/high school life, you took the second position only once. And the cold and reproachful look on your dad's face when you handed to him your Form Two second term report card meant that you had to re-fasten your belt. Not forgetting his snide and sneering statement to you: "You spent the entire term eating fufu corn and *njamnsu* and forgot your studies."

You walked past the General Assembly ground to climb up to the principal's office, on the third floor of the administrative block. In those student days, you could not climb that staircase without properly marshalling your English sentences, weeding them of any traces of Pidgin English or Limbum; without putting on that slightly presumptuous face typical of class prefects, the primus inter pares; nor without removing any assorted dress in case you met Mr Nganjo, the Discipline Master. The latter knew no hierarchy in administering discipline. You entered the secretariat of the principal and there was Short Joe, the secretary. He had served more than ten principals of that institution. Short Joe had an incredible memory for recalling faces and names of former students. You were not the exception. His office seemed technologically updated. Surely, times had changed and the days of manual printing were over. This was the computer age. Formerly, Short Joe single-handedly printed the report cards for the entire school. Visiting your home country from the land of Johannes von Gutenberg, no other person incarnated the printing press (and the typewriter) in your memory better than Short Joe. It was thus not surprising that whenever you beheld your secondary school report cards that you always carried along with you, it was his face that came to mind. Those report cards that preserved the aroma of ink for decades and bore the impeccable calligraphies of various teachers who passed through that school. You still carry some of them along with you, reminding yourself of the tension they used to trigger during end of term declaration of results. Short

Joe symbolised the transition from analogue to digital.

12

Short Joe asked you to wait for a while as there was someone in the principal's office. As you stood in the antechamber, waiting to be received by the principal, the words on the doorpost caught your attention: "Make at least one person happy each day in your life." The modest rectangular poster had sustained the blows of time but the expression was still legible in letter and spirit. Certainly, many successive principals had found it a good moral maxim in a context where occupying an office accorded one the power and pleasure to ask others "to come back tomorrow".

You had entered that office many times in your student days. The most memorable was the day you attended the Disciplinary Council. Then, you were in Form Four. Before 1996, the DC was something that only happened to others. But under the new principal, things changed drastically. People were not only punished for crimes, but also for sins. No one was too holy for the DC. If you claimed you had no sin, you were deceiving yourself and the truth was not in you. It was a period of rigour and moralization. Every teacher became a Discipline Master following a rotating roster system apart from the official Discipline Masters. Campus life became a fertile ground for sagas, akin to Richard Sheridan's *The School for Scandal*.

It was the time of spectacles. DC verdicts were delivered, not during the routine morning assemblies, but during the Special General Assemblies summoned impromptu and dramatically by the principal, sometimes when students were in the middle of a class. Some of the landmark DC cases of those days included the judgment of the members of the Parliament of Aristocrats and Galaxy, accused of promoting occultism on campus; a second cycle student accused of performing magic on campus at night in an attempt to win the heart and soul of a female mate; members of the Boys' Dormitory caught in the Girls' Dormitory during unholy hours, etc. Even dodging from classes, hitherto a negligible infringement of school rules, became a severely punishable crime. Class registers were to be routinely and unmistakably marked and woe betide any class prefect who reneged on his or her duties. And there was the rub. The weekly news bulletin by members of the Journalism Club, under the stewardship of the articulate and intrepid Fresh Prince of Baraki, entertained the school with breath-taking and subversive news reports, some of which earned club members outright dismissal threats from the school authorities.

Your inauspicious DC moment as a class prefect struck when a malignant character sinisterly confiscated the class register and *cahier de texte*, in a desperate attempt to implicate you and your assistant. After about three days of serious search, you discovered pieces of the official documents scattered behind the Boys' Dormitory. The culprit, in a miscalculated gesture of bravado, had written on the torn cover of the Register you found: "Remember the Ghost. This is just the beginning. See you next time". As circumstances would have it, you and your assistant could identify the handwriting of the 'ghost' and made your observations clear to the authorities. The suspect was none other than one of your classmates. So, the three of you, i.e., your assistant, the suspect and you were summoned to attend the DC duly constituted of the principal, the two main Discipline Masters and four members of the teaching staff. It was during those DC interrogations that you realised that some of the teachers whom you had always considered lenient could have been very befitting Judges in a 16th Century Spanish Court of Inquisition.

But the most fearful member of the DC was, as any alumnus of that institution would guess, the then Senior Discipline Master, Mr Nganjo. Whenever he began his sentence with "What I am saying is that heinnn...", what followed was a syllogism to which not even Socrates in Plato's 'Dialogues' could respond with certainty. Even though you and your assistant survived the questioning and were duly acquitted, that was an unsavoury experience, to say the least. The accused was found guilty and was dismissed as per the verdict that was spectacularly rendered one week later. However, three days after the dismissal, he was re-admitted and continued with his classes in tranquillity. He did not even go through the walk of shame or public confession in front of the mammoth crowd of the Assembly ground, as was the case with some dismissed-and-re-admitted students in those days. As a matter of fact, parents of the dismissed students had understood the writing on the principal's doorpost better than the students. "Make at least one person happy each day of your life". The beautyful ones are not yet born.

The teacher who was in the principal's office went out and Short Joe indicated to the principal that there was an alumnus who wanted to greet him. You entered the office without any further protocol. The principal shook your hand and held his right hand on his forehead, in an attempt to recall your name but confessed it had escaped his memory. Short Joe quickly came to his rescue, before closing the door behind him.

"Oh yes! Now I remember. How time flies! Where are you now?"

"In Germany, sir!"

"Oh, that is great. How is Angela Merkel?," he kidded.

"Certainly, she is doing fine, sir," you responded light-heartedly.

At least you had come as close to Merkel's official residence in Berlin as you would never to the presidential palace of Cameroon, the no-go area of the capital city, Yaoundé.

"So, what do you do in Germany?"

"Studies sir, I just finished my PhD."

"Oh my God, you don't mean it!!"

He stood up and gave you a warm and energetic handshake. He called Short Joe back into his office to annouce the news to him "Of course. He was one of our very best!"

You felt proud of this volley of compliments. The principal was certainly taking a break from his busy schedule and you had time to discuss the past. You reminded him of the letters he used to bring to you from your elder sister Nshie who studied in Bamenda at the time, usually with an enclosed one or two thousand francs banknote. He was a Human Biology teacher, a former teacher of Nshie before she moved to Government Bilingual High School, Bamenda.

"I still keep those letters, sir,"

"It is interesting that you still remember. Back then, there was neither Internet nor the flurry of money transfer agencies that you have now."

As you conversed, his ever-radiant and regal mien filled you with a mixture of admiration and anguish. That face reminded you of another face. You tried to forget. You grappled with memory, leery about awakening old pain. You did not know how he would react. But finally, you could not help.

"It is with a heavy heart that I learnt about Yvonne's passing onto glory, sir." You released the words, at first feeling awkward about the glaringly religious overtone of "onto glory" that seemed a bit out of place.

Just at that moment, he got an incoming call and beckoned on you to be patient for a short while as he spoke on the phone. That prolonged the suspense and you felt sorry for bringing up the topic in the first place. You roamed your eyes around the office garnished with sports paraphernalia, trophies and awards; flower vases, the wall clock, three plaques with quotes embossed on them, close to the computer and printer. His office looked beautiful. But nothing could allay the heaviness of the discussion you had just triggered.

"Yes, I am sorry I have a guest now, I will call you back." He dropped the phone, instantly turned to you and said.

"It was a tragic happening. I am still to come over it but I doubt if I ever would. I tried to follow up the case but finally let it go for it was going to cause me more pain and anger."

He went on to describe what his family had gone through as a result of the violent death of Yvonne. Surprisingly, he approached it with astonishing composure and courage. Yvonne was your classmate from Form One to Five. She had a soft brittle voice (certainly a genetic replay of her father's voice) and was a quiet character, except in the company of her female peers. After Form Five she moved to another school in Bamenda. Thus, you lost contact. You tried to reach out but she was out of reach. It is when you were chatting with one of your mutual classmates on Facebook that she broke the news of the untoward and sinister termination of Yvonne's life in Bamenda the week before. So did Yvonne travel on life's common way. But it was the nature of the end that made it more unbearable to everyone who knew her. You visualised the cruel hands of the invertebrate malefactor on her plump cheeks...

> Footfalls echo in the memory
> Down the passage which we did not take
> Towards the door we never opened
> Into the rose-garden. My words echo
> Thus, in your mind.
>
> Go, said the bird, for the leaves were full of children,
> Hidden excitedly, containing laughter.
> Go, go, go, said the bird: humankind
> Cannot bear very much reality.
>
> Time and the bell have buried the day,
> The black cloud carries the sun away.
> Will the sunflower turn to us, will the clematis
> Stray down, bend to us; tendril and spray
> Clutch and cling?
> Chill
> Fingers of yew be curled
> ("Burnt Norton", TS Eliot)

13

In the course of your discussion with the principal, the vice-principal came in and the former bade him to take you around the campus to show you the state of the renovation work that was being undertaken. He was a Maths teacher who had become a Religious Studies teacher in your days by necessity and by conviction. Many of you falsely thought he had been posted to the school as a Religious Studies teacher. You reminisced those days, when he would tell his students in the Ordinary Level Religious Studies Class, in his thunderous but entreating and empathetical voice: "While your concern may be to get A, or B grades in the GCE, my earnest prayer is for you to BE-lieve and be Saved." Many were awed by prospects of the Second Coming, more than the GCE for, after the class, it always felt as if the Second Coming was to take place before the GCE exams. And even if many still sailed through the GCE with their carapace of sin unruffled, a few were surely saved.

He showed you the portions of the establishment where the new administration was carrying out major renovations. They were doing a commendable job. But a Herculean task awaited them, for Dear Side was a shadow of its former self. Cheap Side had also deteriorated, but its demise was not as flagrant as Dear Side, perhaps because the walls of Cheap Side were never painted from the very beginning. It preserved its honour in comparison to the utter downfall of the Dear Side. He that is down needs fear no fall. The storey buildings of Dear Side were in utter degeneration. You wondered what had happened to this great institution that produced all calibres of alumni, scattered all over the world, in different walks of life. The entire nation was deteriorating. On some government structures, even the petals of the flag (symbol of an erstwhile one and indivisible nation) that had faded in solitude under the assault of the burning sun, refused to fly, for want of replacement.

One could say that since 1982, the only thing that was constantly renovated and massaged in that Republic was the Constitution in order to enable the president to rule for life. Every other thing was given a fake facelift on the eve of the National Day. Formerly, this school, with university-like infrastructure, was only comparable to one or two others in the entire North-West province of Cameroon. But it had become a sorry sight. The walls had peeled off and its sky-blue colour had turned into something like pale yellow. The dregs of dry-cleaning water had dripped down the exterior walls, drawing black vertical lines on its faded texture. The roof of the entire staircase that connected the different blocks seemed to be leaking, as seen through the black patches that mapped the decked platform above your head as you moved from one block to the other. The few walls that the new administration had repainted only revealed the magnitude of what still needed to be done. Nearly all the louvres had been broken and poorly shaped plywood served as a degrading replacement. The buildings constituted an eyesore that was in clear contrast to the lush lawns that separated the various blocks and the greenery of the maize stalks that bloomed on the school farm close by. The farm was a symbol of discipline and punishment for many students, but for two people it was a source of life. One of them was the Farm Master, Mr Babah who came to that school as a retrenched civil servant in the mid-1995, but when you met him in the corridors of the school administrative block, he looked even younger than he was back then.

The other person was Farmer Tantoh. When Farmer informed you around 2011 that he was receiving an award in Westminster Palace, UK, you could not help but go down memory lane to his humble beginnings in that school. Many called him "farmer" as a form of mockery, for many students did not understand why someone would choose to be Labour Prefect instead of going in for the more prestigious and juicy posts in the student government. But Farmer was a true son of the soil and due to the way he reacted to the 'Farmer' nickname, it soon turned into an expression of affection. Outside school hours, he spent a great deal of time on the school farm planting flowers and experimenting with all sorts of plants. One of his mates confessed to you that whenever they were asked to form a ridge on the school farm, Farmer Tantoh instead made a bed.

Farmer's footprints could be seen even on the banks of Chua-Chua, an area that harboured stories of purported witchcraft, some of which involved student apprentice-sorcerers, especially from Binju. He converted the area into a touristic site and a flashpoint in his environmental crusade. Despite soaring the heights, Farmer remained a farmer, as humble as water, the source of life which constituted a major dimension of his community projects. One cold foggy Monday morning of 1999, he made a key announcement in the General Assembly. As it was customary, the Labour prefect only spoke after more important members of the students' government and school staff had spoken: "If you wake up in the morning, wondering what to eat, just drink three glasses of water and you would be amazed for how long it can sustain you." Many laughed in public but followed his advice in private, especially the Cheap Side Hungry Ground members, those ones who lacked the basic fiduciary resources to make ends meet with Mami Julie, the legendary puff-puff seller. In a context of the proliferation of fictitious NGOs where some have learnt to talk the talk and not walk the walk without actually doing, he remained a grassroots leader who literarily took pleasure in rooting the grass. Added to his numerous awards, some US partners wrote his life story titled "I am Farmer" and Farmer Tantoh was invited to present the book to more than forty schools across ten states in the US, reaching out to more than thirty thousand school children. While some consider success as a form of alienation, Farmer remained true to himself, and most importantly, to the roots. And his roots were in that school farm.

The vice-principal took you to the Upper Sixth Arts building, the only study hall attached to the Administrative block. The Hall was one of those that had been newly re-painted, at least from the inside. Its brightly painted walls gave you a sense of hope that change was possible in a matter of time. That hall reminded you of the advent of the mobile telephone or MOBILIS as it was called in those days, i.e., at the turn of the new Millennium. Only a few teachers possessed a mobile telephone, not to talk of the students. Your English Literature teacher, Mr Lukong, was amongst the first persons to own a mobile phone in that school. You did not remember the brand but it was either a Motorola or Nokia. Other popular brands at the time included ALCATEL, SAGEM and SONY ERICSSON. During poetry class in which you studied such poems as 'Miniskirt', 'No Coffin, No Grave', and 'Phlora', Mr Lukong was interrupted once in a while by a call. In his naturally composed style, he would unstrap the phone from its sheath under the belt, move out of the class and answer his call. Sometimes, if the network was too poor on the precincts of the hall, he would climb the small mound under the cypress above the Upper Sixth Arts hall for better network. And when he came back, he made no comment about the call, only an "excuse for the interruption". He managed the mobile phone with decorum and gentility. He was one of a kind, when one considered the pandemonium caused by telephones at that time.

Stories were told about a woman who interrupted the sermon in Binju Baptist Church because of her telephone. In a mad rush to answer a phone call, she tripped on her high heels and fell on the aisle, drawing attention from the entire church during a sermon. The ringtone was a clarion call stricto-sensu. Vibration could cause an earthquake with its uproar and to put a phone on vibration mode required expertise, which many did not have. Some phones with quasi tractor structures seemed to have not only antennas but also exhaust pipes and apparently produced smoke as they shook the space around them when vibrating. To receive a call was a great source of pride, a mark of distinction and it meant that one had connections, networks and contacts, both literally and literarily. To answer a phone call, you needed to hush the entire world around you into silence. A missed call was a cause for metaphysical anguish. It was only later, in the android age, that the mobile phone became a means of managing boredom.

14

The vice-principal took you to the storey building which used to host Form Four and Five classes, close to the football field. The building also hosted the Form Three C, a class that made a premature transition from Cheap Side to Dear Side. And you were the lucky ones, the few blue armbands floating in a deep sea of intimidating white. The cheeks of that structure had suffered the blows and ravages of time more than any other. Thick traces of yellowish dry-cleaning water formed a warped network of contours on the walls, especially underneath the balcony. The vice-principal assured you that the structure was going to face the onslaught of the paintbrush in the following weeks. However, as you entered the classroom, you were pleasantly surprised. The inside was rather recently and thoroughly painted, with an appealing and appeasing inner beauty. The walls still emitted the fresh scent of paint, while the benches and desks were well arrayed in a manner not very typical of 'rasta week'. But that inner beauty only entrapped your memory in a whirlpool of agony because, in that building, seventeen Mays before, a voice used to echo that was no more, a voice that spoke about Christ with the same conviction and fervour as the vice-principal himself. A voice that imbibed ambition and hope in the most lacklustre student.

Few teachers had such a holistic approach to education for, even though a History teacher, he used to begin his classes with The Good

News and end with market gardening. He was one of those people who would talk in earnest of how Jesus saved their life, without losing any inkling of their gallantry or sexiness. He seemed like someone whose Jesus had extinguished all the existential butterflies and worms that churn in one's stomach even in one's most blissful moments. A dignified bachelor, full of life, full of vision. He used to refer to his students as "comrade", so you came to fondly call him comrade. He made his students dream, almost literally. He was a clean man. Thus, the interior renovation of that Form Three C structure did justice to someone who was allergic to the least symptoms of inner filth. But the exterior had to be as clean as the interior for he also loved physical cleanliness.

He carefully justified every mark he accorded each student and the returned script usually contained an even longer text as a way of explaining where the student went wrong or right and why. As students, you followed him, intellectually, spiritually and physically. You followed him to carry cow dung for his tomato garden from the Mbororo home close to the school Campus, amidst the extensive veld on the road from Nkambe to Tabenken. It was a voluntary gesture, not tied to marks, but each and every one was there to assist him, even those students inimical to History. Students did so happily, for it was a privilege to converse with such a gracious soul beyond the strictures of the classroom. It was hard to believe that comrade Matthew Ntumfon had died so young through a ghastly accident.

Further afield from the Dear Side were the boys'/girls' dormitories, the refectory and the Lower Sixth Arts hall. That hall was affectionately called the 'Mortuary'. So, when you studied TS Eliot's *Murder in the Cathedral* there, you were basically at home. You cannot say for certain why such a sepulchral nomenclature. Perhaps, due to its isolation from other pedagogic blocks and the fact that, after school hours, it was as tranquil and peaceful as a graveyard. But there was no funereal scent in the Mortuary. Rather, every lesson in that hall was mixed with the intrusive aroma of corn chaff, the main dormitory food, given the proximity of the hall to the refectory. With the effective implementation of Philosophy as a GCE A-Level subject in the school in the year 2001, the Mortuary was immensely transformed. The encounter with Philosophy had a cathartic effect on many a student. Contact with the likes of Thales, Socrates, Plato, Aristotle, the Sophists, Zeno, Cheikh Anta Diop, Kwame Nkrumah, Julius Nyerere, Thomas Paine and John Locke gave birth to the first batch of self-appointed avant-garde public intellectuals.

It was thus understandable that the Lower Sixth Arts class was often a thorn in the flesh of the school authorities, especially the school prefects. You were experts in civil disobedience a la Paine or a la Locke. You rebelled against and boycotted the classes of one of your teachers, leading to a bitter tussle which even the principal could not resolve. The LA5 (Lower Sixth Arts 5) students, in utter disobedience of the principal, had chosen to write the GCE A-Level exams only in Religious Studies, Philosophy and History (or Literature). For the principal, this series was illegal, arguing that Philosophy/Religious Studies were only supposed to be additional subjects to the traditional three-subject series. However, for the LA 5 philosophers, the principal was living in a sort of Plato's world of forms, not to say Plato's Cave. The young philosophers took advantage of the sequestered location of the Mortuary to implant a Plato's Republic, with its own laws and norms, always at loggerheads with the school authorities. Many a time, that Republic opened its doors to other dissidents from the main campus. It was not unusual that during break time, while the rest of the school flooded the school shed for their dose of Mami Julie's puff-puff, the Mortuary, on the other hand, became a lively symposium for Logic, Syllogism, Socratism, Sophism, Democritism, Nkrumahism, etc. Simply put, the Mortuary became the source of life.

15

The front wall of the Mortuary was full of graffiti messages. As you stood there looking at the walls it was clear to you that one name was missing from the litany of graffitied signatures – "Remember so so and so"- engraved by notorious students eager to will themselves into the living archives of that school. That name was Sunjo Fabien. Fabien does not need a "Remember Sunjo Fabien". Like it or not, he would be remembered by any alumnus who schooled in that institution between 1996 and 2002. Fabien was the incarnation of *ndombolo* swag, at a time when the graceful and mellow tones of Congolese rumba had transformed into urbanite fast-rhythm soukous characterised by acrobatic body movements with elaborate choreography. Those were the days of Awilo Longomba, Extra Musica, Koffi Olomide, Mbuta Likasu, J.B. Mpiana, etc. Fabien was part of a generation of Anglophone students who had lived and completed primary school and even started early secondary education in Francophone areas. So, they spoke French (and camfranglais) even more fluently than English.

At a time when the school transformed from Government High School to Government Bilingual High School, this group provided a buffer zone between the dominantly English-speaking students and the fledgeling Francophone section (and also the army, given that their parents were themselves military men that had served in Francophone zones. Some of their *ndombolo* stage props were military wares borrowed from military friends). Even though they had come from areas as diverse as Douala, Koutaba, Foumbot, Yaoundé, Mbouda and even Makenene, they mostly flocked together, dodged together, danced together, developing a distinct idiom and way of life that was very much attuned to the popular culture en vogue. They also had a tendency for provocative assorted outfits as well as a transgression of school rules, as part of a culture of 'strongness', 'strongman' and 'gesteur'. Those were the days of 'La Star des stars', 'Cascadeur', 'Yor' and 'Yoyette'. For example, at some point, some of them would come to class with books in a *nkeng*, a woven bamboo cage used by peasant farmers to transport hens/roosters for sale. But even though they dominated social evening programs with spectacular 'staging', they were some of the most avid bookworms the school has ever known. Again, Fabien stood out.

If you needed to know Fabien's sense of seriousness with studies, meet him after test papers were distributed and he felt he didn't score the best possible mark. His trademark red coat and rugged shoes always drew attention from Cheap Side students and turned him into a mobile touristic site, attracting him several nicknames. When you met him years later in the University of Yaoundé II, you quipped that if some of those his shoes were to be alive, they would certainly be priceless relics in the GBHS Nkambe school museum. Fabien (PhD in Health Economics) burst into laughter, telling you: "Bro, I am now a changed man." Indeed he had changed, but he can never actually change. In his gait, he still walked as if he is bouncing onto the stage, in a shooting position, *position de tir*.

Then there was another group of students from a nearby community known as Tabenken who made the Mortuary experience rather unique. Tabenken jitters between a big village and a small town. In a somewhat benevolent sarcasm, it is often anecdotally referred to as 'Tang-mboh Division', underlining the aspirations of its inhabitants for its administrative status to be upgraded to that of divisional headquarters. An upgrading that has not (yet) occurred, leaving it in a limbo that is visible in myriad social reflexes of its home-grown youth. The story of GBHS Nkambe cannot be told without reference to the considerable number of students from Tang-mboh Division. In the late 90s and early 2000s, waves of Tabenken students migrated to your institution to continue High School after obtaining their O Level in Government Secondary School, Tabenken. Such students from Tabenken who came in Lower Sixth were exceptionally hilarious, gregarious, entertaining and had code names for almost everything. For instance, during boy talk common amongst male students, they had a thousand and one ways of referring to girls. Right in the middle of a lesson, they could plan their after-school drinking spree without anyone having an inkling of what they were talking about.

They had an incredible predilection for *sha* (the local maize brew) and had no qualms carrying parched corn in the pockets of their school jackets or trousers and eating it during classes, despite the enduring aroma and the dry crunching sound it produced. They called each other through whistling sounds and other buccal acrobatics as often the case amongst wanton boys in semi-urban communities. More so, they were known for dodging. But given the proximity of their locality to the campus, a Tang-mboh student could leave the classroom on Friday with the intention of dodging from school and then decide to go on a weekend trip to their home-town/village. They just folded their jacket into their school bag, trekked across the extensive moorland behind the Mortuary and descended the steep Ntfumbang hill into the enthralling arms of the low-lying (*mboh*) village-town, a matrix of untellable mysteries and countless sagas. Suffice to say that despite their apparently jestful, non-conformist and their admirably rustic tendencies, these particular students were incredibly talented and were at the forefront of Journalism, Drama, Environmental and Cultural club activities on campus. Their non-conformism, steadfastness and group solidarity served your batch greatly in its 2001 boycott of and rebellion against one History teacher whom many students considered outrightly incompetent! It is from those generations of Tang-mboh students that emerged the likes of Tamfu Arison, a distinguished member of the Journalism Club who became a reputable news anchor with

the Cameroonian news channel Equinox TV and a freelance con-
tributor to various international news platforms, winning the CNN
Multichoice Award 2014.

Unlike many of the classrooms in Dear Side, the Mortuary had
maintained some form of physical integrity. Its walls reminded you
of the unmistakable Pa Ngeh, your second cycle World History
teacher. He brought World History home to you as if he had lived
with Metternich, Bismarck, Hitler, Napoleon, Washington, Churchill
and Mazzini. Some of the citations Pa Ngeh delivered with great
mimetic precision included: "Italy is a mere geographical expression"
(Metternich) "Here lies Joseph II, who failed in all he undertook"
(Joseph II's self-written epitaph) "He has the heart of a lion but the
brain of an ox" (Italian Count Camilo Cavour on Giuseppe Garibaldi
during the latter's crossing of the straits of Sicily with his Thousand
Red Shirts). You even became addicted to the black colour, not
only because it was 'diplomatic' but also because it was the colour
of Giuseppe Mazzini, the founder of the *Il Risorgimento,* a member
of the *Carbonari* (charcoal burners). He was the prophet of Italian
reunification and a man of strong convictions.

Pa Ngeh's historical narratives were framed in original and
normative syntax. Yet they carried an affective tone that brought
his subject matter to your doorsteps, that made you capture the
rhythm of the Glorious Revolution, the trotting tanks of the First
World War, the conceptual schemes of the Final Solution and the
hot wounds of the Cold War. It was rumoured that Pa Ngeh had
studied in England, but no one knew or could say for sure. Later in
life, when you landed at the Boston airport on the Atlantic coast,
you were seized by the tension that brewed up on that coast on
16th December 1773. But you also recalled how, Pa Ngeh, to clear
the ground for the expression of the gravity of the event, began the
topic by warning you that the Boston Tea Party had nothing to do
with people revelling over tea in a conventional party with friends.
It was rather a group of people rebelling against oppression, an act

that led to the birth of the strongest nation in the world.

The teachers of Cameroon History and African History were equally good. However, while they focused primarily on the GCE, Pa Ngeh wanted students to somewhat relive the history. The rhythm of Cameroon and African History classes was rather too fast and the teachers attempted to cover the entire syllabus within a very limited time. Hence, their history never had the same effect on you as World History. Later in life, you were unsettled by the fact that slavery and the slave trade was taught as a mere GCE topic. In the frenzy of GCE preparations, one did not have time to digest the tragedy of that ignominy. Perhaps it was proper for that period of your young age. But later on, you yearned to learn more, to know more, to understand why a race of people could undergo such misery because of fellow man. Your fervent desire to thrust yourself into narratives of the enslaved was later accomplished when you travelled to Peru for your postdoctoral research and wrote a memoir of your trip, detailing above all, your encounters with Peruvians of African origin; your visit to the ports of arrival in the Pacific and the congenial history of the enslavement of the Red Indians in America.

16

After the 'Mortuary', you went back to the Cheap Side upon the advice of the vice-principal who insisted you should at least address the students of the examination classes who were having a revision class. Though reserved for Form One to Form Three Classes, the Cheapside classrooms could be used for revision by examination classes during rasta week when few students were on campus. Treading stealthily on the lush lawns of Cheap Side was like revisiting the yesteryears when your mind was crowded by the litany of characters let loose from the literary texts you studied. The characters basically lived with(in) you and endowed Cheap Side with an endearing and magical aura. There was Unoma, the young and brilliant schoolgirl struggling against the odds, determined to pursue her education, with her mother telling her father "Unoma must go to school. Do you want her to be like you and I who have eyes but cannot see?" (*Unoma*, by Flora Nwapa); There was also Mbamu, the young lad living with his parents in the banana plantation camp in Mbonge. Locked in a room with a girl by his peers as a means of inducing him to assume the calling of puberty, Mbamu's prudish attitude prevented him from ceding to the snares of the flesh even when the coast was clear for him to act; But in the same text, there was Nkunkum Massa, the character who came back from work earlier than usual, spurred by lust, to catch up with Susanna, providing you young students with your best song in those days which you intoned in chorus as the rain clattered on the Cheap Side roofs:

> *Nkunkum Massa ha,*
> *Nkunkum time e no dey*
>
> *Oh Nkunkum*
>
> *We go for pay oh ha*
> *Susanna lef for house oh*
>
> *Oh Nkum*
>
> *For sika weti ha*
> *For sika e di wait e Johnny oh*
>
> *Oh nkunkum*
>
> *As Johnny e come oh*
> *Susanna take e for house oh ha*
>
> *Oh Nkunkum*

They begin di chop oh ha
The chop e be sweet e plenty

Oh Nkunkum...
(*The Good Foot*, by Peter Nsanda Eba)

There was Rosalind, Celia, Orlando, Touchstone, Duke Senior, coming together in a fairy-tale scene of revelry, after years of mistaken identity, usurpation, courtly intrigues, betrayal and exile, in a text woven in the tapestry of the finest Shakespearean wits (*As You Like It*, by Shakespeare); there was red-haired Tybalt, Juliet's cousin foaming with vengeance against the Montagues and willing to challenge love-sick Romeo to a duel, Romeo whom Juliet confessed to us, "kiss by the book" (*Romeo and Juliet*, by Shakespeare); there was Phileas Fogg with his measured steps, precise actions and enigmatic personality. Succinct and laconic in speech but decisive in action. Not forgetting Passepartout (*Around the World in Eighty Days*, by Jules Verne); there was Scheherazade, Jawan the Robber, Zumurrud (the beautiful slave girl) and Ali Shar in the breath-taking stories of *Strange Tales from the Arabian Night*; there was the homesick soldier, Matthaeus Tina, of the German Legion posted to King George's Yorkshire, who stirred up and gave vent to the pristine algae of love in the bosom of the solitary and shy countryside girl, Phyllis, only for their lives to take a fateful twist typical of Hardian gloomy narrative vision ("The Melancholy Hussar of the German Legion", Thomas Hardy); And there was Ikemefuna, not the Ikemefuna in *Unoma*, Unoma's one-eyed and jealous uncle who once stole a goat. But another Ikemefuna, an innocent boy killed in his prime by Okonkwo in sheer foolhardiness. You came to Cheap Side when *Things Fall Apart* was no longer on the syllabus. But it was one of those books that engrossed and lured you into reading it over and over. Though you ended up not knowing whether it was Okonkwo who wrote Chinua Achebe or whether it was *Things Fall Apart* that wrote Okonkwo, for most of you, perhaps because of your teenage identity, it was the fate of young Ikemefuna that enthralled you in deep and enduring empathy.

Ikemefuna came to represent the shadowed force of unnameable and tragic destiny whose imaginative force was only paralleled by Shakespeare's Hamlet. But unlike Hamlet who had the chance to encapsulate his outrageous fortune in his potent existentialist musing "To Be or Not to Be", Achebe's Ikemefuna was not afforded that privilege. His thoughts, never to be known, remained wrapped in an ill-omened silence. As a move to stave off war with Umuofia after killing Udo's wife, the neighbouring tribesmen offered Udo a young virgin and to the people of Umuofia, they offered a young lad, Ikemefuna in compensation. The elders chose Okonkwo to host the young boy who became part and parcel of his family. Achebe says "He grew rapidly like a yam tendril in the rainy season, and was full of the sap of life. He had become wholly absorbed into his new family. He was like an elder brother to Nwoye, and from the very first seemed to have kindled a new fire in the younger boy." But tradition had to be respected and Okonkwo was not one to be thought of as weak. And the story continued, as Ikemefuna took his tragic exit: "As the man who had cleared his throat drew up and raised his machete, Okonkwo looked away. He heard the blow. The pot fell and broke in the sand. He heard Ikemefuna cry, 'My father, they have killed me!' as he ran towards him. Dazed with fear, Okonkwo drew his machete and cut him down. He was afraid of being thought weak." The last words uttered by Achebe's Ikemefuna, re-echoed in *Chronicle of a Death Foretold* by Garcia Marquez' Santiago, have remained memorable to many readers.

17

You passed in front of the Form One building and met a handful of students, including the Senior Prefect Girls who was organizing the younger students to carry out a task. Though in Lower Sixth, she was quite young, not very different from the other Form One students, unlike during your days when SP Girls were quite mature girls! You took pictures together and they asked you insistently where you were coming from. When you said Germany, they told you they wanted to be like you. You advised them to work hard, to revise their lessons and to be obedient to their parents and their teachers. You told them that close to two decades back, you had entered Form One as a young adolescent moved by a firm belief in the power of hard work. As you conversed with them, you pictured yourself back in that Form One Classroom as you chanted at the top of your voices, competing with the clattering sound of the rain against the window and on the rooftop of the class. Mr Sammy Jato, your Literature teacher had the habit of turning every learning situation into a performance and woe betide anyone who showed any lackadaisical attitude in his class. He was very entertaining and one of the things you remembered about him was the way he would choreograph the three respective rows to sing the different parts of *Swing Low, Sweet Chariot*:

> *Swing low, sweet chariot*
> *Coming for to carry me home,*
> *Swing low, sweet chariot,*
> *Coming for to carry me home.*

I looked over Jordan, and what did I see
Coming for to carry me home?
A band of angels coming after me,
Coming for to carry me home.

Sometimes I'm up, and sometimes I'm down,
(Coming for to carry me home)
But still my soul feels heavenly bound.
(Coming for to carry me home)

The brightest day that I can say,
(Coming for to carry me home)
When Jesus washed my sins away.
(Coming for to carry me home)

If I get there before you do,
(Coming for to carry me home)
I'll cut a hole and pull you through.
(Coming for to carry me home)

If you get there before I do,
(Coming for to carry me home)
Tell all my friends I'm coming too.
(Coming for to carry me home)

The song was a poem in a junior secondary school poetry collection which contained other poems/songs such as "Crocodile Wife" (My father, he married a crocodile wife, she bites! she bites!) and "A Mother's Song" (Some other woman wishes you to be her son, but you are mine, to lie down on a dirty mat with a hungry stomach... But you are mine). It is later on that you understood that "Swing Low, Sweet Chariot", banned in 1939 by the Nazi as one of the harmful and undesirable musical works, became popularised as one of the negro spirituals during the civil rights movements in the United States. It was also interpreted by a wide gamut of artists such as Beyoncé, Elvis Priestley, Joan Baez, Louis Armstrong, Paul Robeson, not forgetting the Smoky Mountain songbird - Dolly Parton.

You bade farewell to the young girls and moved to the office of the vice-principal of the Francophone section of the school. When you left the school in 2002, that section was still tenderfooted, but it had grown over the years. The vice-principal welcomed you very warmly. He was bilingual and you went on discussing in French. Your eyes went to the poster on his wall. It contained the faces of Africa's best writers.

"I can see Ngugi wa Thiong'o over there. He was at my university in Germany last month to receive his Honorary Doctorate Degree."

"You mean he is still alive?"

"Sure, healthy and kicking." He was a bit silent as if doubting me. "Perhaps you are thinking of Chinua Achebe who died last year." You insisted, to clarify the doubts that still seemed to hang on his face.

"I know, but I did not know Ngugi wa Thiong'o was still alive."

"I did my PhD on his novels and I have conducted several interviews with him." You continued, now almost feeling proud, the kind of feeling that goes with the adverb "p-e-r-s-o-n-n-e-l-l-e-m-e-n-t" (personally) in Cameroon.

"And what about his brother, Ngugi wa Mirii". He struggled to pronounce the last name and you helped him out, almost like a specialist of Kikuyu language, to better correct him. Your brief exchange reminded you of your 2012 trip to California to interview Ngugi wa Thiong'o. The visit was a literary pilgrimage to a writer of enormous influence on your entire generation. His intimidating humility completely altered your view of what it meant to be famous. Instead of finding an oracle of a man, you had met someone with a deeply humane touch.

"Not his brother, rather a collaborator." This time, you tried not to seem too corrective. That was a common mistake. Some even thought they were twins.

"I see. I did not know that. But is he still alive?"

"Unfortunately, he died in Zimbabwe in 2008 where he lived in exile. He had a tragic car accident."

"That is awful." He exclaimed.

After inquiring from the vice-principal on the performance of the Francophone section of the school in public exams such as Probatoire and Baccalauréat, you took leave of him.

Then you moved to the corridor of what used to be the Form Two and Three classrooms of Cheap Side. There was a teacher in front of the class. He seemed to be teaching Maths or Physics. You waved at him, indicating you would like to talk to him. He came close to the door with a welcoming smile.

After briefly introducing yourselves to each other, you told him you merely wanted to address some words of encouragement to the students. He gave you the green light. You introduced yourself to the students who put on interrogative but welcoming countenances. You wished them the best in their exams and told them to remain focused on their studies. When you finished talking and after having taken some two shots with the students, you bade them farewell. But one of them shouted:

"Farotage!!"[30]

Not before long, the entire class joined in the chorus. You humbly dipped your hands into your trouser pockets and removed two banknotes of 10,000 frs which you gave to the teacher for the students during break time. The entire class showered all sorts of blessings on you as you walked out of the classroom, elated, but more so, humbled.

As you stepped on the path close to the Form Three B building, about to go back to town, memories of the fallen flashed your mind, of those invaluable souls who made the Cheap Side so dear to

30. It is a jargon current in Cameroon and Ivory Coast, amongst others. It is the act of sharing money generously but also as a sign of showing off.

you and your mates: you remembered Mr Fonta, your Form Three Chemistry teacher, the soft-spoken and almost effeminate gentleman, always in a black top hat and suspenders, the Johnny Cash of your school, the man in black; Mr Ivo, the Form Two PTA Chemistry teacher, who always spoke as if straining his voice, giving his very best for the students; Mr Bongmba Abel, the History teacher with the red Starlet who spoke so gently, a reflection of his character; Mr Shintum, the very rigorous and smart Geography teacher whom everyone feared; Mr Werengie, the charismatic French Language teacher; Mrs Shang Judith, the unassuming Literature teacher whose natural sotto voce echoed on the eaves of the Mortuary (Lower Sixth Arts Hall), bringing out the sinister and tragic tone of the Chorus in T S Eliot's *Murder in the Cathedral*; Mr Valentine, the tireless sports master who used to pronounce 'usually' at the General Assembly as 'jujually'; Mr Tada, the bald-headed Discipline Master with his shiny Manu Dibango buzzcut; Mr Ben Bola, the two-metre tall sports master who was a former National Football Team player. And certainly, the list continued as many of those who gave their best for that institution had travelled to the world beyond:

> They shall grow not old, as we that are left grow old:
> Age shall not weary them, nor the years condemn.
> At the going down of the sun and in the morning
> We will remember them.
>
> They mingle not with their laughing comrades again;
> They sit no more at familiar tables of home;
> They have no lot in our labour of the day-time;
>
> As the stars that shall be bright when we are dust,
> Moving in marches upon the heavenly plain;
> As the stars that are starry in the time of our darkness,
> To the end, to the end, they remain.

("For the Fallen", by Lawrence Binyon)

Hark! This and other poems from the unforgettable *Sheldon Book of Verse* are inseparable from memories of another departed soul. Her name was Mrs Khan Leno Bridget Ngassa, a Sakerette. She taught you literature in Form Four and Five. She was a fine pedagogue and made her students live the literature they studied. She made her students sing, shout, cry, laugh and yearned as they contemplated and analysed the intricate verses of "Come down oh maid" (Tennyson), "La Belle dame sans merci" (Keats), "Dulce et decorum est" (Owen), "The Lady of Shalott" (Tennyson), "Mariana" (Tennyson), "Charge of the Light Brigade" (Tennyson), "The Listeners" (de la Mare), "The Eve of Agincourt" (Shakespeare), "So we go no more a-roving" (Byron), "For the Fallen" (Binyon). With dexterity, Mrs Khan nurtured the seed that Pa Sammy Jato, Pa Want'd (thus named for insisting on the rightful pronunciation of the word 'wanted'), and others had planted in you throughout the Cheap Side days. She dissected with her students the gothic and uncanny interiority of Jane Eyre, the magnum opus of the eldest of the Brontë sisters, taking you through the finicky labyrinths of Jane's deeply troubled but nevertheless humane sensibility as she struggled with rejection, love, self-doubt, and unruly fate.

18

You took the short cut from Cheap Side to the main road leading to Binju. It was a famous path used by dodgers. At the road junction, opposite the entrance to the Government Technical High School, you found a motorcyclist who transported you through Binju to the central town. A great percentage of the student population of GBHS Nkambe resided in Binju. Binju was not just a locale, locality, or location. There was more to it: it was a phenomenon. Those who lived in Binju were bound together by an incredible social glue and social dynamic that was beyond the compunction of some of you who lived in town. For these students, the socialisation that took place on campus always seemed supplementary, for a prior social cementing had already taken place in Binju. They seemed to enjoy many common references, and given that it was the administrative quarter, Binju schoolmates had a better mastery of who was who in town and on campus, in terms of social status: "Don't you know so so and so is the son or daughter of the State Counsel, Magistrate, Director so so and so?"

A girl from Binju was always already 'occupied' before one even thought of anything. Just like the case with Binka, one could not put asunder what Binju had sealed together. Otherwise, it could only be untied in Binju and by a fellow Binjuan. More than solidarity, Binju mates shared a certain sense of complicity and even conspiracy. It seemed that, whenever they took the gravel road to Binju after school hours, a sense of community was formed which bonded them in a unique and interrelated mindset. And it was very striking that non-Nkambe and non-Mbum students entered that social net with enormous ease. As such, Binju welcomed and integrated everyone, despite their ethnic backgrounds. One just needed the rightful Darwinist instincts to assert themselves in that space. Students from other ethnic backgrounds usually talked about Binju in hindsight and nostalgia as if Nkambe was part of Binju and not the other way round. To cap it all, some of them ended up speaking Limbum more fluently than Limbum mother-tongue speakers.

The motorcyclist rode past the Presbyterian Secondary School (PSS) stadium, informing you that a new stadium had been constructed at the outskirts of the town by the rural council. You wondered if the dust of the new stadium could ever gather as many indelible memories as the PSS stadium. The premises of PSS (fondly called *Passassa*) constituted an archive of the socio-cultural history of Nkambe. As the main venue for sporting events, it was also a space of desire, longing, ostentation, social expression, peer interaction, juvenile exuberance, joie de vivre and matchmaking. It was a place of "escorting" and "comportment", expressions that had very specific contextual meanings amongst the student population in Nkambe. As the venue for football competitions organised by school and town authorities alike, it constituted the social intercourse between town life and school life. In effect, for those who attended secondary and high school in Nkambe in the 1990s and 2000s, many of their love stories started, thrived or ended there. Those were the days of the Sisqo dyed hairstyle, the Ja Rule headkerchief, the zengue miniskirt, the SEBAGO (dockside) shoes, the MP3 player/headphones, the Walkman and all sorts of pre-smartphone gadgets. While the games were underway, the fan clubs of the traditional rivals/enemies - Government Technical High School (GTHS) and Government Bilingual High School (GBHS) – would throw jibes at each other in the form of songs, swag and verbal provocations in what seemed like a match outside the match, a match on the touchline. Beneath the surface of that slightly slanting pitch of dusty ground interspaced with patches of lawn, lie priceless memories of sporting heroes that gave meaning to life in Nkambe in the 1990s and 2000s: JPP, Kevin, Gilbert Kalla, MC Hammer, Rahim, Ndao, Lotana, Chijoke, Ndonaah, Namdi, Milton, Kilian, Emile, Boksic, Paddy, Emma, Koude, Chakuna, Roland, Cantona, Rogers, Vally, Njanka, Shey Nko, Lawyer, Atacké, Charlo, Eva, Yakubu, Kenny-Bass, Tado Willi, Diabate, Ngome, Basil, Eric, Ehmah, Makara, Sete. etc. Some of them - Nkeh Ernest, Jato Ernest; Adamu Baba, Isa Bello, Tambang Vitalis and Roland - had fought a good fight and now lie in eternal rest.

That space also brought to mind Mr Nguh Scots, the Biology teacher cum soccer referee. He almost paid the ultimate price due to the emotions that flared up at the end of the games. As a measure of precaution, he often blew the final whistle of the game from the corner-kick spot, poised to flee to the gendarmerie post (the so-called peloton) across the road, for fear of any eventuality. Though football remained the dominant sports, perhaps the most memorable sport figures for many a student were rather the handball prodigies: Sango and Eddie Murphy. The handball pitch was across the road, on the campus of the Government Practicing School, close to the peloton. While football games often went either way and the GBHS school team occasionally lost some decisive games, sending you home with the bitter pills of defeat, the Handball Boys team was the most reassuring of all, thanks to these two sharpshooters. Years later, you were to have an interesting experience with one of them in the Far Northern region of Cameroon.

The bus you had boarded from Maroua to Mora had come to an unexpected stop, leaving a trail of dust behind, in the middle of a sparsely populated hamlet in Mayo-Sava Division, Far North Cameroon. It was one of the most underdeveloped parts of the country, despite being the home of prominent government officials, including the senescent and eternal President of the National Assembly. No wonder, your students used to refer to the division as "Mayo ça ne va pas". Many passengers responded with a chorus of sighs, foreseeing police corruption and harassment. It was about 4:30 PM. and many wanted to arrive in Mora before dusk. Three police agents emerged from a small bar by the roadside. Two of them moved close to the bus and as one asked for the driver's documents, his colleague cross-checked the identity cards of the passengers. They were rather good-humoured and fortunately all the passengers had their regular travel documents at hand. Soon you realised that the face of the third colleague who leaned on an escort motorcycle, following the scene from a distance, looked familiar. In the depths of the extreme north, a near-foreign land for anyone who had spent their entire life in the southern part of the country, it was a miracle to meet someone who knew you or spoke your language. You shouted "Murphy" and waved, sticking your hand and neck out of the half-open window. He turned around and moved closer to the bus, instantly recognising you:

"*Bro, baneke, we lo yo ife a ngong nsarung nfurya!*". ("What a surprise to meet you in this desert[31], my brother.") He exclaimed.

"*Amena bro, me yu hafa sihni i gi ambo mnwe ta waha. Me kwa nkfumbe ni dih moh o to ine Momo.*" ("I have been here for close to five months, bro. I scrape the chalk in a village called Momo"). You responded.

"Scraping the chalk" was a sarcastic reference to a statement by the Minister of Higher Education, Jacques Fame Ndongo, who, during your graduation ceremony from the Ecole Normale Supérieure (ENS, The Higher Teacher Training College) in Yaoundé had referred to the graduates as *les gladiateurs de la craie* - gladiators of the chalk, invaluable pillars of nation-building. Yes, nation builders, even if they had to survive on dust and leftover memories of ministerial speeches wherever they were posted in the national triangle. Especially when they were unlucky enough to be amongst the top of their class. Immediately you mentioned your destination, Murphy bade you come out of the bus, saying his colleague was to travel to Mora an hour later and could take you to your locality before continuing over to Mora. You conceded and notified the driver that you were alighting, letting him know that you had only your hand luggage. You succeeded in extricating yourself from the sardine-packed bus onto the ready embrace of Eddie Murphy. His arms exuded incredible energy and you felt like Lilliput in the hands of a giant. You had grown pale after suffering from malaria some weeks before.

Those arms were a nightmare to the goalkeeper of any team he played against during high school days. You reminisced how his shots would whistle through the net, blasting against the plank wall of the Government Practicing School building, with the mesmerised goalkeeper only realizing the effect of the transient lightning in flashback. You pitied any citizen who would be caused by any undesirable

---

31. 'Desert' here refers to the Sahelian climate of the Far northern region of Cameroon.

circumstances to bear the negative effect of those arms on them. After gulping down two bottles of Castel (commonly known as *Come And See Teachers Enjoying Life*), punctuated by stories from your alma mater and life in the far north, Murphy's colleague drove you for about forty-five minutes to Momo in a brand-new Toyota Carina. It was dusk and you were tipsy, loquacious, full of inspiration and feeling at once light-footed and heavy, like a character in Ekwensi's *Burning Grass*. He left you at the Momo market square, some fifty metres from the compound where you lived. On 19th February 2016 at 8:30 AM, that market square would become the scene of a fatal Boko Haram suicide attack, causing twenty-four instant casualties, wounding one hundred and fourteen.

19

Later that evening, the principal invited you to a snack bar in the vicinity of the grandstand. He offered you a treat of goat meat. Apart from *mthuh sahmbing* (aerial yam)[32], goat meat was one of your most cherished delicacies from home. The hircinous aroma of stewed goatskin was so inviting that it could make one swallow an entire loaf of fufu from a distance even before having any tactile contact with the substance itself. The principal was surprised you were not interested in taking a beer. You told him you were a Bavarian with a difference, perhaps in the same way as you avoided drinking *sha*, the local maize brew, during your school days in Nkambe. As you devoured the goat meat with the vengeful appetite of a reconciled prodigal son, he recounted to you in detail his renovation plan for the school, soothing your initial disappointment in the face of the deteriorating structures of the school. The school was planning to celebrate its fortieth anniversary the following year. As a Form One

---

32. Known scientifically as *dioscorea bulbifera*, it grows in most tropical climates.

student, you witnessed the twentieth anniversary of the institution in 1995 and it was a memorable eye-opener. After witnessing with admiration the spectacular performances of senior schoolmates and the alumni during the anniversary celebrations in the form of theatre sketches, debates, musical interpretations, etc., you were confused about what you wanted to become in life: journalist, musician, medical doctor, actor, politician, lecturer, diplomat…To many former students, the "**I was there**" badge worn by attendants during that occasion remained one of the most evocative relics of their passage in that institution.

You told the principal that, regrettably, you were not going to be back in Cameroon at the time of the anniversary but promised to mobilise some goodwill batch mates and possibly, chip in your widow's mite as a responsible alumnus. Your meeting was brief and he went home immediately after, complaining of a tiresome day.

Later that evening, you visited Pa Ngeh, your History teacher. Surprisingly, he did not have difficulties recognizing you. The man had not changed a bit. You brought as a present for him a bottle of German wine, Dornfelder. For the very first time, you saw him smile. Pa Ngeh could make the entire class shed tears of laughter while he maintained his characteristically neutral face and inexpressive demeanour.

"No student has ever done that to me," he said, with a generous smile.

Honestly, you thought that was an understatement. Certainly, from the myriad of his former students scattered all over the world, he must have received better gestures of acknowledgement. But coming from Pa Ngeh, it meant a lot to you. If Okonkwo knew how to kill a man's spirit, Pa Ngeh knew how to make someone assume their rightful place beyond any sense of self-presumption. His words took you down memory lane to your first class in Lower Sixth, in October 2001. You and your mates were seated in the Mortuary, in your new uniforms, with white armbands - the newly earned second cycle distinction, waiting for the first lesson of the term. The GCE O Level results had made many of you believe that you had crossed the Rubicon. Many were still caught in that peculiar post-GCE swag that made you think the world was your oyster. Pa Ngeh entered the Mortuary through the back door, walked stealthily through the aisle to the teacher's desk. After keeping his leather bag and Philips radio on the table, he put on his spactacles and moved in measured Phileas Fogg steps to the other corner of the hall while gazing steadily at your faces. There was absolute silence, the kind of silence only possible in Pa Ngeh's class. He then walked back geometrically to the centre of the hall, and then passed his verdict:

"The same primitive faces I met in Form Five."

When the entire class burst into laughter, his face did not experience any physiognomic alteration. The students had expected at least a congratulatory phrase from him on their GCE performances. In Pa Ngeh's lexical system, 'primitive' simply meant 'traditional', 'customary' or 'habitual'. No word, phrase, clause, sentence that came out of his mouth was ever casual. On the contrary, his sentences were both historical and historic and there was hardly any distinction between his formal and informal utterances. During assessments or exams, after having separated bench mates and potential partners in crime from each other, he would take about thirty minutes to explain the instructions and the consequences of non-compliance: the distance between the students' sitting positions; the way the responses had to be numbered; the point at which each and every one had to stop writing; the sequence in which the papers needed to be submitted and last, but the most important, which personal renditions of the letters of the alphabet were acceptable or not. Pa Ngeh was convinced beyond doubt that many students failed the GCE because of the way they wrote. So, when the principal organised a counselling session for Form Five and Upper Sixth students a few weeks to GCE time, Pa Ngeh's presentation focused on one theme: handwriting!

As you sat there discussing with Pa Ngeh and his wife, your

eyes fell on the radio set on top of his TV cupboard. It was the same Philips transistor radio which was his faithful companion throughout those years. It was a half-wood, half-plastic, half-steel set. You could not tell if it was there as household memorabilia or as a still functional appliance. Whenever Pa Ngeh stuck that radio set to his ear as he walked under the cypress trees of Nanga Hills to the Mortuary, he was half-removed from his immediate environment. He seemed to belong elsewhere. His radio reminded you of other radio sets linked to GBHS: that of Short Joe, and Pa Forti. The latter used to pass at Cheap Side and signs of his passage would be summarised in the evanescent tones of his radio. As he crossed the lush lawns of Cheap Side, Form One foxes murmured to one another: "that is Pa Forti". You could not come close to Pa Forti if you had not sanitised your English sentences well enough. For him, a wrong sentence was not just wrong, it carried a stench, and he was allergic to that stench.

Looking at Pa Ngeh and the joy that your meeting elicited, even for a taciturn and reserved character like him, made you proud. But you were also aggrieved. Your primary school Headmaster, the first Mr Ngeh of your life, had died in 2007 while you were at the University in Yaoundé.

20

Upon leaving Pa Ngeh's house, you went further close to the St. Rita's College, one of the main technical schools of the town. You recalled your friend, Christian, a German woodworker who taught in that school in the nineties. Christian was a good friend of Richard, a primary school teacher from your village who lived in a luxurious home in a valley not very far from St. Rita's. His home became a meeting point for the three of you. Christian was very jovial and kind, one likely to develop friendship at the very first encounter. He was so interested in the Mbum culture that he was given a traditional title as *Ta Ngwang* of the *Mfuh* Society.[33] During *Mfuh* days, Christian, Richard and you would meet at Richard's house to clear up the remaining jug of palm wine. Though you were not a good drinker, you enjoyed their company and the discussions that Christian usually led, displaying an impressive mastery of local cultural habits and recounting to you several stories about life in Germany. He had lived in other parts of Africa before coming to Cameroon. Every month, Christian supplied Richard with copies of *Deutschland*, a magazine focusing on the political activities of the German Chancellor at the time, Gerhard Schröder and information on German Higher Education Sector. Those copies usually ended up in your hands. Through them, you began to get a grasp of the German post-war political and economic transformation.

Richard died after a protracted illness in 2015. His wife had died eight years earlier when you were still in Yaoundé. In your last telephone discussion with him while in Germany, you asked him if he still had Christian's German contacts anywhere in his archive. He promised to look for them. After your discussion, he tabled a very serious problem before you about his health situation. You sent him some money for hospital bills. Months later, he told you he had recovered and still renewed his promise to look for Christian's address. But that was going to be the last time you spoke with him. Among the things Richard had given you during your interactions were two music Compact Discs: American Hit Parade 1998 and Makoma.

Makoma in particular, represented the effervescence of youth culture, as well as it captured the ambiguity of social identity in an era of religious intensity and uncertainty. Their music was 'godly' in theory but had a 'worldly' swag, and both those who were in the world and those who were out of the world had their

---

33. The Mfuh is a traditional society amongst the Mbum of North West Cameroon. Originally, it was the defensive arm of the kingdom, hence the preponderance of cutlasses and spears that are displayed during Mfuh Dance.

share of Makoma. 'Natamboli', 'Nzambena Bomoyi', 'Napesi' and 'Butunamoyi' were some of their best tracks. But unlike Agatha Moses, the famous Nigerian gospel artist who became a favourite hit both in the church and the nightclub, Makoma was more befitting for youth social gatherings. Your secondary schooldays were characterised by a medley of musical trends such as makossa, zengue, mapouka, ndombolo, zouk, slow jam, RnB and the trending artists at the time ranged from Jean Pierre Essome, Michael Learns to Rock, West Life, Backstreet Boys, Ace of Base, Boyz II Men, Monique Seka, Rachel Mimbo, Bébé Manga, Jocelyne Labylle, Brenda Fassie, Petit Pays, Roméo Dika, Douleur, Benji Mateke, Craig David, Keith Sweat, Shaggy, R. Kelly, Joe Thomas, Sisqo, Destiny's Child, Lucky Dube, Aliya, Dido, Shakira, Jennifer Lopez, Mariah Carey, Christina Aguilera, Whitney Houston, The Corrs, Celine Dion, KC & Jojo, Shania Twain, to ABBA.

Top tracks by artists like Sonya Spence ('Jet plane', 'Where is the love?'), Yvonne Chaka Chaka ('Umqomboti'), Meiway ('Zoblazo) and Chaka Demus and Pliers ('bam bam') came a bit earlier but were quite popular in student quarters in Nkambe. Zaïko, the forerunner of ndombolo, was already in its last days when you entered Form One but its legacy amongst the senior students could be perceived through the distinct hairstyle, dressing style and most especially, the flourishing of social character types with nicknames such as Bolingo, Lokito, Tolambo and Lokassa. On the school campus, you could mistake someone's strutting gait for a physical disability, whereas it was the effect of a specific pop cultural trend. Transient fashion left durable legacies on some students' postures and ways of being as well as those of youth in general. One of the most memorable zaïko interpreters in Nkambe who made his mark in popular clubs like Matignon, UB Relax and Holy War, remains Shey Lokassa!

The Walkman may now seem like a relic of a distant past to some but it had its time and left its mark on your generation. The new android generation may be quite aphasic about anything that preceded it, but only those with short memories will forget the popularity of Walkman in the yesteryears. The Walkman was a major revolution in the entertainment industry, ushering a period of personalised consumption of musical productions. It was the material object of modernity par excellence. It was one of the early technologies that popularised the personalised enjoyment of music in both the private and the public sphere. Sony Walkman emerged in the 1970s and progressively through the 80s and 90s, that music kit was progressively perfected and modernised, enhancing its capacities to provide entertainment while consumers could be multi-tasking. In the 1990s, it was one of the key music technologies that negotiated a perfect transition between the radio cassette and the compact disc. In your alma mater, in particular, the mid-1990s knew a boom in Walkman amongst the student population. For that generation, memories of artists such as Dido ('Thank you', 'White flag'), Melanie C ('Never be the same again'), Craig David's ('Walking away') Shaggy ('Angel'), etc. are umbilically linked to that of the Walkman through which they were both popularly and privately owned and internalised. Before the advent of technological miniaturisation that led to the popularity of kits such as the MP3 player, the Sony Walkman stereo player had influenced an entire generation.

21

As the vice principal had taken you around the campus, specific spaces on campus, brought to mind the names of certain artists, and along with them, certain memories. At Cheap Side, the Form Two C classroom stood for Monique Seka's 'Okaman'. The sound had just been released and your female mates would turn the front of the class into a dance hall during free periods. At Dear Side, the Form Five B classroom stood for Hit Parade 1998: Vengaboys ('Rhythm of the night'), Garcia ('Bamboleo'), D J Bobo ('There's a party'),

Haddaway ('What is love'), Snap!('Rhythm is a dancer'), Corona ('Rhythm of the night'), No Mercy ('Where do you go'), T-Spoon ('Sex on the Beach'), Fun Factory ('I wanna be with you') and Real Mcoy ('Another night'). Music has the magic of capturing the spirit of the time in a way that no other art form or social practice can. The dance step is the acknowledgement of the Dionysian gem in every human: to dance is to throw oneself into a trance, to mix life and death in a transient consciousness of distended self/time in hindsight and anticipation. Music underlines at once the intensity of the NOW moment but also a certain light-heartedness towards life. In music, the body attempts to incarnate time/space and as it responds to rhythm, the corpus re-writes itself as a measure of its kinetic potential. But as you walked through these spaces, you concluded that nothing is as painful as recalling a tone of the past which in turn reminds one of someone who is no more. There is no greater form of solitude.

You went back to your hotel after what was an eventful day of encounters. The hotel was located in the very centre of the town, close to the Old Market. In those days, it was owned by the father of your former girlfriend, Amy. She was tall and of gentle character, with all in her ethereal glow and allure to trigger tremors in the soul of any young college boy. In the mid-1990s, it was alleged that an errant jinx aka Jerome attacked local corn brew (*sha*) drinkers (and drunkards) at night, leaving many people with inexplicable bruises the following day. The saga was so rife that even the *sha* sellers became cautious and paranoid. If by the shape of his face, the clench of his mouth, his overbearing or brilliant quarrelsomeness, the *sha* seller judged that her customer was getting to the fourth stage of drunkenness, she would simply boot him out of her bar at midnight, to avoid the trappings of Jerome. However, there was another, though less (un)popular side to the saga. Some claimed that, after a night of *sha* drinking spree during which he lost his bearings, a *sha* drinker suddenly found himself comfortably home, not knowing how he managed to cover the distance from the *sha* bar to his home. Others said that Jerome disentangled *sha* drinkers miraculously from any late-night brawl after a *sha* drinking session. But stories about the benevolent gestures of Jerome were fewer.

Aliénation

Lorsque les rayons du soleil embrassent le firmament
Nous voilà encore sans armes au gré des ténèbres
Si beau que soit l'accueil du jour à l'aube
Triste est l'approche du crépuscule

Pourquoi le Plaisir est toujours en évanescence
Quand le Chagrin s'érige en permanence
L'errance est de nature réelle
Et l'Idéal reste virtuel

Telle une vague diamantée sur la Côte d'Azur
Telle une colombe sur une branche d'olive
Ainsi qu'un Lys au milieu des prairies
Tu vas me quitter

Amy, peut-être reviendrais-tu, je l'espère
Peut-être ne reviendrais-tu pas, j'le crains
Ton départ m'agonise, tu le devines
Je le regrette, Dieu le sait

Amy, tu seras zéphyr à d'autres rives
Tu seras mélodie à d'autres vents
Tu seras parfums à d'autres airs
Tu seras lune à d'autres nuits

Si ces mots étaient pensés j'te les cach'rais
Mais puisqu'ils sont tous sentis

Je t'en fais ces confidences
G.

The truth is that the saga of Jerome coincided with the advent of the 62nd Infantry Battalion of the Cameroonian Armed Forces in Nkambe that led to a seismic reconfiguration of social relations whose effects could only be captured through anecdotic and surreal narratives. A colony of locusts in the name of soldiers in green berets had invaded the town, bent on consuming the young female offshoots right down to Form One. Though some were men and women of good character, most of the soldiers, rather than reinforcing security, constituted a threat to the security of Nkambe. They were wont to generate brawls from scratch, over any pretext. It was not uncommon for a classmate or teacher to come to school with a swollen cheek or a bandaged arm. But the greatest casualties were moral and social.

> Cursed be the social wants that sin against the strength of youth!
> Cursed be the social lies that warp us from the living truth!...
>
> Every gate is throng'd with suitors, all the markets overflow.
> I have but an angry fancy; what is that which I should do?
> (Locksley Hall, Lord Alfred Tennyson)

The soldiers did not come to fight any major war. In the absence of real war, apart from spontaneous skirmishes in Bakassi,[34] the military men diverted their energies elsewhere. The rhythm and nightlife of Nkambe town changed overnight, especially whenever the soldiers got their monthly salary (usually earlier than other civil servants) and whenever the successive squadrons returned from the

---

34. Bakassi is an oil rich peninsular in the Gulf of Guinea that was at the centre of a deadly boundary conflict between Cameroon and Nigeria. The conflict that led to measured military confrontations since 1981 was finally resolved through the International Court of Justice ruling in 2002 which declared Cameroonian sovereignty over the area. It was effectively handed over to Cameroon in 2007 following the UN-brokered Green Tree Agreement between Cameroon and Nigeria.

Bakassi Peninsula. These returning soldiers seemed to suffer from gargantuan thirst that made them suck the whole town dry. Not only dry of drinks but of many other things. Brawls became rampant in nightclubs as those who had hitherto considered themselves movers and shakers in town got a real match. One either made friends with the new lords or was bound to perish.

If the sporadic skirmishes in Bakassi circulated amongst the students in the form of inflated narratives conveyed by the army fans on campus, many of you were first-hand witnesses and victims of a war of another kind, not less real, not less nefarious. Given that many of the soldiers were from French-speaking parts of Cameroon, communication was a problem, often kept to its basic and functional level. In those days, expressions like "come cook rice" or "come cook spaghetti"; *"tu es mariée?"* - *"Non je suis free"*[35]; *"Je veux boire de l'eau."* - *"Bois-moi"*[36] became catchphrases in town, describing the baiting tactics of the military men to waylay the young girls. They had an edge over you the students, with their sixty thousand francs (about one hundred and ten dollars) salary for the *sans-galons*.[37] That was when Mambo Chocolate and the Special Bread, which hitherto would accompany a declaration of love amongst early secondary school students, lost their value.

The soldiers also had French, a romantic language, but also a language of 'commandement'. When they wanted to terrorise anyone, they used French whether their prey understood it or not. It also happened that even an Anglophone military 'brother' would turn and order the locals in French, both to impress and to cower them. To make matters worse, the camp was not far from the campus. The two were only separated by the Teacher Training College, a school of mainly post-High School adult students. But that was as weak a buffer as the French 1930s Maginot Line against an army that was

35. Question by a soldier: "Are you married?" Answer by a Nkambe girl: "No, I am free."
36. Question by a soldier: "I wish to drink water." Answer by a Nkambe girl: "Drink me."
37. The foot soldier without any epaulets. The lowest ranking military personnel.

after the sweet thirteens of the green Nanga Hills. Many of your teachers, especially your History teacher, Mr Ntumfon Matthew warned against the deadly pleasure of "bearded meat" and its effect on students' education. To no avail. The principal, as usual, was more pragmatic and told the students: "Be patient. Obtain your GCE and after that, you can 'do it' as you like." The stick and the carrot were used. Many resisted.

For others, the spirit was strong but the flesh was weak and even some of the holier-than-thou-student-preachers fell prey. In those days, it was not unusual to find a mate dozing during Maths or History class. Some even came to class with bruised faces, traces of late-night military love. However, surprisingly or perhaps logically, the French subject gained new converts. Some perpetual renegades started doing their homework with impressive consistency, thanks to their faithful backups and surrogates within the framework of "come we stay"[38] policy. Such mates began speaking in coded language and one only heard them talking of "He came last evening" and one needed not inquire about the *he*. The generation of bastards, the rise in the rate of transmissible diseases and school dropouts that flourished in Nkambe are the undeniable legacies of that era.

Thus, you lost your love. But you could not blame Amy, neither are you saying that she was necessarily after greener pastures. Her father was well-to-do, or so you thought. You share the blame for the fact that the pressures of the GCE converted you into a Thierry Gozelin, almost oblivious to the things of the world. Amy sent you a letter just before the GCE to announce her decision. You wondered why she chose only such a moment to pass her sentence. But you were blind to the world and your only god was the GCE. It was painful but that was not your priority. She was telling you matter-of-factly that she had found a *husband* given that you did

---

38. Pidgin expression for "come let us stay together." Use as a nominal phrase, it derogatorily designates cohabitation between man and woman that is not backed by any legal or customary marriage contract.

not "have her time" anymore. You bought a postcard, and in your characteristic calligraphy, penned some few words to her, telling her you still loved her but that you respected her choice. One good turn deserves another. But you found it hard to understand where the strong conviction of getting married came from. She was barely fifteen. In any case, you responded to her with sheer civility. No exchanges of fireworks. No hard words. Love itself has rest. Your friends and conduits started telling you they saw her in town with the military guy, but you said to yourself "I will marry when I want for the 'beautyful' ones are not yet born."

Later that year, in August, the GCE results came out. You succeeded with flying colours. But weeks later, as you boarded the bus to Yaoundé amidst tunes of Westlife, to begin a new life as a university student across the Sanaga, the pangs of separation travelled with you.

During those nights full of memories of times past, you came to the realisation that whenever something happens, something else happens.

ACKNOWLEDGEMENT

I am very thankful to my colleagues and fellow sojourners for reading the very first drafts of this collection and sharing vital insights with me. They include Serawit Bekele, Simon Nganga and Sam Ndogo. The manuscript also benefitted from the keen eyes of my literary comrades such as Nsah Mala, Roger K. Mbianda, Divine Mbutoh, Ndi Blaise, Isabelle Yefon, Ndi Derrick, Meh Innocent, Ras I Mackinzeph, Mbangchia Chester, Muchira wa Gachenge and Stan Diman. I am also grateful for the literary companionship of my senior colleagues like Teke Charles, Victor Gomia, Eunice Ngongkum and Christopher Odhiambo whose comments deeply enriched this text. I equally express my gratitude to Tandap Charles, Nyamngong Januarius, Oliver Jiti and Julius Yerima, who consistently came to my rescue whenever I needed any useful information. I am indebted to the renowned writer, Patrice Nganang who took time off to read through the manuscript and made invaluable suggestions. My publisher showed proof of diligence, thoroughness and insight in a bid to make the manuscript attain its full potential.

Gil Ndi-Shang (Romance Literatures/Comparative Studies, University of Bayreuth) holds a PhD in Comparative Literature from the Bayreuth International Graduate School of African Studies (BIGSAS). He is a member of the Young Colleague Programme, Bavarian Academy of Sciences (Munich-Germany). In the recent past, he has been Research Fellow with the Fritz-Thyssen Foundation and the Alexander von Humboldt Foundation for his literary research in Congo, Peru and Colombia. He hails from the North West region of Cameroon where he grew up before moving to Yaoundé and Bayreuth (Germany) for his undergraduate and graduate education respectively. He is the author of *Letter from America: Memoir of an Adopted Child, State/society: Narrating Transformations in African Novels* and co-editor of *Tracks and Traces of Violence* and *Re-writing Pasts, Imagining Futures*. He is also a contributing co-editor of the poetry volume *Emerging Voices: Anthology of Young Anglophone Cameroon Poets*.

ABOUT THE PUBLISHER

Spears Books is an independent publisher dedicated to providing innovative publication strategies with emphasis on African/Africana stories and perspectives. As a platform for alternative voices, we prioritize the accessibility and affordability of our titles in order to ensure that relevant and often marginal voices are represented at the global marketplace of ideas. Our titles – poetry, fiction, narrative nonfiction, memoirs, reference, travel writing, African languages, and young people's literature – aim to bring African worldviews closer to diverse readers. Our titles are distributed in paperback and electronic formats globally by African Books Collective.

Connect with Us: Go to www.spearsmedia.com to learn about exclusive previews and read excerpts of new books, find detailed information on our titles, authors, subject area books, and special discounts.

Subscribe to our Free Newsletter: Be amongst the first to hear about our newest publications, special discount offers, news about bestsellers, author interviews, coupons and more! Subscribe to our newsletter by visiting www.spearsmedia.com

Quantity Discounts: Spears Books are available at quantity discounts for orders of ten or more copies. Contact Spears Books at orders@

spearsmedia.com.

Host a Reading Group: Learn more about how to host a reading group on our website at www.spearsmedia.com

Also by Gil Ndi-Shang
Letter from America

Inspired by Alistair Cooke's masterpiece "Letter from America" (1934-2004) that depicted the transformation of British culture in the United States of America, Ndi-Shang's text redefines 'America', focusing on the melting pot engendered by African, indigenous, European and Asian cultures in Latin America through the case of Peru, the erstwhile epicentre of Spanish empire in Latin America. It is a reflection on the triangular relationship between Africa, Europe and America against the backdrop of slavery and (neo-)colonialism which continue to define intimate experiences, daily interactions, personal trajectories and human relations in a 'globalized world'. Ndi-Shang probes into the legacies of racial inequalities but also the possibilities of a new ethic of encounter amongst human beings/cultures. The text is based on an intricate interweaving of the humorous with the tragic, the personal with the global, the historical with the current and the real with the creative.

Printed in the United States
by Baker & Taylor Publisher Services